MW01248980

MATINEE
IDOL

MATINEE IDOL

RON BASE

1985
Doubleday Canada Limited, Toronto, Ontario
Doubleday & Company Inc., Garden City, New York

Library of Congress Catalog Card Number 85-15991
ISBN 0-385-25006-1

Interior design by Irene Carefoot
Typesetting by Compeer Typographic Services Limited
Printed and bound in Canada by D.W. Friesen

Canadian Cataloguing in Publication Data

Base, Ron, 1948–
  Matinee idol
ISBN 0-385-25006-1
I. Title.
PS8553.A83M37 1985   C813'.54   C85-099257-5
PR9199.3.B37M37 1985

Library of Congress Cataloging-in-Publication Data

Base, Ron.
  Matinee idol
I. Title.
PR9199.3.B3757M3 1985   813'.54   85-15991
ISBN 0-385-25006-1

For Lynda

You can linger too long
in your dreams.

— Billy Joel,
''Keeping the Faith''

Where's the man could ease a heart
Like a satin gown?

— Dorothy Parker

PART ONE

Part One

PROLOGUE

I t was not until he sat down to write it that the full story of Lyn Lisa Conlon's past began to emerge. It was a story that, as everyone now knows, ended in tragedy and murder. These things have a way of coming full circle: it was also a story that began with tragedy and murder. Actually, it began on a spring night in 1937 when William Conlon arrived in Paris and met Douglas Kenney at a bar known as the Select in the Montparnasse area of the city.

Willy Conlon was a Canadian boy, Toronto born, and thus was narrow-minded, naive, nasty when provoked, as well as being "not badly off," as he was prone to telling people. Willy had what he termed "business ambitions," and there was no reason in the world that he could think of that those ambitions would not be fulfilled. His father was a prominent barrister who once worked in New York for John Rockefeller at Standard Oil. Willy Conlon could clearly recall — at least he told everyone he could clearly recall — summers in the Poconos at the Rockefeller estate.

Beyond those trips, though, Willy Conlon had never been outside the environs of Toronto, a city which, as Willy stated proudly, not only possessed the Royal York, largest hotel in the British Commonwealth, but also the tallest building. The Bank of Commerce building stood an entire thirty-six stories high, and Willy himself had been right to the top. Even so, Willy had to concede that Toronto, colorless, provincial, and bleakly held in the grips of a depression, was not exactly a window on the world. Willy, having escaped parochialism not to mention the worst heat wave in the city's history, was on the lookout for adventure.

Douglas Kenney seemed the perfect adventurer. He had been everywhere and done everything. Willy Conlon was at once intrigued by him and jealous of him. Doug Kenney was wise and worldly and not a little bit mysterious. He was from New York, he said, and he had, two months before, married "the best-looking babe in the city," a twenty-year-old Ohio girl named Lyn Lisa Armstrong. Willy wondered why a man who just married "the best-looking babe" had left her in New York. He did not ask the question, however. Kenney did not seem to invite many questions. He did not flaunt his money, but he was obviously wealthy, impeccably dressed, and known in the best places in Paris.

It was never understood what attracted Kenney to Conlon, although given what subsequently transpired, Kenney may have been in need of a lackey and Willy Conlon was handy enough and naive enough to play the role.

In any event, Douglas Kenney more or less took Willy Conlon under his wing over the next few weeks. Kenney effectively seemed to have missed the Canadian's hair-trigger temper and the spoiled wilfullness that lurked beneath the easily impressed exterior. Or if he saw those qualities, he chose to ignore them.

Doug Kenney was a great talker that spring in Paris. He said he once had drinks with F. Scott Fitzgerald, the writer. He claimed he had dated the actress Jean Harlow. He related how he once ended up in bed with Tallulah Bankhead. He said his wife, Lyn, was one of the great beauties of New York. He laughed and called her "The Ohio Ice Queen." Except in bed, he said. She was no ice queen in bed.

He was less talkative about what he *did* for a living. When quizzed about this by Willy, Doug Kenney gave one of his cavalier shrugs, and said he was in "a service industry."

Finally, one night after a great deal of wine at a bistro in the St. Germain de Pres area, Doug Kenney, in confidence, revealed to his new friend, Willy Conlon, exactly what "service industry" he was involved in: the arms business. What with the Nazis in power, the Italians in Addis Ababa, the civil war in Spain, the world fluttering toward a global conflict, it was a business that was booming as never before. Doug Kenney conceded that for the most part he did not deal with legitimate governments. They were not the people who required his services.

At the moment he was on his way to Algiers to sell weapons to an Algerian nationalist group known as the *Etoile Nord-Africaine*. Would Willy like to come along? He could use an assistant. There was some danger, of course. But the payoff would be worth it. For both of them. Willy considered the proposition. He had come to Europe seeking adventure. This was certainly adventure. He agreed to accompany Doug Kenney to Algiers. It was, as it turned out, a fateful decision.

They arrived in the seaport city of Algiers in September of 1937. Doug Kenney said he had to make contact with a man named Badis, who was attending some sort of Muslim congress. The city in late summer was absolutely torrid. But they had a magnificent suite at the Hotel des Postes. The view from the balcony took in the entire sweep of the waterfront. Doug remarked that Algiers, with its red-roofed villas pressed against the bay, reminded him of Cannes. Willy did not know, since he had never been to Cannes. But the excitement of merely being present in Algiers, well, it was indescribable.

Each evening Doug would disappear for about three hours, returning at 11 P.M. to report things were "coming along nicely." Although precisely what things, Willy could never be sure. One night Doug returned to the hotel with an ugly cut on his forehead. It was nothing, he said; a slight misunderstanding. These things were common in the Algerian heat. They must be accepted.

In the meantime, though, Willy Conlon was becoming bored. If Doug Kenney needed an assistant, he gave no sign of it. There was nothing for Willy to do, except drink too much and become increasingly antagonistic toward Doug. They began to argue, and slowly, imperceptibly, Willy began to hate Doug Kenney. One evening, perhaps realizing he had to do something about the increasing gulf between them, Doug took Conlon along to the house of the man known as Badis.

They traveled along elegant French-style boulevards that came to a halt at the Turkish quarter, or what was more popularly known as the Casbah. The streets abruptly narrowed into dark, confusing alleyways. Willy's nostrils were assailed by the acrid scent of spice and oil. Badis lived in a small, unprepossessing house off a tiny courtyard. He had a long, dark, and pock-marked face, and was jovial enough, welcoming them to *Maghreb* — "the land of the setting sun" — serving tiny Arab dishes known as *mezze*.

The three men were consuming the black olives, wallet-sized pieces of flaked pastry, and kebabs when a slim, dusky beauty was ushered into the dining area. It was then that Conlon met the *Ouled-Nail* Arab girl. He was immediately, and stupidly, infatuated. The girl followed the tradition of the females of her tribe and provided herself as an accomplished courtesan for foreigners with money, before going off with a rich dowry to become an honored wife.

That night at the house of Badis, the *Ouled-Nail* girl serviced Willy with an enthusiasm he mistook for appreciation. He returned again the next evening, and the night after that. Soon he was seeing her every night, and life in Algiers was no longer boring. For his part, Douglas Kenney was vastly amused at the endlessness of Conlon's sexual appetite. He taunted Willy constantly about the girl, called her "that whore." The description was accurate, to everyone except Willy. He was young and inexperienced, and thought much more of her. Worse, he was convinced she thought much more of him.

The last night Willy Conlon saw her alive it suddenly dawned on him that, despite his infatuation and the amount of time he had spent thrusting himself wildly into her supple body, he did not even know her full name. He had never even thought to ask her. What kind of love was that? he later wondered.

Exactly one month later, Willy Conlon arrived in New York and looked up Lyn Lisa Kenney. He found her at her lavish Park Avenue duplex apartment. She was tall, broad-shouldered, and blond-haired. Her oval face had a beauty that in repose was icy and crisp and entirely unforgettable. The coolness of her features was offset somewhat by large eyes that looked constantly surprised by the world around them. Willy Conlon was almost immediately smitten.

Lyn Lisa was also terribly distraught. She had not heard a word from her husband for close to five months. It was Willy's terrible and sad duty to inform Lyn Lisa that her husband, Douglas, the man she loved, was dead.

She was brave about the news, having begun to suspect the worst. Her uncle, who was influential and who had introduced her to Douglas in the first place, had made inquiries through the state department. He had been unable to learn anything about Doug's whereabouts. Now here was Doug's friend Willy from Canada, to confirm everyone's suspicions. It was particularly embarrassing because, although the uncle was aware of it, Lyn Lisa knew nothing of Doug's involvement with the illicit gun trade.

Willy's story was simple enough. Each night Doug went off to the Casbah section of Algiers, returning about 11 P.M. Except one night he did not return. Instead, Willy was awakened at 6 A.M. by Badis, Doug's contact with the rebels of the *Etoile Nord-Africaine*. Badis told Willy to follow him; Doug Kenney had been badly hurt. There were those who suspected Kenney was a *bleu*, a double agent, Badis said. Or perhaps the French discovered he was selling guns to the rebels, and had attempted what they termed an *operation ponctuelle* — an execution.

They hurried through the narrow alleyways of the Casbah to a small house fronting one of the alleys. In a barren anteroom, Willy found Doug Kenney lying on a narrow cot. There was a bullet hole in his chest. His white shirt and suit jacket were stained with blood. He was dead. When he turned to say something, Badis had disappeared, fled into the night, leaving Willy with the corpse of his friend.

Six months after he first visited her, Willy Conlon married Lyn Lisa Kenney. In retrospect, it was hard to say why she did it. She remained very much in love with the memory of Doug Kenney. Her New York friends all were appalled that she would marry a man from *Toronto*. They were further appalled when they discovered she actually was going to live there so that Willy could pursue his business career. They were most appalled, however, by Willy himself. They considered him a bore, and a provincial one at that. He was handsome enough, with dark curly hair, and a strong jaw, standing more than six feet two inches tall. But he drank a lot and became obnoxious when he did. But Lyn Lisa listened to no one. Willy was her link to the memory of Doug. She would not allow that link to disappear from her life. She duly followed Willy to Toronto.

For his part, Willy was absolutely mesmerized by his catch. Lyn Lisa, despite her Ohio roots, was New York sleek, and when he arrived with her in Toronto everyone was totally in awe. What's more, as he confided on several occasions when drunk at his private club, she was indeed the wildcat in bed, as accomplished as the *Ouled-Nail* girl. Except he never talked about her. Never dared mention her.

There was hardly an opportunity to settle in Toronto before World War II broke out and Willy was off to drive a tank around North Africa with the Fourth Canadian Armored Division. By the time the war ended and Willy came home, Lyn was supremely bored with Toronto. It was a glum, claustrophobic city, where everything seemed to be prohibited on the general principle that it might be fun. It was populated by stiff, conservative burghers who worried over religion and drink — particularly when the city actually allowed *cocktail bars* to open on Yonge Street. The hatcheries of hell, someone called them. Everyone was totally obsessed with anything British. Their friends loved to brag they were more British than the British. They sniffed in horror at the immigrants who began crowding into the city at war's end.

It did not take Lyn long to become just as bored with Willy as she was with everything else in the city. Their first child was born in 1945, and if it was not for the dark-haired presence of Malcolm Ashley, his mother would surely have gone mad. As it was, she doted on the boy, spent her every waking hour attending to his needs. The father grumbled that the child was being spoiled. But then the father wasn't paying much attention. He was drinking more than ever, and he was not much of anything in bed. She found herself without friends, interests, or sex. She considered having an affair, but there was no one to have an affair with. There was no one she even wanted to talk to, let alone sleep with. She spent even more time with young Ashley.

Then the nightmares began. Willy would wake up night after night, screaming and trembling with fear. The nightmares caused him to drink even more heavily. One night when he came home very late from his club he hit her. A few weeks later he struck her again. She began to despise him terribly.

It was the drinking, and the remorse that generally followed, that led to the confession. It came one wintry night in March 1950. Willy had had a particularly bad couple of weeks, afraid to sleep because of the nightmares, drinking constantly, too sick from the whiskey to go to work. By this time they were in separate bedrooms, and that night, Willy, overweight and balding now, his face flushed permanently red, stumbled into her room and began to sob. His bad dreams, he said, were of Douglas Kenney. They had started during the war. In North Africa. It was as though his return to that part of the world had forced him to confront the past.

He was a liar, he admitted. And he was a killer. He had murdered Doug Kenney. He told her about the *Ouled-Nail* girl, how he had gone to the house of Badis one night and discovered her in bed. She was naked, entwined in the arms of Doug Kenney. They had laughed at his anguish and invited him to join them. He had begun to carry a pistol for his protection in the Casbah, he said. In a fit of rage, he drew the weapon and fired. He kept firing until the pistol was empty. He didn't remember anything else for a long time. The next thing he knew he was stumbling down the narrow alleyways of the Casbah. The following morning, he got on a plane and left Algiers.

It was not until he reached Toronto that he began to feel the pangs of guilt. The least he could do, he reasoned, was to let Doug's widow know that he was dead. So he created an appropriate fiction, nothing too far from the truth, and traveled to New York. He had not expected to fall in love with Lyn Lisa. But that's exactly what happened. In time, he even came to believe the story he had created. Until he went back to North Africa, that is. Then Doug came to him every night, walking casually toward him across the desert sands, reminding him constantly of the murderous truth.

Oh, God, he moaned. Could she ever forgive him? Only then could he find any peace.

Lyn Lisa Conlon waited a week before she acted. Outside their Rosedale mansion, the wind wailed against the leaded windows. She stood before a full-length mirror in her bedroom and allowed the chemise to slip off her shoulders. Beneath it, she wore only stockings, a garter belt, and high-heeled shoes. She looked properly whorish, she thought. Like one of the women on the covers of those paperback novels that were beginning to proliferate.

She had painted her eyelids purple and colored her mouth with garish red lipstick. She applied perfume behind her ears and beneath her breasts. And then she waited.

Willy, red-faced, pumped full of hope and Canadian Club, slipped into the bedroom. She kissed him tenderly, stripped off his pajamas, then insisted that he be seated in the wing chair in the corner of the bedroom. She knelt between his legs. After considerable work, she gained from him the appropriate erection. He sighed that there was no one like her. She rose up, straddled him, then began slowly to pump up and down atop him.

Willy's puffy head rolled back against the chair. His mouth opened and closed. It reminded her of the mouth of a hungry bass. Then, maintaining her rhythm, she leaned forward. Her fingers slipped away from his shoulders down to the night table she had positioned just behind the chair. Willy began to gasp out indications that he was about to achieve his first orgasm in six months.

Lyn Lisa leaned forward, urging him on. Her fingers

searched along the surface of the table. He announced loudly that he was going to come. Her fingers closed around the butt of Willy's army revolver.

Then Willy began to come. That's it, Lyn Lisa cooed. That's it, darling. Come in me. His mouth gaped even wider. She lifted the gun off the table. Her hand moved firmly around the grip, the forefinger slipping against the trigger. She brought the gun up and around, and shoved its barrel deeply into his waiting mouth. Involuntarily, Willy's teeth closed around the barrel. He tasted the bitterness of cold metal. His eyes blinked open. At that moment, Lyn Lisa pulled the trigger. The back of Willy's head blew all over the chair and the wall.

Behind her, Lyn Lisa heard the bedroom door open. She still straddled her husband's corpse as she twisted around.

She heard a voice call out.

"Mother . . ."

1

"What do you mean he disappeared?" Tom Coward glanced at the digital clock on the bedside table in his Beverly Wilshire Hotel suite. It was nine-thirty in the morning — far too early for a Hollywood crisis.

The voice of the publicist, Kit Parker, was clipped. "That is to say, no one can find him."

"But he is making a movie," Tom said. "His first big Hollywood movie. Remember?" He sat up in the acre of bed. A thin spike of Beverly Hills sunlight, having wiggled through a crevice in the drapes, now crept across the lime-green broadloom. Tom's head throbbed. His mouth was as dry and pasty as a hamburger on Hollywood Boulevard.

"Not this week he isn't," said Kit Parker. "He's closed down the set."

"He's what? When did this happen?"

"A couple of days ago."

"Listen, Kit, a couple of days ago you were telling me Lex Madison was anxious to do the interview. I was telling my syndicate in New York Lex Madison was anxious to do the interview."

"Nobody told me anything," Kit Parker said. Her voice maintained a professional distance. "I'm sure Lex will talk to you, Tom. There's been a delay, that's all."

"Where did Madison go?"

Kit paused over that question for a moment. "No one seems to know."

"Doesn't this strike you as, ah, unusual?"

"I suppose it does, but I'm not that familiar with the mechanics of the business."

"Let me tell you," Tom Coward said. "It's unusual. Lex Madison is a director in the midst of shooting a twenty-million-dollar movie. He disappears. No one knows where he is. That's unusual."

"There's nothing much I can do about it," Kit Parker said defensively.

"Will you call me as soon as you hear from him?"

"Definitely."

"Call me even if you don't hear from him. I can't wait around forever."

"I understand that," Kit said. "It *is* very curious. But then if you ask me, Lex Madison is very curious."

"That's why I'm doing the story. *If* I do the story."

"You'll get the story. Don't worry."

"Keep in touch," he said.

After he hung up, he flipped on the radio. Rick Dees was doing his imitation of Sammy Davis for the KIIS radio listeners. Traffic was not moving on the Hollywood Freeway. There was smog in the valley. As Tom shambled naked past clothes strewn across the carpet, Bruce Springsteen began to sing that he wasn't anything but tired, tired and bored with himself. Tom could understand how he felt. The room was a shambles. His battered Italian leather carryall was pushed in a corner. The nylon suit bag was draped across the table, nearly obscuring the battery-powered Typestar Six typewriter and the Panasonic pocket tape recorder. He had knocked the pile of L.A. papers, the copies of *Variety* and *Hollywood Reporter*, off the dresser, along with his paperback edition of *The Little Drummer Girl*. He had left what remained of the Mouton Cadet open on the top of the dresser, beside the wineglass.

He reached the refrigerator and retrieved the fresh bottle of Mumm's along with a carton of orange juice. He popped the cork in the gold bathroom, the mirrors re-fracting the light into subdued patterns that did not make him look as bad as he felt. Bruce was further informing his audience that you just sit around getting older. There was a joke here somewhere, he said, and it was on him. "Not on you, Bruce," Tom said. "Not on you." He poured a good deal of champagne and a little orange juice into a water glass and downed the mixture in a single gulp. His head continued to throb. He tried another glass and felt better. He studied his countenance, blurred and beaten when viewed at close quarters, in one of the mirrors, and surmised that once again he had drunk too much the night before.

Over his third glass of champagne, he considered the reason for this: Samantha "Stormy" Willis, actress, model, and love of his life. Or former love of his life. That distinction was important. If she was not the former love of his life, he would not have the hangover. Would he? He would not now be considering the possibility of mak-ing a fool of himself by telephoning her and attempting yet again to convince her to take him back. He stared into the mirror. This was not a face, he decided, anyone would take back.

Nonetheless, he carried his glass of champagne back into the bedroom. He turned down Madonna's plaintive wail on the radio, sipped at the champagne once again, gained strength and resolve, and picked up the receiver. The operator came on the line to reassure herself that someone in L.A. really would call Toronto, made sure he was staying in a hotel room, and put him through to Stormy Willis.

Her voice was breathless. "Yes?" she demanded.

"Stormy," he said.

"Tom?" She sounded amazed, as though he were the last person on earth, and she had not expected him to call.

"Yes, Tom," he affirmed. "Of course, Tom. You're waiting for a call from Ronald Reagan?"

"Tom, this is one hell of a bad time to call."

"Is someone there?"

"No. No one's here." She sounded strained, irritable. She did not sound like Stormy.

"What's wrong?"

"There has been a murder."

"A what?"

"A murder. The woman next door is dead. I found the body."

Tom looked at his glass, as though its contents were responsible for what he was hearing. "Body? You found a body? Where the hell did you find her body?"

"Tom, for Christ's sake."

"But you're not making any sense."

She drew in a breath. "I found the body," she explained, speaking very carefully. "I found the body in her apartment. I was supposed to drive her to work this morning."

"Who is her?" Tom demanded.

"For God's sake. Carrie Wayborn."

"Who is Carrie Wayborn? You don't know anyone named Carrie Wayborn."

"I do so," Stormy maintained. "Well, I sort of know her. We talked a fair amount. She lives right next door to this house, Tom. Or lived right next door. I don't know. Anyhow, we chatted about cars. She has a Maserati. I've always been crazy about them, you know that. She gave me a spin in hers a couple of times. Then yesterday the fuel pump on her car went."

"The fuel pump," Tom said.

"That's right. The fuel pump. I offered to give her a lift this morning. She had to be downtown first thing. She had some sort of appointment at the bank. It was really important for the future of her business or something. She owns Intimate Moments."

"I feel ridiculous asking these questions. What's Intimate Moments?"

She sighed again. "Sexual aids."

"Intimate Moments is sexual aids?"

"That's right. She retails sexual aids. That's what she called them. Sexual aids. You know, sexy underwear. Dildos. That sort of thing."

"Good grief," Tom said. "In Toronto yet. No wonder she was killed."

"Tom, this is not funny. Believe me. This is not funny."

"I'm sorry. Tell me what happened."

"She was supposed to knock on my door this morning. Only she never arrived. I waited, then I telephoned. No one answered. I started to get worried then, because I knew how anxious she was to get to this appointment. I went over to her apartment, knocked a few times. I called out her name, and still nothing. I was about to leave, but just for the hell of it I tried the door handle. It was unlocked. I opened the door and peeked in, called her name. Then I went inside, thinking maybe she had slept in or something. The apartment was really quite beautiful. Matelasse cotton sofas. A lovely lacquered Japanese chest. And then I saw her." Stormy paused to swallow. "She was lying on her back along a corridor just off the living room. She was naked, Tom. Actually, she was wearing black chiffon tap pants. But that was it. She was very white. Her eyes were wide open. And bulging. It just looked awful. And there was some sort of dreadful foam around her mouth."

"Foam?"

"At first I thought she was frothing at the mouth or something. But the police say it's not froth at all."

"What is it?"

"Carpet cleaner."

Tom could not help laughing. "Come on," he said. "Nobody kills anyone with carpet cleaner."

"Tom," she said impatiently. "This is not funny. Who-

ever killed Carrie Wayborn squirted carpet cleaner down
her throat. She choked to death on the stuff."
"What did you do when you found her?"
"I thought I would scream. I felt like screaming. But
then everyone expects women to scream, so I thought,
to hell with that. I'm not going to say a word. I just re-
membered that you're not supposed to touch anything,
and backed out of there. I ran here and telephoned the
police. That was a couple of hours ago. It's been chaos
ever since."
"Are you okay?"
"I'm—well, I'm in a hurry," Stormy said. "Listen, Tom.
The police are here. They want to talk again. God, what
a mess. I have to go."
"Can I talk to you later?"
"There's nothing to talk about, really."
"For God's sake, you just found a murdered woman,
Stormy. I want to make sure you're all right."
"Okay, okay," she said hurriedly. "Call me back in a
couple of hours."
The line went dead.

Stormy Willis grew up in Kingston, Ontario, and attended Queen's University, where she was an English lit
major. She was the only person Tom knew who had read
Malcom Lowry's *Under the Volcano* from cover to cover
and actually seemed to understand it. She had entered a
beauty contest in Ogdensburg, New York, as a college
lark, and had won it. The next thing she knew she was in
Los Angeles taking acting lessons from Jeff Corey, who
thought she looked wonderful with that natural white-
blond hair, and those smoky hazel eyes, but did not think
she would ever be a great actress. Stormy was inclined to
agree. She was self-conscious about acting. She could
never shake the feeling that it was rather silly.
Tom met her a couple of years after that. She was in a

movie shooting in Toronto called *Death Elevator*, produced by Tom's friend Alvin Jarvis. Stormy was cast as the promiscuous teenager who was slashed to death just after the credits. It was, she later joked, the role of her career. Tom took her out to dinner and then back to his hotel, where he had the surprise of a lifetime. When he undid her blouse and took off her bra these incredible, gravity-defying breasts popped out into his hands.

He could not believe them. They stood bravely at attention, with large nipples the color of pink Italian marble. She tried to hide them, but he pulled her hands away, fondled them lovingly, marveled at their firmness. Where the hell, he demanded, had she gotten *these*? They were, she admitted, creations not of nature but of cosmetics. She had them "done." She had lived briefly with a skin-magazine publisher. She was young and gullible in those days, not to mention flat-chested, and very self-conscious about it. Particularly in Los Angeles, where sizable bosoms were as plentiful as palm trees. The publisher noted that this was Hollywood, where everything could be fixed. Face. Hair. Voice. Anything. Even tits. He suggested silicone implants. In a moment of prefeminist madness, she had gone along with him. Now she had these gigantic . . . *tits*. And she did not know what to do with them. They were the residue from another time. She felt much differently now. Here, said Tom Coward, directing the left one toward his mouth. I will show you what to do with them.

Frankly, none of Stormy Willis's friends thought she should have become involved with Tom Coward in the first place. They all agreed Tom was charming enough, and there was a certain amount of glamor connected with him and his job. But he was so, well, so *unreliable*, and Stormy was at a time in her life when reliability was becoming more important.

After all, she had had her flings: three years in Los Angeles trying to get work as an actress. A live-in relationship with the aforementioned skin-magazine publisher.
But now she was back in Toronto, having, understand-
ably, soured on Hollywood. She was in demand as a
model, and she did the odd acting part to pay the rent.
She had had her frivolous years. She still had the big
knockers to remind her of them. Her friends recognized
that what Stormy now sought was *substance*. There appeared to be no substance at all to Tom Coward. For one
thing, he was not even in town three quarters of the time.
While everyone wrestled with a mortgage, Tom defined
his life with the perimeters afforded by a first-class hotel
room. Someone joked that Tom never drank from a water glass that he did not first have to free from a waxed-
paper wrapper. Someone else laughed that Tom Coward
could not possibly live in an environment without twenty-
four-hour room service.

He was a hotel gypsy. If he was in Los Angeles, then
one could leave messages at the Beverly Wilshire. In New
York, he refused to stay anywhere but the Plaza. Dallas?
The Loew's Anatole. San Francisco? They knew him at
the Fairmont.

When he was in London, Tom preferred Claridge's. In
Paris either the Crillon, the Ritz, or the Georges V. In the
south of France, he took nothing less than the Hotel du
Cap at Eden Roc, although during the film festival at
nearby Cannes he would, in a pinch, stay at the Carlton.
It was awfully noisy, but all the waiters knew him on the
terrace, and he was always assured of getting a table.

It was not where Tom Coward stayed, it was that he
never stayed anywhere for long. Tom Coward, Stormy
herself once conceded, was a nomad, moving from hotel
to hotel awaiting the next interview with the next celebrity,
always restless, always rumpled, always unwilling to
settle down.

Initially, none of that mattered. Tom was fun, and Stormy, even though she sought substance as an antidote to the insubstantial life she had been leading in California, still appreciated fun. There was something, even his critics agreed, terribly romantic about Tom; a big lug constantly outfitted in a leather jacket, and a snap-brimmed fedora who insisted on drinking champagne and orange juice for breakfast each morning.

But after a time, one began to look for something beyond the merely romantic. When you did that with Tom Coward, there was nothing. Not ambition. Not commitment. None of the qualities that eventually were demanded of most men. After a while, Stormy found the champagne just plain irritating. She thought he drank too much, and stayed out too late, and he didn't show up when he was supposed to.

Tom had made an attempt to clean up his act. He had even said he was ready to settle down. After all, he was now thirty-three years of age, and it was time he was more responsible. He and Stormy found a lovely old house with gabled windows in the Beaches area of Toronto, just north of Lake Ontario. The house was a bit of a wreck, and it leaned precariously toward the big brick apartment building where some time later Stormy would discover the body of Carrie Wayborn. They would fix up the house, Tom announced, with that rakish grin he could haul out so reassuringly on such occasions.

They no sooner moved in than he was off to Israel for a week to do a piece on a fading movie star, leaving Stormy with a paintbrush and a lot of wallpaper. She had drawn two strokes across a wall when she decided she did not like this at all. The frivolous plaything of a skin-magazine publisher, the would-be Hollywood starlet, had not died as easily as she imagined. Besides, being the child of solid middle-class parents, she still felt this sort of thing came under the category of men's work.

It was not that their life went from bad to worse. It was that over the course of their year together it never quite got to good. Fun on occasion. Certainly lively. But never *good*, as in, we have a *good* life together. Sometimes, the rare quiet times, Stormy would sit with Tom by the fire in their tiny living room, watching that unhandsome but attractive face of his. It was a long, white face. A face, she concluded, that had been in too many movie theaters, too many bars, and too many strange beds. It suggested in its ruggedly formed lines and creases that it was somehow older than its thirty-three years. And somehow younger, too. It was a face that had tried hard never to become an adult, yet somehow had been pushed into it. Tom's face summed up Tom as well as anything that could be said about him. Tom would never grow up. Yet Tom was grown up. That was the paradox, and Stormy found it increasingly difficult to deal with it the longer they lived together.

What happened next, Stormy's friends stated, was inevitable. Stormy, as was her wont on Saturday mornings, was standing in the checkout line of her neighborhood Family Food Fair, flipping through the latest edition of the *National Enquirer* — also her wont, although she declined to admit to anyone that she even looked at it. There, on page fifteen, in living color for Christ's sake, was Tom Coward. He hung fondly onto the elbow of the former Olympic pentathlete turned ABC television personality, Constance (Connie) Armitage. Connie, blond and freckled, with her tanned and freckled tits (not nearly as nice as hers, Stormy noted) hanging out of something suede and chic, was described as being with an "unidentified escort." She was arriving for an opening-night party at the Hard Rock Cafe, providing the cameras with what Stormy described as a big horsey grin. As for the "unidentified escort," Stormy snorted, she could certainly identify him. What the hell was this particular escort, who was supposed to be in Los Angeles, doing in New York? All night long she pictured Tom's stubby fingers lifting those freckled tits out of Connie's suede-and-chic something. Stormy boiled.

Tom, as he always did, had an explanation: he had gone to L.A. to interview Connie Armitage, only to discover she was in New York. The date at the Hard Rock Cafe? It was not a date at all, he protested. Merely the pursuit of the story. But Stormy could not be placated. She ended up doing something she had never done before: she slapped him hard across the face. The damage was done, and it was not to be easily undone.

2

Tom had a long cold shower and some more champagne, and emerged from the bathroom, glass in hand. On the radio, Rick Dees was doing his Jimmy Stewart impression. Traffic was backed up on the Ventura Freeway. The temperature was headed up to ninety degrees. Everything was perfect in southern California. Back in Toronto, though, Stormy Willis could not talk to him because she had found a dead body. Maybe he already had had too much champagne. His Stormy, after all, did not find dead bodies. He managed to wait an hour and three quarters before he called her again.

At first he got the answering machine. "Hi, this is Stormy Willis. . . ." But then she picked up the receiver.

"Tom? Just hold on." She clicked off the machine.

"I hate answering machines," Tom said. "Are you all right?"

"A little shaky, I guess. This is all just starting to hit me. God, Tom. I've never even seen a dead body before, except on the news. And the police. They keep asking me questions. Now they want me to go down to the police station. I mean I hardly knew Carrie Wayborn. They keep asking me about her boyfriends and that sort of thing. I don't know what to say. I don't know anything about boyfriends. Everybody is worried that some sort of sex maniac is loose in the neighborhood, one who goes around killing women with rug cleaner. Apparently whoever killed Carrie screwed her first. At least that's what this sergeant told me. It's not public or anything. But they found semen in her vagina, and in her mouth too. Ugh.''

"You don't like semen in your mouth?''

"Not mixed with rug cleaner, I don't. Thank you very much.''

"Is there anything I can do to help?''

There was silence on the line for a moment. "You could give me a little breathing space, Tom.'' The voice was not unkind, but the statement was offered flat, without adornment.

"Well, I'm worried about you, that's all. It's not every day someone you know finds a body. Do the police have any idea who killed her?''

"They don't seem to. They think it was someone who knew her. Because, you know, she had sex with him and everything. The police keep saying that most people are killed by people they know. That's why they want to find out about her boyfriends. Apparently she had a very active social life. *Very* active. In fact, she sounds like your kind of girl.''

"I'm talking to my kind of girl,'' he said.

"I'd better get going,'' Stormy said. "I'm late as it is.''

"I miss you,'' Tom said.

"Don't miss me, Tom,'' she said. "Please don't miss me. You didn't miss me when it counted. Don't miss me now. Okay?''

"We're still friends?''

"We're still friends,'' she agreed.

"Then there is hope.''

The silence rumbled along the line.

Originally, they were not supposed to break up for good. There would be a "cooling-off period" (his term). He had to find out "what it is he wanted" (her term). They had in her words (his?) "drifted apart.'' They were — his words (hers?) — going to "live apart in order to get back together.'' He was not sure, he told himself, whether

he was ready to ''settle down,'' to ''make a commitment.''
In the end, all the carefully employed buzzwords didn't
make any difference. He left for New York and more as-
signments, swinging the tape recorder and the overnight
bag over his shoulder. She did modeling jobs and the odd
acting stint, and stayed alone in their house. He said he
would call her every day. He called her twice a week for
two weeks. Then Stormy didn't hear anything from him
for three weeks. When she heard from him again, she
didn't want to hear from him.

Tom had a day in Toronto before flying off to Los Angeles to talk to Canadian director Lex Madison. He called
Stormy for lunch. Yes, she said quietly. It was time they
talked. They met at the Courtyard Cafe. She was dressed
in electric blue, an outfit that could not hide the lush
contours of her body. She was inspected avidly as she
was escorted to the leatherette banquette. The brass and
the ferns glittered under the huge skylight. Stormy
wrapped a long strand of hair around her finger, ordered
a glass of white wine, and told Tom Coward that she was
in love with someone else.

Tom was stoic. ''When did this happen?''

''Recently.''

''Obviously recently. I mean a month and a half ago
we were living together. So it had to be recently.''

''A couple of weeks.''

''You're in love with someone you met two weeks ago.''

''Yes.'' Flat statement.

Stormy's friends said that if it had not been Ashley
Conlon it would have been someone else. But it *was* Ashley Conlon, and the women who knew Stormy, friends
who otherwise were sane and sound and not easily
swayed by male charm, tended to get weak at the knees
when his name was mentioned. It was all very well to be
liberated, they agreed, but they were now into their thirties and a trifle concerned about spending the rest of their

lives alone. They were therefore willing to reassess their opinions on the institution of marriage. And if you were Stormy, with this pale Madonna's face and a body that would stop the traffic — even if the two most obvious parts of it were a trifle fabricated (this from the catty friends) — why not go for the best?

Ashley Conlon was wealthy. There was talk of family money. He was also a partner in one of the big Bay Street law firms. He drove a Porsche, dressed in Italian designer clothes, and looked like, well, everyone thought he was cuter even than Richard Gere. Sexier than Mel Gibson. In other words, very cute and very sexy. Stormy was not quite so easily swayed, at least not initially.

She met Ash Conlon at one of those chic urban Sunday brunches where smoked salmon is consumed on a pine deck overlooking an alley. White wine was sipped from long-stemmed glasses. Everyone was divorced or separated, bonded together into curious middle-aged friendships that had to do with loneliness and the banalities of once again living a life on one's own.

They talked a lot about movies, Stormy recalled later. Ash was crazy about movies. He loved the old stars. Gable. Bogart. Tracy. Flynn. Gary Cooper. The matinee idols. The guys who commanded the screen. The women were all right too, Stormy interjected. Bette Davis did a pretty good job of holding onto the screen. Sure, sure, he said. But they don't make men like that any more. Men don't have faces like that any more. That heroic, larger-than-life quality. It was like Patty Hearst's mother said when her daughter was kidnaped. What was that? Stormy inquired. If Clark Gable were still alive this would never have happened. They both had a good laugh.

The next day he called, and in a purring masculine telephone voice asked her to lunch. They had a romantic meal at Fenton's Garden Room, among the oleander blossoms and the bougainvillea. She had poached eggs with

shrimps, mushrooms, and cream sauce. She didn't notice what he had, because by the time the lemon cheese-
cake arrived they were discreetly holding hands. And she
was crazy about him.

"Maybe you're confused," Tom said hopefully. He was
eating salad with chicken. She was consuming salad with
salad. They were not holding hands.

"I'm not, Tom," she replied. He hated that firmness in
her voice. "Not about this, anyway. We haven't gotten
along, Tom. I haven't seen you for almost a month. Three
quarters of the time I don't even know where you are. I
think you're in London. You phone from Los Angeles."

"But I love you, Stormy."

"That isn't enough. Just saying it isn't enough. You
know that. You announce your love on the way to the
airport. That's not love. That's a holding action so you
can get out of town without a hassle."

"I'll change," Tom said. He did not sound convincing.

"Tom," she said earnestly, leaning forward, searching
his face with those fathomless hazel eyes. "I don't want
you to change. I want you to give up on this. I think it's
best for both of us. It's the healthiest thing to do."

"It's healthy to go running off with a guy you've known
for two weeks? Stormy, there is a crazy streak in you,
there really is. You want to be a middle-class housewife.
Except you end up getting your breasts done over, and
living with a skin-magazine publisher. You're capable of
impetuousness, and you know it. And that's a dangerous character trait."

"Tom, you're talking about a woman who existed a long
time ago. Besides, I want to be with him. I want to see if
it works. *I have* to see if it works. We're certainly going
nowhere together."

"Are you going to marry him?"

"I don't know."

"Have you talked about marriage?"

Pause. ''Talked about it? Yes, we've talked about it. We've made no decisions. But we've talked. We talk about everything.''

He sat there in the cramped leatherette banquette, studying her closely, taking small mental snapshots to study later in hopes of discovering a flicker or a waver, some sign that she was putting him on. The view of her placid, invigorating beauty began to moisten and blur. This surprised her even more than it surprised him. She did not think he had a tear in him.

''Tom,'' she said gently, reasonably. ''You don't want responsible. I want responsible.''

''Tell me you don't love me any more,'' he said.

She said nothing. The hazel eyes swung away from him.

Tom shaved, dressed, finished off the champagne in the water glass, then took the gold-and-glass elevator to the lobby. French tourists strayed across the wine-red carpeting. He strolled around to the newsstand. Gray-haired old gentlemen in Lacoste shirts waited momentarily to be seated in the Cafe of the Pink Turtle, a coffee shop that contained no signs of pink turtles.

In the newsstand, he viewed himself in ghostly black and white as the cameras hanging over the magazines picked him up and cast his image on the little television screen that sat on the glass-topped counter beside the salesgirl. He did not look happy. He paid for his copy of *Daily Variety*. The woman gave him a cheery smile and, like everyone else in southern California, ordered him to have a nice day.

He went into the coffee shop. The gray-haired gentlemen now leaned over tables talking closely together, hatching movie deals that would never get across Wilshire Boulevard. The waitress who escorted him to his seat had a single request: please, have a nice day.

Tom gritted his teeth, ordered black coffee, and opened

the paper. Movie production was up 20 percent this year. But the studios had spent two hundred million dollars more making movies than the public spent to see them. Tom glanced around. Nobody seemed worried about the shortfall. There was yet another shake-up at 20th Century Fox. Someone had just signed a three-picture pact at Universal. That is, there was a three-picture pact if the first picture was a hit. If it wasn't, the three-picture deal would disappear faster than a table for lunch at Ma Maison.

The coffee arrived as Tom began to read Army Archerd's column. The Canadian director Lex Madison was well into production of his biggest feature to date, Army reported. The producer, Arnold Berne, was quoted as saying that, contrary to rumors, this was not a horror picture. It was a psychological suspense thriller. That meant there was no killer hacking up promiscuous teenagers. Army said production on the picture was ten days behind schedule, and there were reports Madison and Lea, his wife of three years, had separated.

Army then went on to remind his readers that Lex, at the age of thirty-nine, was something of a *wunderkind*. His low-budget horror pictures, produced mostly in Toronto, had taken on cult status in the past few years. As far as Army was concerned, Lex had made the best picture ever to emerge from that land of ice and snow. It was titled *Zoom-Zoom*, and stood as the definitive statement on troubled youth in the alienated sixties. There was no mention that the author of the definitive statement on troubled youth in the alienated sixties had disappeared.

But then neither had Army received the news that Tom Coward, ace reporter of the totally frivolous and inconsequential, was sitting in the Cafe of the Pink Turtle, with a terrible hangover, sipping black coffee, and feeling sorry for himself. Not all the news was fit for print, he guessed.

3

'He has returned," Kit Parker announced breathlessly over the telephone. "Lex is back."

It was three days later, and Tom was burning by the pool. He wore cheap plastic wraparound sunglasses. He lay on the yellow chaise longue in a latticed and arched ersatz Mediterranean setting, keeping a close eye on the water spurting out of the fountain and into the azure blue of the pool. He pretended not to be watching the beauty in the wet T-shirt and the red-and-white striped bikini bottom who lounged at the pool's edge. Her boyfriend, a man of enormous girth, smelling of cigars, suntan lotion, and money, glared at the world from behind mirror-lensed sunglasses.

"Where was he?"

"Toronto."

The beauty got up, rearranged the bikini bottom across a voluptuous behind, and went over and flicked water at the gent with the girth and the money. He said, "Fuck, Sherry," and tumbled off his chaise longue.

"What was he doing in Toronto?"

"Off the record?"

"Certainly."

"I think he went back up there to see if he could get back together with his wife, Lea. Judging by his mood, he failed."

"His mood is bad?"

"Lex's mood is always a fragile thing. One moment he's your best friend, and the world's most charming guy.

The next moment he's acting as though he could be happy operating a death squad in El Salvador. Mercurial. That's how I would describe our Lex."

"Great," Tom said without enthusiasm.

"Anyhow, you can find out for yourself tonight. At Lex's beach house in Malibu. He'll talk to you there. Can you get out there yourself? Barry Manilow is at the Universal Amphitheater, and I managed to get some tickets."

"Lucky you," Tom said.

"About seven o'clock," Kit said. "Lex is expecting you. I'll give you the address. Can I be honest with you?"

"Aren't you always?"

"Lex doesn't trust the press."

"Good old Lex."

"He may have Tina out at the house, that's all."

"Who is Tina?"

"Tina is Tina Deni. Tina is the star of the movie. Tina has a snub nose, big tits, and no class."

"Sounds like my kind of girl."

"Lex is worried you might write about her."

"I can't write about her if I don't see her."

"I mean he doesn't want anything that appears in print to interfere with the possible reconciliation of his marriage."

"I think that's called having your cake and eating it, too," Tom said.

"No, no, darling," Kit said. "That's called Men in Hollywood. Anyway, Lex is definitely eating his cake. Tina Deni was born so the Lex Madisons of the world could eat."

Tom Coward knew this much about Lex Madison. He had been born in the west end of Toronto. His father was a tailor and his mother a housewife who loved the movies. Almost every week she took her Lex to the pictures, usually at the old Loew's theater. Lex was fond of saying that he never wanted to be anything but a filmmaker. One of the great memories of his childhood was the moment when he divined that actors do not by accident end up in front of a camera, mouthing words that just happened to turn themselves into a story. Someone had to write those words and induce those actions. From the beginning, Lex decided he would be one of those people.

He started out making eight-millimeter movies starring his dog Captain and two little girls who lived next door. Occasionally, even his mother, Delores, would make a guest appearance, all fluttery and self-conscious. His father, a grim sewer of cloth, thought the whole enterprise ridiculous, his son's fascination frivolous and, what's more, a waste of time. More to please his father than anything else, Lex enrolled at the University of Toronto in the 1960s, halfheartedly intending to pursue a career in law. He had absolutely no interest in the subject; film increasingly was his obsession.

He founded a film society at a school that barely acknowledged the existence of celluloid, in a country that was cold and cultureless and imported its entertainment. The film society was called the Rear Window Society, after one of Lex's favorite movies, an Alfred Hitchcock thriller that starred James Stewart and Grace Kelly. It was about a man who peeked in windows. That, of course, was what movies were all about — a man peeking into a window and being continually amazed by what he saw.

But Lex wanted to do more than just look in the window. With the help of a couple of fellow students, he put together enough money to make a low-budget horror-movie spoof that he called *Schlock Treatment*. It was made for fifteen thousand dollars, and to the immense surprise of everyone involved, the picture was picked up by a small distributor and eventually grossed about five million dollars at the box office in Canada and the United States.

By that time Lex had dropped out of university. His

father had died, and there was no one to tell him not to get into the movies. With the proceeds from *Schlock Treatment*, he made a more ambitious film that attempted to deal with the turmoil of the sixties. The movie, which he titled *Zoom-Zoom*, caused quite a stir when it was shown to various producers and studio heads in New York and Los Angeles. It was deemed too raw and frightening for commercial release, and ended up in small art theaters that showed movies at midnight on the weekends.

Nevertheless, *Zoom-Zoom* was recognized as the work of a talented young director and writer. In 1969, Universal Studios signed Madison to a three-year contract. He toiled on the Universal sound stages, which were, in reality, factories, churning out television shows in much the same assembly-line fashion the large auto makers manufacture cars.

Madison learned to shoot fast, within a clearly defined time limit and budget. If a director on the lot went over on either time or budget, then he was removed. Simple as that. Lex never went over. He never made a mistake.

All the same, after two years, there was nothing left to learn. He got out of his contract and went back to Toronto, where, in the early seventies, he made a series of horror pictures that made money at the box office, made Madison quite rich, gained him an enormous cult following, and saddled him with a reputation for making ultraviolent films that shocked and offended large numbers of people. There was, critics pointed out, a great deal of hostility and anger in Lex's movies, particularly where women were concerned. Lex tended to dismiss that sort of talk as nonsense. Nevertheless, he remained one of the most controversial young directors working just outside the Hollywood mainstream. Now, with his new movie, Lex was wading into the mainstream once again. There was more than a little interest in how he would accomplish this.

Tom thought of these things at twilight as he parked his rented Firenza just off the Pacific Coast highway and walked down to Lex Madison's beach house. It was a rickety-looking two-story structure, shoehorned among the other homes that elbowed for narrow space along the twenty-seven most expensive miles of beach in the world. The Malibu colony was the demonstration of success, the acknowledgment that you could afford the minimum two million dollars it cost for a lot that measured no more than thirty by one hundred and twenty-five feet. This is where Lex now camped while he made another run at Hollywood.

Madison opened the door himself.

"Tom, hello," he said cheerfully. "Come in. Come in." He led the way through a tiny courtyard garden choked with bromeliads, cyclamens, and grapefruit trees. Lex pointed out the grapefruits. "We just pick 'em off the trees in the morning, and you've got your fresh-squeezed juice. Never get that in Toronto, I'm afraid."

He was all muscular energy barely held in check. His baldness made him look older than thirty-nine, but added to the impression that he was stripped down for action. The skin was pulled taut across his cheekbones, making his eyes seem all the more reptilian. He was friendly enough. But it was not a friendly face.

He wore a white flowing caftan that made him look like a particularly divine Ben Kingsley as Gandhi, or perhaps the not-so-benevolent leader of some weird southern California religious cult. He appeared to be naked beneath the robe. He carried a glass of white wine in his hand. As he gestured, some of the liquid slopped over the side and onto the caftan. The god had stained himself.

"Shit," he announced to the Santa Monica Mountains behind him and the azure-blue Pacific in front. On a bad day the mud could come sliding down from the mountains, the septic tanks could back up into the ocean, and a world-famous movie director could spill wine on his caftan. There was no justice, Tom thought.

Inside the house, Lex turned to him. His eyes were fierce, sitting dark and round like stone marbles beneath heavy lids. The stone marbles were burning. They were eyes that could peer into the infinities. He's coked to the eyeballs, Tom concluded. Lex allowed a small smile to play around his brown, hard features.

"Glad you could come, Tom," he said. "I thought this would be more pleasant than the set. More time to talk."

The room was low and wide, and it looked out through sliding glass doors at the ocean. There was a mirrored fireplace, shelves full of books, a lot of big ferns and lovely white flowers in delicate vases.

"Anyhow, it's just about over now. We've got a few more days of principal photography, and that's it. Then I go back to Toronto and start editing."

"Are you happy with it?"

"Happy?" He seemed to taste at the word, as though it were something quite foreign to his experience. "I'm perhaps too close to it, Tom, to be anything but relieved that it's over. This has not been an easy shoot. Not because it's a difficult movie logistically or anything like that. But there has been tremendous pressure from the studio. And of course there was the five-day shutdown. Forgive me. I'm not being much of a host here. Would you like a drink?"

Tom accepted white wine. Lex threw himself onto a low couch near a lacquered coffee table, and bade Tom draw near in an adjoining easy chair.

"I wanted to ask you about the shutdown," Tom said, producing a notebook.

Lex made a fluttering motion with the hand that was not holding the wineglass. "Script problems," he said. "The studio decided it wanted a PG rating. I thought we were going for an R. A number of scenes had to be toned down. I have, well, a reputation I suppose for a certain amount of carnage on the screen. The studio is concerned about that. We had some communications problems. I thought we'd better close down and get them settled before moving on.''

"What happened?''

Lex gave out another one of his tiny smiles. "We got them settled.''

"Do you think your reputation for movie violence hurts you?'' Tom asked.

"Look, I'm trying to tell stories in the movies,'' Lex said, a trace of irritation showing. "I'm trying to keep an audience hooked. There are certain ways of doing that. I've chosen the ways that keep an audience scared and a little bit titillated. We go to the movies because we want to have our emotions aroused in some way. Ivan Reitman makes you laugh. I like to scare the pants off you. I don't think there is anything wrong with that, any more than there is anything wrong with taking a ride on a roller coaster.''

"But the studio is obviously concerned.''

"They don't want a horror picture. They want a psychological suspense thriller.''

"Is there necessarily a difference?''

"In their minds there is. As I say, that's why the set was closed down.''

"There are reports you went back to Toronto.''

His eyes narrowed. "Where did you hear those reports?''

"I can't remember,'' Tom said.

From somewhere in the house, a telephone began to ring. Madison's eyes flicked away, then turned, bright and luminous, to Tom.

"I just felt I could write better in Toronto,'' Madison said. "Away from the studio.''

The telephone continued to ring. Madison seemed more tense now.

"Could you?'' Tom asked.

"Could I what?"

"Write better."

"I got the work done," Lex said tightly.

"It's just that there was some thought you went back to Toronto to try and patch things up with your wife."

The muscles in Lex Madison's face began to throb. The telephone stopped ringing.

"These are personal questions," Madison said. "I don't want to be unfriendly, Tom. I really don't. But this is not the point in my life when I want to discuss that sort of thing. I went back to Toronto to write. I wrote. We are continuing to shoot what I think will be a fine picture for the studio. Period."

"I'm sorry," Tom said. "It's a bad habit of mine. Asking the wrong questions at the wrong time."

Lex seemed to make a physical effort to shake himself back into a jovial mood. He forced another smile.

"Forget it," he said. "I'm a little uptight, myself. Why don't we both have another glass of wine?"

He got up from the couch just as a door off the living room burst open. A stunning young woman in a white-satin teddy flew in.

"Oh, Jesus, Lex," she wailed. Snub nose. Big tits. And no class. Tina Deni had made her entrance.

Lex looked genuinely horrified. "Tina, for God's sake—"

"She phoned again!" Tina howled. "That voice. Always that voice. Jesus. I can't take it any more. I can't."

Lex's skull looked as though it would burst right out of its skin. "Tina, please. Go into the other room. I'll be there in a moment."

"I'm sorry, baby, but I can't stand it. You promised she wouldn't call again."

Tina's wide eyes were wet and red, her mouth trembling, gearing up for more anguish. Lex didn't give her the chance. He grabbed her by the arm — Gandhi manhandling the playmate of the month — and swept her out of the room.

Tom got to his feet, stood there uncertainly. Lex hurried back. He looked ominous, all traces of the laid-back Malibu friendliness disappearing under the darkness.

"I'm afraid you're going to have to leave, Tom."

"We haven't talked much," Tom said.

"As you can see," he said between his teeth, "there has been an emergency. A personal matter. I have to take care of it."

"Maybe we can get together later."

Lex Madison curled his fist. "Get the fuck out of here," he hissed. "I've had about enough of this."

"I'll see myself to the door," Tom said cheerfully.

Lex Madison stood in his living room, outlandish in his caftan, looking less frightening than pitiable. The anger, flaring off his face, failed to hide the hurt and the anguish. Tom stopped at the door. Madison came up behind him.

"Look," Tom said, "in case you're worried, I'm not going to write anything about this. You may not think so, but I've got some idea of what you're going through."

Madison's face softened somewhat. "I thank you for that," he said quietly.

Tom opened the door and walked out without another word.

An hour later, Lex Madison snorted one line of the coke on the coffee table, then another. He sat back and drained his wineglass while Tina took the glass straw from him and did the other two lines laid out on the table. They both were naked. The house was in semi-darkness. Lex could hear the crash of the Pacific against the beach outside. This was better, he thought. No problems at moments like this. He was sorry about Coward. Every time he thought he had his temper in control, he managed to lose it. But maybe Coward understood. Maybe he understood that a man could still want his wife back, and need a little something on the side to hold him together. Tina pressed herself against him.

"I'm on the space shuttle," she murmured. "Now all I need is an Atlas rocket to get me into orbit." She giggled and wrapped small fingers around his penis. "Here's one now," she reported breathlessly. Twenty minutes later, they were on the floor, their writhing images reflecting off the mirrored front of the fireplace. Then the telephone rang again.

"Don't answer it," Tina said, trying to catch her breath.

"It's probably Don," Lex said. "He was going to call with the schedule changes for tomorrow."

He picked up the receiver. It was not Don with the schedule changes.

"Killer," the voice said.

"Who is this?" Lex said, knowing damn well who it was.

"It's your conscience, hon. The voice that knows you killed Carrie Wayborn. The voice that knows what a murdering bastard you really are."

Lex flung down the receiver. The effects of the cocaine were beginning to wear off, leaving him in that no-man's-land where the villains lurked everywhere. Oh, shit. He was lost.

"It was her again. Wasn't it her?" Tina lay on her back, staring up at him, ripe and ready, but scared as hell.

"Forget it," Lex said. "Forget everything. Get me some more coke."

"We've done enough, baby. I feel all strange."

"Look, just get me some more," he shouted. "Jesus Christ! Do as I say."

She scampered off as the words began to play back: *I know you did it. I know you killed Carrie.*

4

The next evening Tom Coward met his friend Alvin Jarvis, the producer, for drinks at the El Padrino bar, in the Beverly Wilshire. Saddle cinches acted as partitions between the banquettes, and a cozy Spanish darkness enveloped everything. It was the best place in the world in which to drink a margarita.

Tom had brought Stormy here on their first or second date in Los Angeles. She sneered at the Mexican saddles and the oil portrait of hotel owner Hernando Courtright, astride a white stallion looking, in his *charro* outfit, for all the world like the Cisco Kid. The El Padrino was too Old Hollywood for her. But she was the aspiring actress then, and she made a profession out of being hard to please. Or so Tom thought.

Still, he could not now walk into the place without feeling a twinge of nostalgia. Alvin, of course, wanted to hear about Lex Madison. Alvin never did like Lex, resented his success, and took unabashed pleasure in hearing the bad news about him.

"Horror movies are dead," Alvin said disdainfully. He had ordered a double bourbon and soda from the tall, long-haired waitress who somehow managed to pretend they did not exist.

"Lex says this isn't a horror movie," Tom said, after he ordered a glass of white wine.

Alvin chose not to hear this. "The kids are sick of that slasher shit. Physical movies, that's what the kids want now. Tits and ass."

"This from the creator of that horror classic, *Death Elevator.*"

"Listen, don't knock *Death Elevator.* We made it for five hundred thousand dollars. Grossed twenty million. But times change, and you have to change with them, Tom. Now the youth audience wants teenage girls showing off bare tits and making out with guys in cars with Duran Duran singing in the background. Go with the flow, I say. That's why I'm making *Buns.*"

"What the hell is *Buns?*"

"*Buns* is lots of bare asses. That's what *Buns* is. It is also my latest production. We've got a great script. We start shooting in Toronto in two weeks. *Buns* will be a bigger hit than even *Death Elevator.*"

Alvin signaled the waitress for another drink. Alvin's father sold books. He discovered that if you built bookstores that looked like supermarkets you could attract an awful lot of people who otherwise would never go into a bookstore. He also discovered that most books did not sell. Therefore, they could be bought up cheap and sold cheap in the bookstores that looked like supermarkets. This simple knowledge had made Alvin's father very rich indeed. Alvin's father had wanted Alvin to go into the book business. But Alvin had too much taste to sell old books in places that looked like supermarkets. He decided instead to make movies featuring slasher killers and horny teenagers. He was making a fortune.

"Anyway, I haven't been back to Toronto since those crazy tax-shelter days in the late 1970s. Christ, I never met so many Canadian dentists in all my life. They were all anxious to invest their money in movies and get a big tax writeoff. They all thought Richard Harris was a star. Crazy times."

"I may go up to Toronto," Tom said.

Alvin looked at him narrowly. "Why would you go back

to Toronto? I thought you were fed up with Toronto. Toronto is dull. Toronto is provincial. I believe those are accurate quotes from you."

Tom shrugged. "Lex Madison is from Toronto. I thought I might follow that up. Talk to some of the people who used to know him there."

"Yeah. Right." Alvin finished his drink. "Stormy wouldn't have anything to do with this, would she?"

"What would Stormy have to do with it?"

"Maybe you might go back there to try for some sort of reconciliation."

"The thought never crossed my mind."

"Okay, but if you're looking for an excuse to go to Toronto and get Stormy back, you could talk to a fellow named Arthur Grinton. He hosts some sort of local movie show up there. I was on it a couple of years ago, talking about the art of the B movie. Anyhow, he told me he used to know Lex at school."

"I'm not looking for an excuse to get Stormy back," Tom said. He wrote Arthur Grinton's name on the back of a coaster and deposited it in his pocket.

"I liked Stormy," Alvin said. "I really did. She was sweet, and she was vivacious. And she had the greatest pair of tits God ever created."

"God had nothing to do with it," Tom interjected.

"But she wanted you to settle down."

"What was wrong with that?"

"You tell me, Tom. You're the one who couldn't settle down. Hey, kid, we're a couple of drifters, and you know it. The goddamn middle class is constantly snapping at our asses. So far I've managed to elude it. They almost got you, though. Your little house near the lake. Home at five. 'Jesus, dear, I forgot the fucking quart of milk. Here, I'll run up to the store.' You could handle that about as well as I could. Which is to say you couldn't handle it at all."

Tom merely snorted at this. The waitress arrived with fresh drinks.

"Thank you, darling," Alvin said, giving her a leer copied the world over by independent movie producers. She returned a disdaining look that could only mean one thing: she was the only waitress in the greater Los Angeles area uninterested in a movie career.

Not that Alvin held out much promise of movie glory. He was squat and balding. A vague scratch of beard trailed hopefully around the bottom of his face. His uniform was simple and unchanging: windbreakers, Lacoste shirts, Lee jeans, and Frye boots. Alvin didn't own a suit, perhaps because there was no place, really, to hang it. He was, as he said, a nomad, moving restlessly through the first-class hotel rooms of the world. He was far too hyper for anything more permanent. He was in constant motion. Even when he was at rest his leg jerked up and down ceaselessly. He looked constantly for the next jolt in life, the next diversion.

"Okay," he said. "On the phone you promised to tell me about this guy Stormy is so crazy over."

"I think she is going to marry him."

"You think she is going to marry him? Who is he?"

"He's a lawyer, Alvin. If you can beat that. A goddamn lawyer."

"They make the best husbands. Does he have a name?"

"Ashley Conlon. Stormy says he is tall, dark, and handsome."

Alvin lifted his eyebrows and whistled softly. "You're kidding."

"You know him?"

"I know him," Alvin said grimly.

"Come on, then. What do you know?"

"He confuses me, I must say. There are certain decisions about Ash that I haven't been able to make."

"What decisions?"

"For instance," Alvin said, "I can't decide whether Ash Conlon is a bigger cocksucker than he is a crook. But I do know one thing for sure."

"What's that?"

"That he is both a cocksucker and a crook."

They debated about where to eat. Tom wanted the Mandarin or Mr. Chow's. But they settled on Spago on Sunset Boulevard, because Alvin wanted to be seen—he said. Although given the windbreaker and the beard, it was somewhat doubtful that anyone would want to see him. Paul Mazursky, the director, was at the next table, and didn't even glance up when Alvin sat down. Apparently he never had seen *Sorority Girls' Nightmare*. Alvin glanced hungrily over at the bar where a luscious blond sat waiting in something by Bill Blass. A moment later she was joined by a rock-jawed hero in a lightweight Perry Ellis suit. Alvin turned away and concentrated on ordering a bottle of Pouilly Fuisse from a waiter who had short brown hair and blazing green eyes, and who wanted to be in the movies. He looked longingly over at Paul Mazursky's table as he skittered away to get the wine.

"Tell me more," Tom said.

"About seven years ago I got involved in a deal to turn some romance novels into a series of movies. You know, the sort of thing where the girl is a fucking virgin until the fade out. Real women's fantasy stuff. I was dubious about how it would ever work on film, but what the hell. The money seemed to be there. We floated a stock option on the whole package. Now the trouble with those kind of financing deals was that in order to raise money you had to spend a lot of it. Ash Conlon was advertising himself as a lawyer and a financier. He got involved not only in selling units, but later as representative of those unit holders when it came time to sell the movies.

"Well, we shot the movies, and they were absolutely

terrible, and the problem was, as it always was in those days, getting distribution. Nobody wanted to touch it. I was still green. I had yet to learn that you never, never show a studio executive the finished product. You only show him the rushes. That way if it goes down the toilet, there's an out. The executive can always say, 'Gee, the rushes looked great.' Anyway, all we got out of these romance movies was a few foreign sales. The point is that the money never got into the hands of the unit holders or anyone else.''

''Where did it go?''

''If I could answer that question I could resolve the half dozen lawsuits still floating around from the fucking thing. However, I have my suspicions. My strong suspicions.''

''And those are?''

''I think Conlon took the cream off the top. So do a lot of other people. Well over three hundred thousand dollars in foreign-sales money supposedly came in, and only about fifty thousand dollars of that money is accounted for.''

''Do you know anything about his background?''

''Not much. He seemed to have a lot of money. He was very sure of himself. I thought he was a jerk, though.''

''Why did you think he was a jerk?''

''Because he never did anything except run around in expensive suits getting his hair cut and his nails done. Oh yes, he was also busy working out at his health club. He used to drive me crazy. I wouldn't have thought he could take time away from his busy schedule to steal money. But there you go.''

At the bar, the Perry Ellis suit moved away from the Bill Blass girl. Alvin got up from the table.

''Where are you going?'' Tom demanded.

''Business,'' Alvin said. ''Being a producer is something

you have to work at 24 hours a day. That blond at the bar would be perfect for *Buns*.''

"How do you know she wants to be in the movies?''

Alvin was genuinely taken aback. ''Are you kidding? Everyone wants to be in the movies.''

5

It took a couple of days for Kelly Langlois to find the right pigeon. At night she wandered around the Air Canada terminal at Los Angeles International Airport, sleeping fitfully on one of the hard plastic seats along the concourse. When she spotted him, she immediately knew she had found her man. He was tall and heavy, and it looked as though he wore a hairpiece. It hovered in tight black curls above a soft pink face that the thick handlebar mustache did not help much. He also wore a lemony leisure suit, with a wide-collared shirt that was open at the neck to reveal a couple of gold chains and a patch of hair. When she slipped onto the bar stool beside him in the lounge, he smelled of English Leather cologne. A real swinger. He even helpfully displayed his Air Canada ticket in a breast pocket, just to reassure her that he was headed for Toronto.

She told him, after he ordered her the Wild Turkey on ice, that she used to hang out with a lot of rock groups in Toronto. He asked her if she ever had met Kenny Rogers, and she managed to keep the smile fixed. No, she had never come across Kenny in her travels. Bob Dylan, Mick Jagger, Rod Stewart, sure. But not Kenny Rogers.

By this time he was aware there was no bra under the man's silk shirt she wore. The faded blue jeans adhered to her buttocks. Even though her features were hard and dark and a trifle worn around the edges, there was about her still this incredible bubbling witch's brew of sexuality. She did not often turn it on for men any more. But when she did, it still worked. And it worked now with Johnny. That was his name, he said. Johnny Karras. Greek extraction. No surprises there. He was divorced. No surprise there either. And he was vice-president of some computer-systems outfit. Most of the guys in suits at LAX, she imagined, worked for computer outfits.

Johnny Karras ordered her another drink and put his hand on her knee. Then he admired her scuffed cowboy boots. She bought those in Nogales the day she brought the six kilos of cocaine across the border for Pepe, just to show him she had what it took. Since then, she had acted as a middleman for him, making sure certain people in pop music around the Sunset Strip area got the cocaine they needed, and sometimes even the heroin. But, of course, she didn't say anything about the dope. Nor did she say anything about Carrie Wayborn, even though Carrie was the reason she had to get up to Toronto as soon as possible. If she hadn't been snorting so much shit lately, smack included, the ticket wouldn't have been any trouble. As it was, though, she was broke, crashing with a couple in an apartment behind the Hyatt On Sunset. Mainly she was staying there because the woman really dug her, and the guy didn't mind. He was much more into dope than he was into sex. But then just about everyone she knew these days would rather dope than fuck.

Pepe, that son of a bitch, refused to advance her anything until she made some of the deliveries she promised him. But she couldn't do any of that right now. Her friend Carrie was dead, and she had to do something about it. She couldn't just stay put in L.A. delivering little glassine bags to guys with long hair in recording studios. She had to do *something*. So here she was at LAX hitching a ride east from a creep with a toupee and a big hairy hand moving higher along her thigh.

''Too bad you're not flying to Toronto,'' Johnny Karras whispered into her ear.

"Who says I'm not flying to Toronto, hon?" She looked at him, all dark and smoldering. Then she pecked him lightly on the mouth and her legs closed in on his hand. "Mmm," she said. "Feels good. Are you saying I'm not flying to Toronto?

"No, I'm not saying that."

"What are you saying, hon?"

"I'm saying I'd love you to fly to Toronto."

"Then fly me to Toronto."

"This is crazy," he said, in a way that suggested the craziness was delightful.

She continued to hold his hand between her legs. "Now listen, hon, I want you to help me. I have a .38 caliber pistol in this leather carrying bag here, and also a gram of cocaine. That's so we can party when we get to Toronto. For now, though, we're going to have to put the gun and the coke in your overnight case there, and check it through."

"You've got a gun?" His soft face radiated incomprehension.

"Come on," she said reassuringly. "This isn't safe old Toronto. A girl has to protect herself out here. You can understand that."

"Sure," he said in a voice that was trying to look on the brighter side of the whole matter. "The crime out here is unbelievable."

"There you go." She kissed him harder this time, gave him a little more heat, and ran her tongue into his mouth. He began to breathe like a bellows, and she let her hand slide up his leg. After that she took his tote bag into the ladies' washroom. She went into one of the cubicles, put the cocaine and the gun into his bag underneath the latest issue of *Penthouse* magazine. She sat on the toilet, had a pee, flipped through *Penthouse*, and read a letter from a guy who had been blown off by a sexy attendant while on a flight to Australia.

Johnny Karras checked the bag through to Toronto when he turned in his ticket and purchased two first-class seats on a 727. On board the plane, they both ordered champagne, and she rubbed her breasts against him.

"You're something else," he whispered to her.

"You're a doll, hon, you really are. As soon as the plane takes off, and the movie starts, I'm gonna put a blanket over us. Then I'm going to pull out your cock and jerk you off. How do you like that?"

"Jesus Christ," he said. She could almost see him beginning to draft his letter to *Penthouse*.

When the plane landed in Toronto, they took a cab to his condominium apartment in a complex that overlooked the waterfront. There was a white shag rug, a glass-topped coffee table, and a great view of the Toronto Islands and Lake Ontario. There were also paintings of nude women on the walls, and an RCA home-entertainment system, of which Johnny was particularly proud.

He demonstrated it was possible to tape a television show on his VCR unit, while at the same time recording a hit song from a radio station, while at the same time listening to Neil Diamond singing "Cracklin' Rosie." Yeah, she thought, "Cracklin' Rosie." Right. Sure enough, he did have lots of Kenny Rogers albums. Kelly found all his albums beside the home-entertainment system, when she padded nude out of the shower. He sat on the leatherette sofa, also nude, and inspected the .38 pistol.

"You don't have any Talking Heads records do you, hon?" she called out to him.

He looked up. "Huh? Uh, no. Talking Heads. Never heard of them."

She threw aside a Barry Manilow album, stood up and fiddled around until she found a rock station on the radio, adjusted the volume, and went to the sofa where Johnny Karras was pointing the pistol out toward the lake.

"I've never even held one of these before," he said.

"Yeah, hon. Well, be careful. It's loaded."

He looked at her in amazement. "Loaded. You mean bullets?"

"That's what you put in it all right, darlin'."

Later, in bed, he grunted and jerked on top of her, and she faked all sorts of violent moans, sent up some real wolf howls. All the time he was thrashing away with her, she thought of Carrie. She thought of the years they spent together, the nights exploring each other's bodies. She thought of Carrie dead in this town. She thought of avenging Carrie. And that thought, held carefully just off the end of her nose, at the point where the countenance of Johnny Karras would otherwise hang, helped her make it through the night.

Everyone loved Toronto. The American tourists came up in droves on the weekends from places like Cincinnati and Detroit, the guys in polyester, the women still clinging to memories of Farrah Fawcett in the way they did their hair. They marveled at the city's lack of crime, its pristine demeanor, its clean streets, the civility. It all made Tom Coward uneasy.

He leaned over and looked out the porthole. Toronto the Good gleamed off the wing tip, a flat gunmetal circuit board creeping up from the edge of Lake Ontario. He thought of the natives moving restlessly below. Torontonians were curious people, arrogant in their pride of place—after all, Americans like the city, it must be good—and suffering at the same time from a fierce inferiority complex.

It was a town run by provincial villagers who feared God and sin in equal measure. It was a society scared of itself, and thus it kept itself firmly in check. There were laws governing everything, special-interest groups constantly on the alert for social infractions, a keen sense that the citizens, straight and sober though they were, nevertheless were up to no good.

The result was a city lacking in originality or excitement. There was no decadence, therefore no edge, no speed or energy. You walked out on a street in New York and you could feel the adrenalin pumping. You walked out on a street in Toronto and you worried about leaving a candy wrapper on the pavement.

Once again he was back, and he was miserable. Confronting the city forced him to confront his feelings about Stormy. And as Stormy would have told him, he disliked confronting anything, let alone his feelings. He loved her; he was sure of that. And he was someone, he concluded, who needed love more than he liked to admit. He had no anchor, and he required one. Stormy had provided the weight for him, and he simultaneously liked it and pulled against it. God, he thought as he waited for his luggage at Lester B. Pearson International Airport, whatever happened to worrying about the next destination, the next drink, whether the girl across from you at dinner would spend the night? And what the hell was her last name anyway?

For the moment, he would play a new role, that of the knight in shining armor. His lady was involved with the wrong man, of that he was certain. The least he could do was swing down from the yardarm and save her from the fate worse than death.

Besides, there was the Lex Madison story to pursue. Lex would be back in Toronto anytime. Maybe he would be more amenable to a chat here, away from hysterical starlets and curious phone calls. In any event, he was a good story and a convenient excuse.

The royal-blue limousine, a Fleetwood Cadillac with smoked-glass windows, was waiting for him just outside the arrivals area. The driver was a young, energetic John Travolta look-alike named Louis. He wore a dark chauffeur's cap with a shiny visor, and, despite the heat, a black three-piece suit, as well as leather racing gloves and aviator-style sunglasses with gold rims.

"Louis, yeah Louis," he said. "They want me to refer to myself as Louis, you know, like I wear a tie to bed and everything. But you can call me Lou, Mr. Coward."

"Okay, Lou," Tom said, as Louis held the door of the Fleetwood open for him.

"That's great, Mr. Coward. Just great. You mind if I call you Tom?"

"That's all right, Lou. Just call me Mr. Coward."

At these prices, Tom thought, I might as well get a "Mr. Coward." Besides the insistence on formality had the effect of shutting up Louis for the duration of the drive into Toronto. It took them about forty minutes to reach the Windsor Arms Hotel, a small, vine-covered edifice that had yet to learn the anonymous ways of the big corporate hotels. Tom always stayed at the Windsor Arms. The Courtyard Cafe was just off the lobby, as was the Twenty-Two bar. The management knew him and catered to his every whim.

"Mr. Coward," the clerk behind the desk said, as Louis piled Tom's luggage on the floor. "The assistant manager would like to have a word with you."

He wants to welcome me, Tom thought. How nice. The assistant, a calm, European-looking man in a herringbone jacket, cleared his throat.

"You are, of course, always welcome here, Mr. Coward."

"I'm always delighted to be here," Tom said.

"Yes, well, the last time you visited us I'm afraid there was a slight problem."

"I paid the bill," Tom said indignantly.

"Oh yes," the assistant manager said. He looked a trifle embarrassed. "But there was an incident involving a young woman."

"What young woman?"

"The one without any clothes on."

"Ah," Tom said. "That one."

"The one pounding on your door at three o'clock in the morning."

"I was not responsible for that," Tom said. "I was just as surprised as you were."

"Be that as it may, Mr. Coward. We here at the Windsor Arms hope that such an incident will not occur again."

"You have my word on it."

The assistant manager provided a gracious smile. "That is all we need."

A bellhop looked hopefully at Tom's luggage. "I want you to take this stuff upstairs," Tom said. "Then I want you to get hold of room service and have them stick a magnum of champagne into the refrigerator in the room. Mumm's. And some orange juice as well." Tom gave the bell hop a two-dollar bill. The bell hop looked at the two dollars, and he looked at the amount of luggage, and he made a low, unfriendly growling noise deep in his throat. "Jesus Christ," Tom said, and handed him another dollar. Louis was waiting by the door.

"Will you be needing me any further, Mr. Coward?"

"Check with me in a couple of hours, Lou. I'm going into the bar for a drink."

"Hey, Mr. Coward, I could use a beer. It's damn hot driving that car around, lemme tell you."

Whatever happened to the quietly serving classes, Tom wondered. "Sorry, Lou. No drinking on the job."

Tom left Louis, who still had a frown on his face, and went into the Twenty-Two bar. The place was half empty. A little man in a brown jacket, his black hair slicked straight back, glanced up sharply as Tom leaned against the bar.

"Hey, Artie," Tom said to the bartender. "How are you?"

"Good, Mr. Tommy. Now that you back, very good."

"Hey, man. It's real good to see you."

"Now maybe you pay your tab."

"Tab?"

"Two hunnert dollars. Outstanding."

"Jesus, Artie, I'm sorry. I forgot all about it." He pulled a wad of money out of his pocket. "You take it in American?"

"You give me two hunnert American, you have about eighty dollars credit in here, Mr. Tommy."

Tom handed him the money, ordered a glass of wine and a telephone. He dialed the number for Arthur Grinton that Alvin had given him, and made an appointment to talk to the television host the next morning. He put the receiver down, and a voice said, "Tom, how are you?"

He turned and a tall, lanky brunette swept down and brushed at his cheek with her lips.

"Hi . . ."

"You don't remember me. It's Kathee Whelan."

"Of course," he said, trying desperately to remember who she was. Then it clicked. New York. The model. Leather slacks. He was supposed to phone. "I was supposed to phone," he said.

"But you didn't," she said.

"I'm unreliable."

"So I've heard. What are you doing in Toronto?"

"A story. How about you? Can I buy you a drink?"

"I'd love one. But I've got a costume fitting. I'm in a movie. The last time I saw you, you promised to buy me dinner."

"You're in a movie? That's terrific. I'll buy you dinner."

"You're in luck, bunny. I happen to be free tonight."

"Where are you staying?"

"Here."

"Me, too," he said. "I'll pick you up at eight."

"Make it seven-thirty, and you've got yourself a date, bunny."

"The leather slacks," he said. "Don't forget the leather slacks."

Her eyes became wider. "You remembered."

"Of course."

She pecked him on the cheek and was gone. Artie added more wine to Tom's glass.

"You remember, Mr. Tommy? You remember what?"

"You got me, Artie," Tom said. "I can't remember what the hell it is I'm supposed to remember."

He actually picked her up at seven-forty just so he wouldn't look too anxious. In fact, he wasn't anxious at all. He would just as soon have curled up in his hotel-room bed feeling sorry for himself and contemplating the idea of perhaps phoning Stormy. But then maybe it was better if she didn't know he was in town just yet. Not until he caught the lay of the land, so to speak.

Kathee wore the leather slacks and looked stunning. He decided to take her down to the Courtyard Cafe, where he could make the appropriate impression. The maitre d' gave him a cold eye as the two of them walked in. He led them to one of the leatherette banquettes, and as Tom slid in, the maitre d' leaned forward.

"No trouble tonight, eh, Mr. Coward?" he whispered.

"Trouble?" said Tom. "What trouble?"

"You know what I mean," the maitre d' said. He departed, leaving a nasty little smile and two menus. A white-coated busboy hurried over and began pouring water.

Kathee's eyes had gotten big. "What did he mean by trouble?"

"I don't know," Tom said. "I may have caused an untoward scene or two the last time I was here."

She looked at him over her menu. "You cause untoward scenes?"

"Constantly. Tell me about the movie."

"It's called *Buns*. Starts shooting next week." She leaned forward conspiratorily. "I'm not supposed to say anything about it."

"Oh," he said.

"Would this be . . . off the record?"

He was all innocence. "Of course."

"I've always wanted to say that," she said. "Off the record. If I ever get to be a big star, I'll tell everyone everything is off the record."

"When you get to be a big star, you won't even talk to me."

"Do you think not?"

"Well, you'll give me lots of problems," he promised. "I'll have to talk to your New York publicist, and she'll have to phone the west coast PR firm that represents you, and they'll have to huddle with the publicity department at the studio that's producing your picture. It will be very complicated. It will be easier to arrange a meeting with Yassar Arafat."

She clapped her hands together gleefully. "Oh, I love that idea. I love the idea of being complicated, and difficult to get to. At the moment, I sometimes think I'm too easy to get to."

He raised his eyebrows. "That's interesting."

"Not *that* way, silly. Although sometimes I worry about that, too. No, I mean I sometimes think maybe I should be holding out for the great roles, you know. Like Ophelia or Blanche Dubois or something like that. I ask myself, would Sally Field do *Buns*?"

"Well, you've got to eat."

"Exactly. That's what my agent tells me. Besides, they make a movie such a big deal that you're happy just to get any old part. Even in something like *Buns*."

"Who do you play in *Buns*?"

"I'm the Camp Crocodile nympho."

"The what?"

"It's about all these guys at summer camp, right? And I'm the nymphomaniac who's always trying to seduce them. Only I never get to seduce any of them. Something always happens. It's all supposed to be very funny. I mean if I was really making it with a bunch of teenage guys, I wouldn't do the movie. At least that's what I tell myself."

He was about to say something reassuring when he saw the two of them walk into the restaurant. He would later replay the scene often, and it always would be swathed in a golden light, the two of them emerging out of it, like a television commercial for perfume. Stormy Willis and Ashley Conlon. He had never seen two people look quite so good together. They positively shimmered. Everyone in the restaurant noticed it, even Kathee Whelan. When she spotted Ash Conlon her eyes once again grew large.

They were escorted across the restaurant, far enough away that Stormy Willis did not notice her ex-boyfriend sitting there looking like a fool. Not that she would have noticed him if he'd walked over and sat down beside her. She had eyes only for the tall, striking man who led her by the hand. He stood, Tom reckoned, about six feet three inches tall, and he wore a dark double-breasted Giorgio Armani suit, gleaming Bally shoes, a striped tie Tom was sure was by Jeffrey Banks. Most movie stars do not look like movie stars. Ash Conlon looked like a movie star.

His hair was black, falling just so around his ears, curling in thick waves over the collar of his shirt. How do some people get hair like that, anyway? Tom wondered. His face was almost delicate it was so finely chiseled. A few years before he would have been a sulky pretty boy. Age added a certain masculinity to the face. His cheekbones were superbly formed, serving to square the jaw and emphasize the small pout of a mouth, the narrow line of the nose, and the precisely set almond-shaped eyes. Even the eyebrows tapered off exquisitely. He smiled at Stormy and revealed teeth that were perfectly straight and startlingly white. Capped, Tom thought.

"Wow," Kathee said. "What a hunk." Tom cocked an eyebrow at her. "You're cute, bunny, really you are," she hastened to add. But the appearance of Stormy put a damper on the evening. Tom spent some time stewing over whether he should go over to say hello, thereby demonstrating his maturity and showing that there were no hard feelings. But he had no inclination to demonstrate his maturity; and there were hard feelings. He picked at scallops sautéed in tarragon and champagne, and drank a good deal of white wine.

His last sight of Stormy and Conlon as he left the restaurant with a by now miffed Kathee was of the two of them talking into each other's eyes, their hands intertwined. They were close, self-absorbed lovers. How, he wondered later, did one break into that? What the hell was he doing here, anyhow?

"Um, I have a busy day tomorrow, Tom," Kathee said when they got to her room. "Costume fittings, that sort of thing. I'd really like to get a good night's sleep."

"Sure," he said.

"Thanks for dinner, bunny." She sounded a little sad.

"I'll call you," he said.

"Sure," she said.

Tom went back to his room and fell into a fitful sleep. All night long Stormy rose up in his nightmares, pleasuring herself on the body of Ashley Conlon, a body that for his nightmare seemed to have been sculpted by Rodin, every muscle taut and dramatically obvious as he heaved to accommodate her. Tom awoke with an ugly grunt and sat up in the silent, darkened bedroom. He had spent too many nights alone in dark hotel rooms around the world, he thought. His body was drenched in sweat; the sheets on the bed were damp.

He went into the bathroom, showered under hot water, dried himself carefully, went back into the bedroom and stared at himself in a full-length mirror. The years of easy living stared back at him. "Okay, Tom," he said to the mirror, "maybe you should work out a little bit. Lift some weights. Do some pushups." The thought depressed him. He tried pulling in his stomach. It did not pull in very far.

"Never mind, Tom," he said to the mirror. "You love Stormy Willis, and that's what counts. That's what makes the difference." He looked more closely at the mirror. Now that was curious. That big, overweight guy staring back at him, he had tears in his eyes. Very curious indeed.

6

Arthur Grinton, "Mr. Old Movies" as he was known locally, carefully poured tea from the small pot he kept in his office into the cup he provided for Tom.

"So you're doing a piece on Lex for a number of American publications? My my," he said. "American publications. My goodness, Lex really has come a long way, hasn't he? American publications, indeed." Arthur Grinton could not have been much over forty, but he gave off a jolly, avuncular air that was aided by a bald pate and thick military mustache, the ends of which he tugged at constantly.

He wore a green blazer and gray slacks, and what looked to Tom to be an old-school tie, although precisely what old school he couldn't say. Grinton proceeded to pour his own tea. When that was finished, he sat down opposite Tom in his cramped little office. There was barely room for the two of them and a metal desk, filing cabinets, and some shelves that contained movie reference works: Halliwell's *The Encylopedia of Film*, *The History of the Talkies*, *The Films of Roger Corman*, *My Life in Pictures*, by Charles Chaplin, books of film criticism by Pauline Kael, James Agee, and John Simon. Everything about the room marked him as a film nut. The mustard-colored walls were adorned with movie posters: Bogie and Ava Gardner in *The Barefoot Countessa*; Renee Soutendijk in *The Fourth Man*; Clint Eastwood in *Sudden Impact*; Kurosawa's oil rendering for the Cannes Film Festival.

"Well, just let me tell you, Tom — do you mind if I call you Tom?"

"Not at all," Tom said. He looked dubiously at the tea.

"Well, *Tom*, just let me tell you, Lex is a wonderful fella. Just a wonderful fella. We've tried to get him as a guest on my movie show. Yes, yes, talked to him a number of times. But you know how it is, Tom. He is so busy out there in Hollywood. Home in Malibu. Goodness. Malibu. Can you imagine? Our Lex Madison in Malibu." He paused for breath. "You've talked to him, of course."

"In Los Angeles. Yes."

"Los Angeles. You don't say. You talked to him there. Why that's wonderful. I tell you, makes me shudder to say that word. Yes, indeed. City of Angels. Los Angeles. I get out there once a year, mind you. We're trying to line up an interview with Buddy Rogers, in fact. You remember Buddy Rogers? He was in — what was that picture? Oh, dear. And I'm supposed to be a trivia buff, too."

"*Wings*, wasn't it?" Tom said helpfully. He sipped at the tea. It tasted awful.

"Of course. Of course Tom. You had me there. Yessir. You had me there. Anyway, he was married to Constance Talmadge. Oh dear, Tom. What a beauty she was, my goodness — "

"Uh, wasn't Buddy Rogers married to Mary Pickford?"

Mr. Old Movies threw his head back and slapped the open palm of his hand against his forehead. "Of course! Of course! How could I be so silly. Oh, dear, Tom, what you must think of me. Oh, dear indeed. And you're here from American publications, too."

Tom put the tea to one side. "You were at the University of Toronto, weren't you, when Lex started up the Rear Window Society?"

Grinton managed to recover somewhat. "Oh, yes. Goodness yes, Tom. I was there. Certainly. I was taking a fine-arts course, yes indeed. But I was like Lex. I was more interested in going to the movies than I was in going to school. That's all it was really, an excuse for us not to go to school.''

Tom made a note. ''What kind of guy was he back in those days?''

''Kind of guy. Let me see.'' Arthur Grinton chewed anxiously at his lower lip. ''Quiet. That's it. Quiet and introspective. Thoughtful. Certainly he was not at all flamboyant, not the type you would think would make movies, oh no. I suppose in another age he might have been what you would call bookish, Tom. Except I don't think I ever saw Lex with a book.'' He chuckled at that and tugged at the edges of his mustache.

''Did he talk about making movies?''

''Did he talk about making movies?'' Arthur Grinton studied the ceiling. ''Did he talk — Tom, that's the curious thing. Now that I think about it, Lex never talked about making movies. I mean we all talked about going to Hollywood. That was the place to go, you see. Still is. There must have been, what? Twenty of us? Yes. Twenty members in the Rear Window. And we all were crazy about movies. We were very influenced by that auteur stuff. You know, Truffaut, Godard, Fellini, Resnais. They were all the rage then. Lex would somehow get his hands on these movies, a lot of them never shown in Toronto before, and he would screen them endlessly. He studied everything — what's the right word here, Tom? — intently. That's it. Intently. *Intense.* That's what I remember most about him. This intensity of spirit.''

The door opened and a heavyset woman, her small mouth fiercely set, her hair pulled back into a severe bun, swept into the room. She was pale and chubby in a denim skirt and a red sweater. She threw some papers down on Arthur's desk and glared at him.

''Here is the background material on the Delores Del Rio festival.''

Grinton appeared not to notice her anger. ''Oh, that's just wonderful, Helga. Grand work. Just grand.'' He rubbed his hands together. "I've been wanting to do this for years. Everyone loves Delores Del Rio. Let me tell you."

The woman rolled tiny green eyes. "God," she murmured.

"Now, Helga, this is Mr. Tom Coward. He's working for American publications. Doing a story on my old friend Lex Madison. Tom, this is our Miss Volkmann."

Our Miss Volkmann limply shook Tom's hand. "How do you do?" she asked. She turned to Grinton. "Did you look at that material on the Fassbinder films?"

"Miss Volkmann is our resident foreign-film buff, Tom," Arthur Grinton said. "Werner Fassbinder, that dead German chappie, is one of her favorites."

"*Rainer* Werner Fassbinder," she snapped. "And he's hardly a dead German chappie. He happens to be the most important filmmaker to come out of the New German Cinema. We have an opportunity to run four of his early films, Arthur. We have an opportunity to make a contribution to people's cinema consciousness. Are you going to ignore that opportunity?"

"Oh, dear me," said Arthur Grinton with a nervous chuckle. "Can we talk about this later? Mr. Coward here is in the middle of interviewing me."

"I would like to talk about it *now*, Arthur. I have to let them *know*."

Arthur had risen from his desk and was opening the top drawer of one of his filing cabinets. "Later, Helga. We will talk about it later." He glared at her. She glared at him. After a moment, she turned and stomped out of the office.

"Oh, dear, Tom," Grinton said. "I don't know what to do about her, I really don't. We ran a couple of foreign films last year. *Seven Beauties* was one of them. Lina Wertmuller, you know? Well, I must say, my audience didn't like that at all. Oh, dear no. There were letters of complaint."

"Many letters?"

"Oh my, yes. Lots of them. Three or four at the least. People who are shut-ins rely on those lovely old black-and-white films to transport them away. Fassbinder won't transport them anywhere except to Berlin. If you're shut in and miserable, Tom, the last place you want to be transported to is Berlin. Let me tell you."

He turned back to his filing cabinet and began leafing through manila folders. "I've got something here I think might interest you. Now where were we?"

Tom sighed. "Lex Madison. I think we were talking about Lex Madison."

"Of course we were. Certainly. Intensity of spirit. That's it. He was never one to talk about his aspirations; he sort of kept to himself. The rest of us, though, all we did was yap, yap, yap." He pulled a folder out of the cabinet. "Maybe that says something about Lex, and about us. We all wanted desperately to be in the movies, Tom, but we never did very much about it. Lex did something. He didn't just blab away. He *did* something."

"You have your TV show," Tom said.

Grinton snorted. "My TV show. Oh, dear. Well, I cling to my dreams, Tom, small as they are. And I show my movies. But it's really just an extension of the movie worship we indulged in at college. None of us, I don't think, ever expected it to go any further than worship. Except Lex, of course." He put the manila folder on his desk and opened it up. "I just wish I knew we were supposed to take it seriously, Tom. It was just a lark, that's all, before we got on with the more serious business of life. But Lex, he thought the serious business of life was making movies. That's the difference, I guess. I wish I had known that. I wish he had told me it was possible to take them seriously."

"So you weren't around when Lex made *Schlock Treatment*, his spoof of the horror movies?"

"No, no, Tom. That was after the Rear Window had

more or less disbanded. I guess we were really strong for only about a year. I remember being surprised that Lex had made a movie. As I said, he spoke so little of any ambitions along those lines." He opened the folder up. "I used to keep all sorts of dope around on the Rear Window. I was sort of the recording secretary, heh, heh. But over the years I've lost a lot of it."

"What about *Zoom-Zoom*?"

Grinton looked up from the folder. "What about it?"

"Did you know Madison when he made the movie?"

"Goodness no, Tom. I had graduated by then. Was out teaching English in one of the suburbs. Trying to get nasty little fellows with pimples on their noses to read *The Red Badge of Courage*. Not easy, let me tell you." His eyes took on a faraway cast. "Can I tell you a secret? I always wanted to be an actor. I even auditioned for a couple of parts on stage locally. Never got them, though. I don't know. Maybe I just never put enough into it."

He was going through photographs, yellowed newspaper clippings, mimeographed sheets the Rear Window Society issued to advertise the week's screenings.

"Silly old faded memories," Grinton said with a bitterness that surprised Tom. He handed Tom a photograph. "This shows a bunch of us together. It's just about the only photo I have in which Lex was featured. He never liked having his picture taken."

The photograph showed a half dozen young people all posed around a sixteen-millimeter movie projector. There was no mistaking them for anything but 1960s college students, captured just before a whole new youth culture that included long hair, Beatles music, and grass swept in to change them forever. Even Lex Madison, with hair here, appeared ineffably sophomoric.

"Now this is interesting," Arthur Grinton said, tapping a well-bitten nail against the photograph to indicate the girl standing beside Lex. Raven hair fell well past her shoulders, framing a face that radiated sensuality. She was not terribly pretty, but you would notice her in any crowd. Lex had thrown a proprietory arm around her. "This is the girl, who starred in *Zoom-Zoom*. Apparently Lex was very much in love her. I wouldn't have thought he was in love with anyone. But he was crazy about Kelly. Kelly Langlois. That was her name. She was in *Zoom-Zoom*."

But Tom was no longer looking at Kelly Langlois. His gaze had drifted to a tall, curly-haired kid with a sober boyish face who had his arms around a second girl. This girl had a short bouffant hairdo, and a full figure. She leaned back against the tall youth, and she smiled into the camera. The smile was at an angle, curiously provocative.

"Who is this?" Tom demanded.

"Let me see," Grinton said. He picked up the photograph and studied it closely for a moment. "Oh dear. I'm not good at names. Curly hair. Thought he was James Dean or somebody. All the girls were crazy about him. Never knew him very well. Cameron? Catlin? Dear me. Dear. Dear."

"Conlon?"

Grinton looked at Tom, surprised. "Yes. That was it. Conlon. Ashley Conlon."

"He was a member of the Rear Window?"

"Yes. Why? You know him?"

"I know of him," Tom said. Tom looked again at the photograph. Ashley Conlon stared back at him. His young, clear face showed nothing.

"Now I do know who this is," Grinton said. He pointed to the young woman folded into Ashley Conlon's arms. "This poor girl is Carrie Wayborn. Such a shame. Such a darned shame, Tom. I don't suppose you know anything about it, just coming in from Los Angeles, but she was murdered, you see. In her apartment. It's the talk of the town, Tom. Talk of the town."

"I know about it," Tom said vaguely. He could not keep

his eyes off the photograph. He could not stop studying Ash Conlon holding Carrie Wayborn in his arms as she leaned back against his body.

"Well, you are informed about us up here, I must say, Tom."

Long ago in school, Carrie Wayborn looked very happy to be with Ash Conlon. His arms held her tightly. Stormy Willis was now in those arms. Stormy Willis lived next door to Carrie Wayborn. It was Stormy Willis who had discovered Carrie Wayborn's body. Where did Ash fit into all that?

"It looks as though Ashley and Carrie were pretty chummy," Tom said.

"I don't know about that," Arthur said. "I mean I wasn't particularly involved in anyone's personal life."

"Can I borrow this? We may print it with the story."

Arthur Grinton looked dubious. "As long as I get it back. It's the only one I have."

Helga Volkmann came back in. "Arthur," she said, "I just have to speak to you. Those people are on the phone. They want to know about the Fassbinder films. They want to know if we want them."

"Dear me, Helga." Grinton was exasperated. His face reddened. "Tell them no. Tell them we don't want your Fassbinder."

"Jesus Christ, Arthur," Helga said. She was near tears.

"I'd better get going," Tom said.

"I'm sorry about this." Arthur Grinton indicated the now trembling Helga.

"He's a great filmmaker," Helga sobbed. "You run Randolph Scott movies, and you ignore a great filmmaker. You are an idiot."

"Here, here," Arthur Grinton shouted as Tom left the office, "I won't have that sort of talk. Not from an employee I won't."

"I'm not an employee," Helga sobbed. "I'm a film archivist."

"You're a pain in the rear end, young lady! That's what you are!"

Tom quietly closed the door behind Mr. Old Movies and his Miss Volkmann.

Louis the chauffeur was waiting for him outside, hatless, filing his nails as he leaned against the Caddy.

"Don't you have a chauffeur's cap, Lou?" Tom said as the driver scampered to open the door for him.

"Ah, for Christ's sake, Mr. Coward. I wear the goddamned thing and people think I'm a chauffeur."

"That's because you are a chauffeur, Lou," Tom said. "Put on the cap."

"Ah, shit," Lou said.

In the royal-blue interior of the car, Tom settled back against the seat and listened to the quiet purr of the air conditioning. He took the photograph out of the manila envelope with which Arthur Grinton had provided him, and studied it. He wondered what Stormy knew about this. Did she know her new boyfriend was once intimately acquainted with her murdered next-door neighbor?

7

A lvin Jarvis's party to celebrate his latest motion-picture production was held in the backyard of the neo-Victorian house Alvin rented in what is known as the Annex area of Toronto. A fluttering blue-and-white marquee had been erected and the chichi masses were already present when Tom arrived, the women showing lots of chic skin in thin summer frocks, the men done in various pastel shades that put him in mind of *The Great Gatsby*.

Alvin had selected twelve female extras, outfitted them in short-shorts, high-heeled "fuck-me" pumps, and miniscule halter tops, dubbed them the Bun-Bun girls, and set them loose to pour champagne and serve hors d'oeuvres. The champagne, Tom discovered to his horror, was Canadian.

"Where's the good stuff?" Tom demanded when Alvin passed by, escorted by two comely Bun-Bun girls with plump breasts falling out of their halter tops.

"What do you mean good stuff," Alvin demanded. "This is the good stuff. Who's the punk in the funny hat wearing racing gloves?"

Tom turned and saw Louis avidly watching the Bun-Bun girls. "That's my chauffeur."

"Chauffeur, Jesus."

"I hate driving," Tom said. "Do you have any Mumm's?"

"Fridge in the kitchen. But, for Christ's sake, do it on the sly."

Tom found a magnum behind the Stilton cheese, and poured himself a glass. Kathee Whelan came in with the world-famous director Bobby Putnam.

"I'm a little bit tipsy, bunny." She licked at Putnam's ear and noticed Tom. Her eyes became narrow. "Oh. Tom. How are you?"

Tom lifted his glass, and Bobby Putnam pumped his hand. He was a large man with a shock of dirty-blond curls. He wore a denim shirt open to the waist to reveal a vast stomach.

"Thomas, old duck. Haven't seen you since Cannes."

"*Horror Chamber Shocker* was a big hit in the marketplace," Tom said.

"A cult picture," Bobby laughed. "Now I'm directing *Buns*."

"*Buns — The Masterpiece*," Tom said.

"That's it!" Bobby roared. He pulled Kathee against him. "We're gonna make this young lady a star, we are."

"I'm a little tipsy, bunny," Kathee repeated.

"That's okay, darlin'." He winked at Tom. "I hear tell Alvin's hiding the good stuff in the icebox. Canadian shit for the investors. Good stuff for the creative help."

"I've got to find a bathroom," Tom said.

"Upstairs," Bobby said, as he poured champagne for himself and Kathee. "Try not to piss on the floor."

There was plumply upholstered wicker furniture in a hallway, and the sitting room was done in muted tones. The second-floor corridor was wall-to-wall fuchsia. He opened a door and discovered a bedroom with floor-to-ceiling windows on two sides that looked down on the marquee in the yard below. He tried another door across from the bedroom. A dark-eyed woman, her summer silk hiked up around brown thighs, squatted on the toilet.

"Well," she said.

"I'm sorry," he said.

"You might have knocked."

Tom closed the door, sighed, went down the stairs, and discovered Prudence Caldwell at the bottom, leaning against the banister.

"I've gotta quit going to these goddamn affairs," she said. "Everyone's starting to say the same things over and over again." She was a little bullet of a woman, dressed always in black, her hair sheared short and turned to the color of straw at sunset.

"I heard you were out of the gossip business."

"That's right dear. Back on police. Twenty-five years in the business, and I end up where I started."

"I'm sorry to hear it," Tom said.

She shrugged and retrieved a glass of Canadian champagne from a passing Bun-Bun girl. "It's newspapers, Tommy. What can I say? Welcome back, incidentally. Alvin told me you were in town. Meant to call and all that. Been tied up on a murder thing. Listen, I heard about you and Stormy. Sorry. I always thought you two were a swell couple."

"Everyone's breaking up this year," he said. "It's all the rage."

"I hear Stormy and Ash Conlon are an item."

"You know Ash Conlon?"

"Let's say I know his family. His mother was Lyn Lisa Conlon. Does that name ring a bell?"

"No. Should it?"

She made a face. "You kids, honestly. No sense of history. Back in 1950, dear, Lyn Lisa Conlon made love to her second husband one night, and while he was recovering from the orgasm, she popped a gun into his mouth and pulled the trigger."

"She killed him?"

"No, dummy. He recovered and lived a long and happy life with two mouths instead of one. Of course, she killed him. It was a big story. Her second husband had admitted to Lyn Lisa that he had knocked off her first husband years before. In Algiers of all places. Juicy stuff. I was working for a Fleet Street rag at the time. They sent me over to cover the story. I never went back. Great yarn. The rich blowing each other's brains out. The public eats it up."

"How old was Ashley at the time?"

"I dunno. Maybe five years old."

"What happened to him when his mother went to jail?"

"Who said anything about jail?"

"You just said Lyn Lisa Conlon killed her husband."

"True enough, and there were only twelve people in the whole town that weren't convinced she was guilty. Unfortunately, they happened to be on the jury."

"So she got off?"

"Brilliant defense lawyer. Guy named Porter. He convinced the jury that the two of them made love, then Willy Conlon put the gun in his own mouth and pulled the trigger."

"But why?"

"Remorse, apparently."

"What happened to mommy?" Tom said.

"After that she became a recluse. Nobody ever saw much of her, although lots of people tried. She moved to Mexico and died there of cancer about ten years ago."

"Sounds like a cheerful subject." Tom turned. The woman from the upstairs bathroom stood on the stairs behind him. She had green eyes and a cynical mouth, and dark-brown hair that fell thickly to her shoulders. Someone told her as soon as she was old enough to understand that she was beautiful, and nothing had happened to dissuade her of the truth of that original statement. She tossed her head, and the hair shook itself off the shoulders. She knew she was being inspected, and chose to make the process as easy as possible for the inspector.

"Lea," Pru Caldwell said. "I didn't know you were here. Do you know Tom Coward?"

"We've met." The cynical mouth possessed a lovely British accent and a trace of humor. She offered him a long brown hand. He took it. The handshake was firm.

"Good to see you again," Tom said.

"You know Lea Madison?" Pru Caldwell said.

Tom looked at her. "You're Lea Madison?"

"Shouldn't I be? Actually, I shouldn't. I'm the *former* Lea Madison."

Pru looked at Tom. "If you know her, how come you don't know who she is?"

"Can I buy you a drink?" he said to Lea.

She regarded him for a moment. "That would be nice," she said finally. "But let's get outside. Stuffy in here."

She moved down the stairs, and Pru said, "Tom, I have to talk to you some more. Don't leave without checking in with your Auntie Pru."

Tom watched Lea Madison's tightly molded rump challenging the expensive silk of her dress as he followed her out through the kitchen.

"Hold it a minute," he said. He opened the refrigerator, found the Mumm's. "This is better." He poured her a glass, then got one for himself. Alvin came into the kitchen, looking a trifle bleary.

"Jesus," he said, "I'm up to my ass in Bun-Bun girls." He saw Lea and said, "Lea, I didn't know you were here."

"Nobody knows I'm here. I should have hired a couple of trumpeters to announce my arrival. Hello, Alvin. Good to see you. Did you read the script I sent you?"

Alvin helped himself to some of his champagne. "Yeah. I read it."

"And?" She had a way of arching her right eyebrow that brooked no foolishness.

"What can I tell you Lea? It's nicely done. But — "

"But?"

"It's nice. Sweet. But not commercial. The world wants *Buns*, Lea. They don't want that sort of stuff. Listen, we'll talk later. I promise. There's a guy from the bank out there and he's trying to stick his tongue down the throat of a Bun-Bun girl. I gotta get back.''

Lea gave him a fleeting smile as he hurried out. She looked down at her champagne glass.

"You've got a script?'' Tom said.

"Doesn't everyone?''

They wandered out into the yard and stood at the edge of the entrance to the marquee. It was early evening and the party was going full tilt. Someone had put on a David Bowie album and the Bun-Bun girls were dancing with the investors.

"I don't have a script,'' Tom said.

"You somehow don't look like an investor.''

"I'm not.''

"What are you?''

"A journalist.''

The glass barrier dropped down as soon as he said that. "Oh,'' she said.

He swallowed hard. "I'm doing a story on Lex.''

"And you just *have* to talk to me.''

"I didn't even know you were going to be here,'' Tom said.

She regarded him suspiciously. "Thanks for the champagne,'' she said. "I have to be going.''

"Can I drop you anywhere? I've got my chauffeur here.''

"You're a journalist. And you've got a chauffeur.''

"I hate to drive,'' he said. "I'm only in town for a few days.''

"Thanks, anyway. But I have a car. No chauffeur. But, what the hell, a single girl makes do.''

"I probably deserved that.''

She smiled and the cynical mouth was gone in a flash. "You probably did,'' she said. "See you.''

Tom was left with a champagne buzz, swaying slightly to David Bowie singing "China Girl.'' Alvin Jarvis appeared, rocky on his feet, despite the fact he was balancing himself against a petite Bun-Bun girl who was about to fall out of her halter top. He tugged at Tom's arm.

"Come with me," he ordered. He leaned against the Bun-Bun girl. "To the library, Darlene."

Alvin and Darlene staggered into the house, dragging Tom behind. They all entered what should have been a book-lined study, except the shelves loomed skeletal and empty around the room. There were a half dozen *Reader's Digest* condensed books propped up forlornly. You could read James M. Michener's *Tales of the South Pacific*, the short version, while you wondered where the books were. Appropriate that Alvin Jarvis, the bookseller's son, would rent a house that had a library without books. But Alvin was paying no attention to such ironies. He was pawing through one of the drawers in an old-fashioned rolltop desk.

"Here it is," Alvin announced gleefully.

"Here is what?" Tom said.

Alvin held up a gun. Tom blinked a couple of times. The Bun-Bun girl gasped, and the color drained out of her face. Abruptly, she was not leaning against Alvin. His support gone, he faltered. The gun described circles in the air.

"Where the hell did you get that?" Tom said, when he found his voice.

"My protection. I'm gonna blow Bobby Putnam's brains out with it. Where the fuck is he?"

Tom went over and patted Alvin on the shoulder. "You can't do that, Alvin," Tom said, his voice friendly.

"Yes, I can. He wants to put giant fucking rats in my movie."

"Alvin, where are you going to find giant rats?"

"He wants to dress dachshunds up in rat costumes. Can you believe that? This is about good clean kids getting laid at summer camp. This is *Buns*. A tits-and-ass picture." He pulled Darlene toward him. "We need Darlene's tits." He buried his face in her cleavage. Tom took the opportunity to pluck the gun from Alvin's limp fingers. Alvin raised his head. "We do not need dogs in rat costumes."

"Beddy time, Alvin," Tom said. He looked at Darlene. "Why don't you take him upstairs?"

"Yeah," Alvin agreed, "Let's go upstairs. But first lemme blow Bobby Putnam's brains out."

"First go upstairs. Then blow his brains out."

Darlene looked at him imploringly. "Please, honey. Come with Darlene."

The anger drained out of Alvin as quickly as it had risen. He wrapped his arm around Darlene and allowed her to lead him out of the study. Tom waited until they were gone, then went over to the shelves and balanced the gun behind the *Reader's Digest* condensed books.

Then he went upstairs. Alvin was on his back in the bed. His pants were down around his ankles. Darlene had her top off, displaying what it was Alvin wanted for his movie. She raised her head.

"He'll be okay," she said.

"So I see," Tom said.

She gave him a wink as he quietly shut the door.

Downstairs, Prudence Caldwell was waiting. "I've been looking all over for you. Where've you been?"

"Sorry, Pru. Medical emergency. Dr. Coward had to make a house call."

"All right. Now pay attention. You know that murder I was telling you about?"

"Yeah," Tom said. "The murder you're covering. What about it?"

"A woman. She was killed in the Beaches, right next to where you used to live."

Tom looked at her. "Carrie Wayborn," he said. "You're talking about Carrie Wayborn. Stormy found her."

"I'm well aware of that," Pru said. "I've been trying to get hold of Stormy for the past few days. Apparently she's out of town on some modeling assignment. I'm doing a follow-up piece on the murder. It's been a couple of weeks now and the trail's grown cold. Police baffled, that kind of thing. I'm just about to drive out there for a sniff around. You don't know anyone who resides in that apartment building, do you? I mean you did live right next door."

"Sure. Old Laura Crawford Dougall. I used to carry her garbage out all the time."

"Do you think old Laura Crawford Dougall knows anything?"

"Well," Tom said "we could find out."

"That's what I wanted to hear," Pru said.

They found Louis. One of the Bun-Bun girls was propping him up as he threw up over the rear fender of the Fleetwood.

"I think he's had too much to drink," the Bun-Bun girl said.

"I think you're right," Tom said.

Louis looked up. His John Travolta face was deathly white. "Sorry, Mr. Coward." He threw up again, then collapsed on the ground.

"What are we going to do?" Pru Caldwell said.

"Let's get him into the back."

"Who's going to drive?"

"I will."

"You're going to drive your own chauffeur-driven limousine?"

"And I hate driving," Tom said.

The Beach, as it was called by the veteran residents, is in the east end of Toronto. It is bounded on the west by a racetrack and on the east by the border of a tractless and unappealing swatch of early suburbia known as Scarborough. The Beach, as its name implies, flows up from the sandy shores of Lake Ontario, north as far as an industrial byway known as Kingston Road.

Within these informally held borders is what amounts to a small town, its streets tree-lined and for the most part peaceful, as though calmly awaiting the return of Andy Hardy. He will never come, although certainly Andy's WASPishness survives. To the west are ethnic melting-pot neighborhoods, but here the semidetached houses and clapboard cottages have recently been commandeered by upwardly mobile professionals. There are lots of journalists and broadcasters, a large crowd of actors and models.

Tom thought the whole area a resting place for unreconstructed hippies. Stormy loved it. And she particularly loved the narrow two-storey brick house they found just south of the main thoroughfare, Queen Street. Tom parked the Fleetwood in front and looked out at the house. It had not changed except that the hedges Stormy forced him to plant along the front of the porch had perished, exactly as he predicted they would.

In the backseat, Louis stirred and groaned.

"I don't think Lou wants to be a chauffeur," Tom said to Pru. She merely snorted and opened the passenger door.

They got out and went up the walk to the Beachcourt Apartments, the scene of the murder of Carrie Wayborn. Even in the twilight, he could see how much the building had changed. When he and Stormy moved next door it was a dilapidated joke, a temporary holding pattern for teenagers and university students on their own for the first time and much given to arriving home at three o'clock in the morning to pee on the street.

Soon the renovators had arrived. While Tom and Stormy watched, the facade was sandblasted and the paint stripped from the doors to return them to their natural oak. The kids left, and the young trendies, the Yuppies who inhabited the cozy little restaurants that had sprung up in such profusion along Queen Street, had become the new residents at Beachcourt. Their Volkswagen Rabbits and Toyotas and Honda Civics were parked in front of what remained, after all the gentrification, a five-story building shrouded by huge maple trees. The maples got their revenge. They continued to pour a sticky sap down on the foreign imports.

Laura Crawford Dougall had survived the kids, and she endured the Yuppies from an aerie perched atop the building. Her apartment was surrounded on all sides with leaded-glass windows so that she had the view of the lake everyone else coveted but could not possess. She remained a relic of another time in this area, a time when the neighborhood was old and solid and sure, and no one ever moved out.

They found her at home and anxious to entertain. "Thomas Coward, as I live and breathe," she said, when she opened the door. "The press has arrived just in time. I've recently returned from a glorious engagement at the Burt Reynolds Dinner Theater in Jupiter, Florida, where I knocked 'em dead in a production of *40 Karats*. I am now prepared to give interviews. As long as you're not from the *National Enquirer*. Burt told me not to talk to the *Enquirer*. He said it would be bad for my career."

She had once, she said, been a contract player at RKO. But whatever it was about her that RKO found attractive had been lost to age. Now she was a small, stout woman, with white hair and a puffy, jolly face. Only the extravagantly colored kimonos she wore gave any hint of the former screen siren.

Tom introduced her to Prudence Caldwell, who was dazzled.

"I used to read your gossip stuff, Miss Caldwell," Laura Crawford Dougall said. "You gave life to this dull, dead city. No wonder they took it away from you. You dared treat people as celebrities. We will never have a culture here unless we can do that."

Laura led them into a magnificent art-deco apartment, festooned with framed covers from *Movie Mirror* and *Screen Gems* magazines. Linda Darnell smiled out at the world. Dick Powell gave everyone a merry wink. Victor Mature posed with a newly lit cigarette casually held between slim fingers.

There was a white baby grand piano in a corner. On the piano there was a photograph of Gary Cooper in a silver frame.

"I went out with Coop back in the thirties," she said when Pru picked up the photograph. "It was just after he broke up with Clara Bow. I was a contract player at RKO at that time. My mother had brought me out to the coast from Toronto herself. She said, 'Laura, you're the most beautiful little girl I've ever seen. It's only right that you become a movie star.'

"Coop was a wonderful guy. But the things he used to do with Clara Bow. Shocking. The talk of Hollywood. He wanted me to do those same things, and I never would. He respected me for that, I'm sure. He was crazy about me, after all. Then he met Lupe Velez. She was, ah, Latin, and there was nothing she wouldn't do. And I mean nothing. In my innocence I didn't stand a chance. Anyhow, they were wonderful days, just wonderful. But it's like the song says, Miss Caldwell, *these* are the good old days. Out of nowhere I'm offered this wonderful part at the wonderful Burt Reynolds Dinner Theater. Burt was there opening night. He came backstage afterward and kissed me" — a bright red nail pointed to a spot on her cheek — "there. It was a tremendous two weeks. I'm back. I'm exhausted. I'm tremendously happy."

She insisted that they seat themselves on an overstuffed peach-colored divan, while she bustled around serving coffee and liqueurs.

"When did you get back?" Tom said as he accepted coffee served in a delicate bone-china cup and saucer.

"I returned to Toronto yesterday," Laura said.

"Then you didn't know anything about the murder here." Pru sounded disappointed.

"I heard about it as soon as I got back. I couldn't believe it. Poor, poor Carrie."

"You knew her?" Pru asked.

"Of course. She lived right underneath me. She used to invite me down to tea. I told her all about Gary Cooper. She was fascinated, naturally."

"What was Carrie like?" Pru had a spiral-bound notebook on her lap.

Laura issued a deep sigh and pulled at the edges of her kimono. "That is a difficult question. After all, I didn't know her at all well. But I heard lots. I mean she was right underneath me, and this building's acoustics are terrible. One could hardly be unaware of her lifestyle."

"What sort of lifestyle?"

"She was a girl involved with a great number of men, Miss Caldwell. Now I'm not a moralist, and I am not a prude. But I do believe our Lord and God Jesus Christ put women on this earth to please men — and to watch themselves very carefully. I do think Carrie Wayborn pleased men. I do not think Carrie Wayborn watched herself very carefully. She was like Clara Bow. She was ready to take on the entire football team. More's the pity, because she really was a very nice young lady in many ways."

"Recently, where there any men in particular?"

"Oh, she never discussed her affairs with me at all. Our relationship was really quite superficial. But, you see, I *hear* things up here, and occasionally, because, after all, I am surrounded by these windows on a small world, I *see* things."

"So there was a man?"

"An absolutely gorgeous man, Miss Caldwell. What

they call today a hunk. Tall, dark, and handsome. I saw her walk him out to the car one night. A beauty. Like a young Ty Power. And I should know, because I once dated Ty Power. A real gentleman. Now they write about him and they say he was a homosexual. Are they kidding? This was a man. A real man.''

Pru was scribbling notes furiously.

"But I don't think they were getting along very well.''

Pru looked up sharply. "Oh? What makes you say that?''

The red-enameled nail pointed again, this time to her ear. "Because, as I say, I *hear* things.''

"Okay. What did you hear?''

"I heard the two of them arguing. Violently arguing.''

"The same man? The hunk?''

"I'm almost certain, yes.''

"What were they arguing about?''

"What does anyone argue about? I could not *hear* the specifics. But it sounded to me as though they were arguing about money. He was supposed to give her money.''

"And this was before you left for Florida?''

"A month ago, I think that was it. It really got quite nasty and angry.''

"That would have been perhaps a couple of weeks before Carrie was killed.''

"You think this man may have been the killer?'' asked Laura Crawford Dougall.

"It's certainly possible,'' Pru said. "Tell me, Mrs. Dougall, have you told the police any of this?''

"How could I? I just got back.''

Pru Caldwell closed her notebook. "Mrs. Dougall, I want to thank you. You've been a tremendous help.''

"I always try to co-operate with the press,'' Laura Crawford Dougall said. "Many people in show business despise the press, I know. But I think the press is important.'' She looked fondly over at Tom. "Besides, I happen to be crazy about this young rascal. Have you seen Stormy lately, Tom?''

''I just got back to town myself, Mrs. Dougall.''

''You know it's such a shame about the two of you.'' She wagged a finger at him. ''She wanted you to settle down, Tom, you know that. She wanted you to settle down and you wouldn't. I understand that. I understand wanderlust. But it's not good for a relationship.''

''I know,'' Tom said. ''I'm trying to mend my ways.''

''That was the problem with Errol Flynn. He could never settle down. You took one look at that rakish grin of his and you just *knew* he would never settle down. But, oh, he was a charmer, if I do say so. Never dated him, although he did ask me out. But his reputation! Goodness. They say he had teenage girls up at his house constantly. And two-way mirrors. Of course, they also said he was a Nazi. How ridiculous. If Errol Flynn was a Nazi than Ty Power was a homosexual. And Ty Power was no homosexual. He was a man. And there aren't many of those left any more.''

Outside, it was a warm late-summer night. A breeze came up from the lake and shook at the maple trees. Prudence Caldwell turned to Tom.

''What do you think?'' she asked.

''She's quite a character.''

''Never mind that. I think I've got one hell of a story. The police have no description at all of any suspect. Now we have one. The Heartthrob Killer.''

''The what?''

''Heartthrob Killer. It's perfect. Of course, there are a few things I have to check out first. It would be interesting to find out if Carrie was having financial problems. But what a story. And I've got you to thank, Tom.''

''Yeah,'' Tom said distractedly.

''Anything wrong?'' Pru asked.

He was looking past the Beachcourt Apartments at the

sagging pile of a house that he and Stormy used to live in. It was dark. Nobody was home. He started toward the limo.

"No, nothing's wrong," he said.

He dropped Prudence off at her apartment, then headed uptown toward the Windsor Arms. *Tall, dark, and handsome.* If he was going to describe Ash Conlon in one sentence, that's how he would do it. A hunk? That, too. Sure. He was a hunk. No doubt about it.

Stormy Willis was crazy about him. Ash Conlon had gone to school with Carrie Wayborn. Suppose he was seeing her on the sly? Hopping out of Stormy's bed and running next door to Carrie's. According to Mrs. Dougall, Carrie wasn't adverse to a little hanky-panky.

Suppose further that something had gone sour. Suppose — just suppose — Ash Conlon killed Carrie Wayborn. Why would he do a thing like that? All sorts of reasons. Maybe she was going to tell Stormy he was fucking her. Maybe he got mad because she was yelling at him. He filled her mouth full of carpet cleaner. This was all nonsense, of course. But suppose. Just suppose.

In the back of the car, Louis the chauffeur stirred and groaned. He sat up, pale as a wafer.

"Mr. Coward," he mumbled.

"Take it easy, Lou," Tom said. "I'll have us at the hotel in a few minutes."

"Mr. Coward, I think I'm gonna be sick," Lou groaned.

"Oh, shit," Tom said. He pulled the limo over to the side of the road.

8

In the darkness, Lex Madison fumbled for his keys. He stood on the porch of the small, midtown house he had rented for the next couple of months, and tried to unlock the door. Shit! He could not believe it. Having to rent a house in *his* town. It was unbelievable. But Lea got their old place, then turned around and sold it without even telling him. It was her way of signaling that the marriage was over. She had gone out and bought what she termed "her own place." Jesus Christ, but she had gall. Her own place, indeed.

He finally got the key in the lock and went inside, where he snapped on some lights, threw the single overnight bag he had brought with him from Los Angeles on the sofa, and went upstairs to the bedroom, intending to change into a robe, maybe snort a little something — although, Christ, he had to be careful with that stuff — and get a good night's sleep. In the morning, he thought, as he went into the bedroom, he would start editing the movie, safely removed from those fucking jackals at the studio.

"Don't turn on the light, hon."

He was halfway through the door leading into the bedroom. There, on the queen-sized bed with the quilted pink coverlet, lay Kelly Langlois. She did not have any clothes on.

"Hello, Lex," Kelly said. "I've been waiting hours. Never thought you were going to get here."

"I'm sorry about that, Kelly," Lex said calmly. "The

flight was delayed out of Los Angeles." He glanced
around the bedroom. Just stay cool, he thought. No sense
in getting all riled up. The new Lex, the Lex he wished to
cultivate, would not blow up like the old Lex. He studied
her for a moment, noticed that her body had survived
the years extraordinarily well, then said, "You should
have let me know you were coming. Then you wouldn't
have had to break in here."

"That's okay, hon," she said. "Turns out I'm a real cat
burglar. Smashed one of the panes in the back door with
a brick."

"It's been a long time, Kelly," he said.

"Too long, hon."

"Not long enough."

"Aw, come on, babe. I got myself all hot and bothered
for you and everything." She shifted on the bed and put
her hands between her legs. "You used to love it like this."

"So we'll fuck."

"One for old times sake, hon."

"And then what will we do?"

She removed her hand from her crotch. "Then we can
talk about Carrie."

"Then it was you phoning the beach house."

"I may have dialed once or twice. Shake you up a bit,
hon?"

"Kelly, Kelly," Lex said. "You're still crazy after all these
years."

"I think you killed her, hon. You or Ash. I'm not sure
which. That's what I'm here to find out."

"Go lie in his bed, then."

"In good time, hon. Right now I'm more interested in
you."

"If you want to know whether I killed Carrie, the answer is no. I haven't seen her for years."

"That's bullshit, hon, and you know it. She was after
you for money. Pulling in the old markers. She told me

so herself. I talked to her just a couple of weeks before she died. She told me what she was up to."

Lex didn't say anything for a moment. Then he said, "I told her to fuck off."

"That's better. That's more like my Lex. Maybe Ash told her the same thing. I figure if she got tough one of you might have gotten a little carried away. Which is why I am having to take time out from an active business life in the greater Los Angeles area in order to get to the bottom of this."

"I don't think you've got enough of a brain left after all those drugs to get to the bottom of anything dear," Lex said nastily.

"You don't think so, Lexy? Don't kid yourself. I know the buttons to push. With both you and Ash."

"Maybe then, Kelly. Not now." He took a step closer. "Come on. I want you out of here."

She reached casually for the leather shoulder bag that was on the floor beside the bed. A moment later, she was drawing out a brutal little snub-nosed revolver. He stood very still when he saw the gun pointing at him. She rose off the bed.

"Why don't we finish it right here?" A cheerless smile curled around her mouth. "Nobody even knows I'm in town. They'll find your body, and they won't have a clue who did it. I'll bet you've got some blow around here, sexy Lexy. Make sure the cops find that, and maybe it's a drug deal gone sour. Right?"

Lex swallowed a couple of times. "It's like I said. I didn't kill Carrie. She made some nasty noises about money, that's true. But I didn't kill her."

Kelly raised the gun up, and he thought she was going to kill him right there. He began to tremble. She pulled back the hammer on the revolver.

"Oh, Jesus, hon," she said breathlessly, "it would be so damned easy. So goddamned easy."

"Please." His mouth felt very dry. He had difficulty getting that word out.

"I hope it is you, Lex. You know that? I have dreams about killing you. But I can wait, hon."

She bent down and scooped her clothes from the floor and held them against her torso. "What I'm going to do is go downstairs. I want you to stay right here for the next ten minutes or so, until I'm out the door. That's my boy. And don't worry. I'll be in touch."

He collapsed onto the bed, his face slick with sweat. *Jesus. Oh, Jesus. Jesus.* He sat there, shaking, until he heard the door close below. Then the rage started building, the fury at Kelly and his own impotence when it came to dealing with her. He saw it in her eyes, though. She *would* have killed him. In the bedroom, he let out an anguished howl, shook his head furiously. He tried to regain some calm. Maybe a little blow. That would settle him. He would do just a bit, and then he would be able to see things much more clearly. He could decide how to deal with Kelly Langlois.

"*Darrrr-ling!*" Kelly's voice reverberated through the apartment as she came in the door. "Your little wifey poo is home. I'm gonna put on the pot roast, hon. How's about a martini before dinner? I'm gonna slip into my baby-doll pajamas and ride your big fat cock."

She went into the living room, stepped around the pool of blood on the white shag rug, and went over to the home-entertainment center her John-O was so proud of. She extracted a tape from her shoulder bag, and popped it into the tape deck. Mick Jagger filled the room, screeching out, "She's the Boss."

"I hope you don't mind, hon," she said to Johnny Karras. "I mean this is better than Kenny Rogers. And shame on you, babe. I was going through your records, and I found *Andy Williams' Greatest Hits*. You've gotta get rid of that shit, you really do."

Johnny stared at her from the brown leather Lazy Boy where she had left him after she stuck the long paring knife between his ribs. He stared at her sightlessly, his mouth partially open, as if to express surprise that after he had kicked her ass all over the apartment last night, she might want to retaliate like this.

"Them's the breaks, baby ducks," Kelly said, bending over and planting a kiss on his cold, hard forehead. She supposed it was her fault. She did suggest that they freebase the coke. But then who knew that freebasing a little coke would turn him into such a violent maniac? Live and learn, she thought as she crossed the room to the telephone.

Someone picked up the receiver on the other end after three rings. A female voice said hello, and Kelly said, "Ashley Conlon, please." She waited a moment, and then Ashley came on the line.

"Who's the cute young thing, hon?" Kelly asked. "Would she care to know that you're not quite what the advertising claims?"

There was silence on the line.

"I know you can't say anything, hon. She must be standing right there wondering who I am, right? Don't fret, babe. I'm not gonna tell her anything. Not yet. But I do need your help. Well, I need either your confession or your help. If you did kill poor Carrie, then I think I should know. But if you didn't, and I don't really think you did, you can help me nab the culprit. You know? Just like a Nancy Drew mystery."

The line went dead. Kelly sighed deeply, looked over at the corpse of Johnny Karras, and winked conspiratorily. "I think we've got 'em on the run, John-O". She dialed again. When the receiver was picked up, she said, "Hey, Dude," taking her voice down to the old throaty growl.

" — Kelly."

"How are ya, hon?"

"For Christ's sake. Where did you spring up from?"

"Everywhere. Nowhere. You know me, darlin'."

"Are you in town?"

"Sort of."

"On the quiet?"

"Sort of."

His laughter slid down the line. "Same old Kelly, for God's sake. Still in the movie business?"

"Are you kidding? I was never in the movie business, Dude. I was just, you know, *there* for a little while."

"Well, you may not be in the movie business, but I sure am. I'm a production manager now."

"Whatever that is, hon, I'm happy for you. I'm happy for anyone who's got their shit together in this day and age. But listen, hon. I need a favor from you." She glanced over at the corpse of Johnny Karras. "My, uh, boyfriend and I just broke up. I need a place to crash for awhile. A private place, Dude. Somewhere where I'm not gonna be hassled."

"Same old Kelly," he laughed. "I've got something for you, though. I'm on this movie. A teen exploitation thing called *Buns*. They're opening the old Lakelot Studio, down by the water in the west end, to do the interiors. Remember the Lakelot? We did the *Zoom-Zoom* interiors in there."

"Sure, hon, how could I forget it? I was the *mooo-vieee* star."

"There was a little apartment there. In fact, I bunked in it for a couple of weeks when we shot *Zoom-Zoom*. It's not much of anything. Bedroom. Sitting room. Shower. But it's okay. I dunno whether anyone even remembers it's there. Anyway, I went up on one of the catwalks the other day, and lo and behold, there it was. Little dirty, but you could clean the place up, no trouble. And it's private. No one has to know you're there if you don't want them to."

She was delighted, of course. "Good old Dude," she said.

"That's okay, Kelly," he said. "You was good to me back when Credence Clearwater Revival was making all the sense you needed." They went through a lot of shit like that before she could get him to the point where they made arrangements to meet and pick up the key for the place.

When she hung up, she went into the kitchen and found a pair of rubber gloves. Then for the next two hours she cleaned up the apartment, obliterating any trace of her presence. She got the glassine bags of cocaine and emptied one of them around the body. Then she polished the handle of the paring knife, and the portion of the blade that was exposed.

She found three hundred dollars in tens and twenties in his wallet, found another five hundred dollars in a desk drawer, decided against the jewelry in his bedroom or any of the credit cards. Finally, she gathered her shoulder bag, took one last glance around, and blew Johnny a kiss. He sat there in the Lazy Boy, just staring back at her.

"Fuck you, hon, if you can't even say goodbye. And after all I did for you, too." She laughed and closed the apartment door carefully behind her.

9

Just before nightfall, Stormy Willis jogged steadily along the boardwalk. The lake adjacent to the boardwalk was a gray sheet bunted against the rumbling thunderclouds that moved along the horizon. A few sea gulls, sensing the coming rain, fluttered close to inspect the lake surface, as though suspicious of its placidness. Reassured, they veered away and headed inland for safety.

A few raindrops struck Stormy on the arms and shoulders. That was enough to send most of the joggers home. There were a couple of other diehards, guys in short shorts with great legs and headbands and lots of sweat. Nothing like Ashley, of course. Nothing as good as that.

The rain began to fall steadily now. But Stormy decided to go another mile. Have to keep in shape for that man of mine, she thought.

She was warm and dazzled just thinking about him. Horny, too. God, how he could fuck her. She was absolutely wanton for him; she surprised herself, having come to believe she was beyond that sort of thing. The rough passion could not last, Stormy told herself. A couple could not go on fucking themselves silly forever. Could they? But then the possibilities with Ashley were endless. There was no darkness on their horizon. Was there?

She slowed to a fast walk, and suddenly the adrenalin was swamped by a wave of depression. Okay. So there were a few things that made her uncomfortable. She wished, for example, Ash was not quite so picky. Everything with him took on a certain perfection. Nothing out of place. Not a hair. Not even a crease in his custom-made suit. She noticed his neck, the unbroken brown smoothness of it, and marveled that there were never razor burns, not a nick or a cut. That kind of perfection was wonderful in the movies. That was, after all, one of the reasons you went to the movies. You wanted perfect people in a world where everything turned out all right. But in life it wasn't possible, and it worried her that Ash pursued the impossible.

She had watched him stand before the mirror for what seemed like hours, inspecting his face, running his manicured fingers over it, checking for lines. He studied his body constantly, a quality-control inspector seeking the smallest imperfection and acting on it immediately.

Then, there were his absences. He was out of town three or four times a week. Usually in New York. But then he always called. Unlike Tom, he never got too busy. Or forgot. Or any of the other countless excuses Tom dredged up. Ash had made it clear that she could not call him at the office. Some sort of company policy. But he always called her. And he was delightful. He perhaps lacked Tom's throwaway charm, but he was caring, and he talked about things with her, and they actually shared experiences. Tom never talked about anything, shared little. At least that's how she now chose to remember their relationship.

It was raining harder. Lightning flashed, and the darkness was alive, shaking her out of her reverie, and making her wish she had decided to go back before the storm hit. More lightning. It cut down through the sky and outlined the old bandstand, a green-painted pavilion with a sloping shingled roof which stood in the midst of the park area on the land side of the boardwalk. She turned and headed for the structure. The rain was pelting down now, soaking her to the skin. The wind was picking up with a surprising fierceness. It mingled with the sound spinning out from the pavilion. What was it? She strained to hear.

Good Lord, it was. Buddy Holly. "That'll be the day, when you say goodbye . . . " Then the words were gone, swallowed in the wind and the darkness. She reached the base of the bandstand and hesitated. She looked up to the top of the stairs. A figure leaned against one of the posts. He wore a leather jacket, and a fedora pulled down over his eyes.

"Tom," she said.

"Come on up," he said cheerfully. "You're soaking wet."

The interior was dark and damp, the rain thudding against the roof, wooden floorboards creaking as she moved across them. A yellowish light reached them through the rain. The light came in over the railing, across the cracked wooden floor, and caught the bottle of champagne he had set down beside the two plastic cups and the portable tape deck where Buddy Holly was just launching into "Peggy Sue."

"When did you get into town?" she asked.

"A few days ago," he said. "I'm doing a story. Here." He handed her a towel.

"Don't tell me," Stormy said. "You made it rain."

"It was easy. A wave of the magic wand."

She removed her headband and ran the towel over her face and hair.

"Would you like some champagne?"

"Are you still guzzling that stuff?"

"Sipping. Just sipping." He filled one of the plastic cups and handed it to her. She took a sip. "Mmm. Hits the spot." She looked at him closely. "How are you, kiddo?"

"Great," Tom said.

"You've put on weight."

"Too much room service."

"I've heard that before."

"I'm thinking of settling down," he said. And he laughed.

"I've heard that before, too." She joined his laughter.

He touched his cup to hers. "Here's looking at you, kid," he said.

"God," she said, "the number of stunts you charmed your way out of with that line."

"It doesn't work any more," he said.

"I know," she said.

Buddy Holly began to sing "True Love Ways." He sang, "Sometimes we'll sigh, sometimes we'll cry." Tom put his cup down and took her in his arms.

"Here," he said. "Like old times."

"Oh, Tom," she said, exasperated, loving, resigned. "I'm soaking wet."

But she came to him. He swirled her around in the bandstand. The light caught at her, outlining the length and sweetness of her face, the water dripping down the upturned nose. How many times had he kissed the tip of that nose?

"Sometimes we'll sigh,
Sometimes, we'll cry,
And we'll know why,
Just you and I,
Know true love ways."

She leaned against him. He pulled her in, wrapped himself right around her. Instinctively almost, she snuggled against his shoulder. They danced in the music and the memory. The rain stopped, and the mist started to come in, and the bandstand was the world's most romantic place, and he was dancing with the girl of his dreams.

Then the music died. She turned and walked away from him, went over to the railing, leaned against it. He followed her. She looked out at the lake.

"Why are you here, Tom?"

"You know, to do a story."

She looked at him, gave him the knowing smile.

"You're up to old tricks. The whirlwind romance. You're a past master. Champagne. The right music. The next thing is the expensive restaurant where the waiters know you. Then the lovely hotel room, the bellhop winking conspiratorily. I've been through it before, remember? I'm a veteran. It's hard to resist."

"Maybe I'm fighting fire with fire."

"But Ashley doesn't fight, Tom. He's romantic, too. But he's solid and good and reliable. I know where to find him, and I know what to expect."

"I'm worried about you, that's all."

"Tom, there is nothing to worry about."

"I don't think you know what you're getting into."

"With Ash, you mean?"

"You don't know anything about him. How long have you known him? Three weeks. A month at the most."

"Tom, I know him."

Then he told her what she did not know. He told her that Ashley Conlon cheated on a movie deal. He told her that Ashley's mother was tried for the murder of his father. He told her Ashley Conlon knew the murdered Carrie Wayborn, had dated her in college.

"Did he tell you that?" Tom demanded. "When you told him your next-door neighbor had been killed, and you found the body, did he tell you that she was an old girlfriend?"

"Tom," she said quietly, "it's stopped raining. I have to go."

"Aren't you going to discuss any of this?"

She turned to him, eyes flashing. "I don't have to discuss anything with you, Tom. None of it matters."

"How can you say that? The man is a stranger, and you know it."

"But he's a stranger I'm getting to know, a man I care about. Deeply. Your coming back to town and digging up a lot of gossip isn't going to change that. Who do you think you are, anyway? Poking around in my life? What right do you have to do that?''

He shrugged helplessly. ''I don't have any right, I suppose. Look, Stormy. I've made a lot of mistakes, I know. But I care about you.''

''Then for heaven's sake, let me go. You wanted me to let you go. You wanted to play the king of the vagabonds, and you didn't want me sitting at home whining. Do the same favor for me. That's all I ask.''

''Okay,'' he said. ''But just tell me one thing. The night she was murdered. Were you at home?''

''Yes, that's what made it so scary.''

''Was he with you?''

She paused for a moment. ''Yes.''

''All night?''

''Yes, all night. Yes.'' Her face was fierce once again. ''What's all this about, Tom? What are you trying to get at?''

''I just think you should be careful, that's all. Just be careful.''

''You can't be serious. You can't believe Ash had anything to do with Carrie Wayborn.''

''I didn't say that.'' Tom held up his hands. ''Don't put words in my mouth.''

''I don't have to,'' she said. ''Jesus, you really are crazy. It's not just a rumor. You really are crazy.''

''Now there is one other thing. Are you going to tell him about this?''

''This? You mean this asinine conversation with a lunatic in a bandstand, in the middle of a rainstorm? I don't think so.''

She turned and went down the stairs. At the bottom, she stopped and called up to him. ''Tom,'' she said. ''This is it, okay? I want you to leave me alone.''

''What?'' He held his hand to his ear and leaned farther over the railing. ''What? I can't hear you. What did you say?''

"I said, 'You're crazy.' " Then she turned and ran off into the darkness.

The telephone jangled into his left ear at eight-thirty the next morning. Tom rolled over in bed and stared at the blue-flower print wallpaper. For a moment, for the life of him, he couldn't remember where the hell he was. That had happened to him before, leaping up for the New York morning only to discover it was an L.A. afternoon. "Well, that was a pleasant wild-goose chase we went on the other night," Pru Caldwell said.

"What wild-goose chase?"

"Just for the record, Laura Crawford Dougall was born in Owen Sound, Ontario. She spent the first twenty-five years of her life there before she moved to Toronto, worked for Bell Canada as a switchboard operator for the next five years, then married a dentist named Dougall. She then stayed home for fifteen years or so, raised three kids, and read too many movie magazines. Her husband died eight years ago. She never dated Gary Cooper or Tyrone Power. She did take the Universal Studios tour a couple of years ago, her daughter says. But otherwise she has never in her life been on a back lot. She was in Florida, all right. Daytona Beach. A fair hike from the Burt Reynolds Dinner Theater. Somebody oughta punish that lady. Cancel her subscription to *People* magazine or something.

"Thank Christ I checked her out before I wrote the story. All that bullshit about hunks with curly hair who look like Ty Power leaving Carrie's place late at night. Jesus. My career, such as it is, would have gone right down the toilet."

"Wait a minute, Pru. I never said Laura didn't entertain certain delusions of grandeur. But that doesn't necessarily invalidate what she heard going on below her, or saw out her window."

"It does in my books, darling. Anyway, it's all water

under the bridge. I'm onto another murder. Some computer vice-president, a swinger type, was found sitting in his apartment with a knife between his ribs. Drugs are involved. The police found cocaine. Anyway, thought you should know the truth about poor old Laura.''

"Hold on a minute," Tom said. He swung his feet out over the bed and onto the floor. He rubbed fiercely at his scalp. "Did you find out anything else about Carrie Wayborn?''

"Sure, lots of stuff. I found out that her mom's name is Rebecca. She lives at 531 Church Street. And she doesn't like to talk to the press. At least she wouldn't talk to me.''

Tom made notes as she spoke, the telephone jammed between his ear and his shoulder. "Anything else?''

"She was, in fact, having financial problems. She wasn't nearly as flush as everyone thought. The sexy-lingerie and rubber-dildo business apparently had fallen on hard times. At least it had gone bad for her. The staff had no idea she was in bad financial shape until they started looking at the books. Why are you so interested in all this?''

"Stormy's involved," Tom said. "That makes it fascinating.''

"You're going to solve the murder for her? Give it to her as a Christmas present?''

"Besides," Tom said, "I'm bored. Dull work awaiting the return of the great Lex Madison.''

"Do your job, then. Go around and interview his estranged wife.''

"I don't think Lea Madison would be interested in talking to me.''

"Good grief," Pru said with a groan. "I hope you know more about journalism than you do about women.''

"She's not involved with anyone?''

"There are rumors. Supposedly, she was catting around on the side with some guy, and Lex caught her at it. But it's just a rumor.''

"Do you have her number?"

"I thought you'd never ask."

"One more thing about Ashley Conlon," Tom said after he jotted down Lea Madison's phone number. "Any idea what law firm he works for?"

"Sure. Big one. Bunting, Crossland, McWhirter and Associates. You can watch the money growing on the trees along Bay Street from their offices. He handles entertainment law for them. He got the firm into the movie-investment business a few years ago. Acting as the middleman. The movies lost money. But I hear he made a bundle. Why? You going around there to challenge him to a duel?"

"That's not a bad idea," Tom said.

He hung up, showered, shaved, got dressed, and dialed Lea Madison's number.

"It's Tom Coward," he said.

"Ah," she said. "The washroom pervert."

"How are you?"

"Not talking to reporters."

"How about eating with them?"

"Are you calling for a date?" She sounded surprised.

"Yeah. I'd like to have dinner with you."

"Do you still have the chauffeur?"

"Of course."

"Good," she said. "I only go out with men who have chauffeurs."

"I'm not surprised," he said.

The walls of the reception rooms at Bunting, Crossland, McWhirter and Associates were painted a soberly expensive corporate gray. Original Canadian art hung everywhere: coureurs de bois made their way overland delivering furs to the Hudson's Bay Company. John A. Macdonald, Canada's first prime minister, rose up in Parliament to rail against American imperialism. A fisherman cast his net into the Bay of Fundy. A Quebecois farmer tapped the syrup from one of his maple trees, while mom and the kids waited in the horse-drawn sleigh in the background. It was traditional stuff, Tom mused, as the receptionist, who had colored her hair to match the walls, fussed about. It was work that passed as art in a corporate world. It allowed the firm's lawyers to feel less guilty about going home at night and watching the Buffalo newscasts.

"Now what did you say your name was, sir?" the receptionist politely inquired. She sat at a large black onyx-topped desk. Nearby were low-slung black-leather sofas. Current copies of *Maclean's* magazine and *Saturday Night* were stacked neatly on the coffee table.

"Diver," Tom said. "Richard Diver. New York *Times*. New York *Times* business section. I telephoned earlier today for an appointment with Harold Bunting."

Tom wore his best gray-worsted business suit, black knit tie, black Oxford wingtip shoes. His hair was slicked back, and he had gotten one of the bellhops to dig up a pair of horn-rimmed glasses. He could barely see through them, but they did the trick. The receptionist was obviously impressed.

A few moments later he was ushered into Harold Bunting's huge corner office by a secretary who appeared to be a clone of the receptionist, right down to the hair color. As he crossed the threshold he stumbled against the deep pile carpeting. Damned glasses, he thought. The secretary gave him a cool eye.

"Whoops," Tom said.

There was no corporate gray in Harold Bunting's "room," as he called it. There was lots of dark oak paneling, as well as heavily draped windows that overlooked downtown Toronto. Silk lampshades and silver cigarette boxes sat atop side tables. You could have organized a curling bonspiel on the vast gleaming mahogany table behind which Bunting reclined in a huge leather chair.

He rose as Tom entered, the epitome of a silvered and refined Canadian establishment that had all but disappeared in the past few years. His blue pinstripe suit was impeccable, his gray brush of a mustache as carefully clipped as his manner. He radiated ruddy good health, offered a firm handshake, and a quick inspection of his visitor. The steely gray eyes reached a quick conclusion: a young man dressed for success who was not successful. In short, a newspaper reporter.

"Let me just say, sir," Tom gushed as they shook hands, "that is one mighty fine suit you're wearing there. That didn't come off the rack at Brooks Brothers. No way."

Harold Bunting looked down at it, as if noticing the pinstripes for the first time. "Why, ah, thank you," he said. "No, it's not Brooks Brothers, I must say. I get all my suits at, ah, Anderson and Sheppard in London."

"Savile Row, I bet."

"Thirty Savile Row, yes. Fred Astaire also gets his suits there. Never seen him in there, of course." Bunting settled back in his chair, cleared his throat, as though to signal a shift in the conversation. "It's not every day we get a visit from a representative of the New York, ah, *Times*, ah, Mr. Diver. What can we do for you?"

"Thanks for seeing me on such short notice, Mr. Bunting," Tom said as he seated himself. "As I explained on the telephone, I'm on a very tight schedule up here."

"Glad to be of service to our American media friends, of course," Harold Bunting said with dignified good humor. "Although I'm a little in the dark as to what it is you're after."

"I'm doing a story on the business prospects for the movie industry up here," Tom said. "You know, with the Canadian dollar the way it is, things are mighty attractive for American filmmakers. Unions are co-operative. Crews are good. Everyone speaks English. And the telephone system works."

Bunting cleared his throat. "Well, ah, Mr. Diver. That's

all well and good. But I'm afraid we don't have very much to do with movies.''

Tom made himself look surprised. He flipped open his notebook and began checking blank pages. "Oh, but I thought you did. I'm told one of your employees, let me see here, yes. Ashley Conlon. He's represented the firm in a number of movie ventures.''

"That was several years ago, and our involvement, ah, such as it was, ended then. It was not a pleasant experience at all for us, I'm afraid.''

"In what way?''

"There are several lawsuits still pending from that particular, ah, situation, Mr. Diver. I'm not really at liberty to discuss it. Besides, I don't know many of the pertinent details.''

"Perhaps I could speak to'' —he checked the notebook — "Mr. Conlon.''

"That won't be possible, I'm afraid.'' Bunting now looked distinctly uncomfortable.

"Why not?''

"Mr. Conlon has left the firm.''

This time Tom did not have to force himself to look surprised. "How long ago?''

"Five months, I believe.'' Bunting looked to the ceiling for guidance. "Yes. Five months.''

Tom snapped his notebook shut and slapped it down on the mahogany desk top. It made Harold Bunting jump.

"Okay, Harold,'' Tom said. "Do you mind if I call you Harold? I think we'd better get this on a one-to-one, eyes-only basis as quickly as we can. Don't you?''

"I beg your pardon?'' The steel-gray eyes were starting to look distinctly worried.

"Come on, pal. We can go off the record at this point. But let's quit playing around. You know why I'm here. My sources tell me you're a very wise bird in the woods, Harold. My sources tell me you were tipped off a couple of days ago that a member of the *Times*'s investigative-services team would be coming up here to see you.''

Bunting made a face. ''Investigative services?''

''Yeah, Harold. Investigative reporting. You know, like Watergate. I know Carl Bernstein personally. Drink Miller High Lite with him. He's a hell of a guy, Harold. An inspiration to all of us.''

''Goodness,'' Harold Bunting said. He ran his tongue around his lips.

''Now our information in a nutshell is this: Ash Conlon skimmed thousands, maybe even hundreds of thousands, of dollars off the top of a number of movie deals this firm was involved with during the late seventies and early eighties. There has been an internal investigation in this office. Stop me when I get off the track, Harold. Internal investigation. It took some time, of course. Because you were thorough. You didn't want to point any fingers at the wrong people. Finally, though, you turned up all sorts of—what should we call it? Let's be polite, Harold: inappropriate behavior. Good term, huh? Inappropriate behavior in Ash Conlon's dealings with the clients of this firm. You call him in. It's very discreet. You lay the facts in front of him. You ask for his resignation. All very hush-hush. No one gets hurt.''

Tom sat back. ''The cards are on the table, Harold. Tell me if I've dealt you the right ones.''

Harold Bunting looked at him in absolute astonishment. His mouth opened, then closed. He shifted the perfectly formed Windsor knot of his maroon silk tie against the collar of his pale-blue cotton shirt. ''We are talking, ah, off the record? You said we were talking off the record.''

''Harold,'' Tom said firmly, ''we are talking off the record.''

''Well, it was nothing like the amounts you suggest, Mr. Diver. Nothing at all. Mostly it had to do with Ash's incompetence. I know there was that nasty business with the romance films several years ago. But he wasn't being dishonest so much as he was being stupid. We're still fighting the lawsuits over that one. No, Mr. Diver, Ashley's not a crook. Not really. We became, ah, tired of him. That's all. He is a man with a tremendously high regard for himself. Unfortunately, we in the end were not able to share that same high regard. We tried for a long time. Believe me. He certainly looked the part of the bright young mover and shaker. But he just could not manage it. We quietly asked him if he wouldn't like to resign."

"And he agreed that he would like to resign?"

"I, ah, don't think he had much choice," Bunting said.

Tom arranged his features into a look of doubtfulness. "You seem an honest man, Harold. A truthful man. But my sources are pretty damn good. You wouldn't object to my talking to this Ashley Conlon myself. Would you?"

"Of course not. In fact, ironically enough, you're the second person this week who's been in touch trying to locate Ashley. He's listed in the phone book, as far as I know. But we'll be glad to provide you with his address and phone number."

Tom narrowed his eyes. "Someone else is looking for Conlon? Don't tell me someone from the Washington *Post* is onto this."

Bunting held up a reassuring hand. "No, no, Mr. Diver. Nothing like that. It was a woman. Someone who used to go to school with him."

"Oh, yeah? What was her name?"

"Langlois, I believe. Kelly Langlois."

"Okay, Harold, If you had said Sally Quinn, then we both would have been in big trouble."

"I doubt it, Mr. Diver," Bunting said with a smile. "I don't think you're going to find much of a story."

Outside, on Bay Street, Tom took off the glasses and breathed a sigh of relief. Not bad, he thought to himself. Not a bad performance at all.

"You should have seen me in there, Lou," Tom said as he approached the limousine. "I was wonderful. They thought I was from the New York *Times*."

"That's a newspaper. Right, Mr. Coward?"

"Jesus Christ, Lou."

Louis looked chagrined. "No offense, Mr. Coward. But sometimes I wonder where you are from." He held the door open. "The company's on my ass about the bill."

"It's only been a week, Lou."

Louis got behind the wheel. "They like to be paid by the week."

"Tell them not to worry. Tell them I wear white suits and have a silver spoon hanging around my neck. They'll think I'm good for the money."

Louis sighed, and eased the car into the choked traffic. Young men behind the wheels of Tempos paused respectfully and allowed status into the street.

So, Tom thought, Ash Conlon had been fired more than five months ago. And Stormy still thought he was the successful young lawyer going off to Bay Street each day to pursue the ancient tenets of capitalism. But if he wasn't going off to Bay Street, where was he going? Tom thought for a while longer and decided he liked being the play actor. Let's see how far it could be taken. He leaned forward and gave Louis the address of Carrie Wayborn's mother.

10

The city was closing in on Rebecca Wayborn's small, nondescript red brick house. There was a sagging green porch fronted by a dusty swatch of ground that in downtown Toronto stood in for a lawn. The house was being nudged by high-rises and trendy restaurants and parking lots operated by fierce-looking men with turbans. Her house was one of the last remnants of a solid middle-class residential district that was now almost extinct.

Tom pounded on her screen door with an authority he did not feel. Almost immediately, as if someone had been waiting on the other side for him, a voice called out.

"Who is it?"

"Mrs. Wayborn?"

"What do you want?"

"Dick Diver here, Mrs. Wayborn. I was at school with Carrie."

The door opened a cautious crack. He could just make out the dark outline of a head.

"What is it you want?" The voice was harsh, roughed up by a lot of cigarette smoke.

"Like I said, Mrs. Wayborn. My name's Diver. Dick Diver. I've been living in New York for the last few years. Just got back a couple of days ago and read about Carrie in the newspapers. I can't tell you how shocked and sorry I am, Mrs. Wayborn. It's just terrible. You expect that sort of thing in New York. But not in Toronto."

The door opened farther as he spoke. Rebecca Wayborn peered out at him from a gaunt, troubled face. It was the face of a lonely aged woman with a daughter who had gone wrong. Confusion lurked in the corners of her narrow eyes.

Tom produced the appropriate look of subdued agony. "I—I didn't know what to do. I didn't want to phone. I thought if I came around . . . I shouldn't be bothering you. We don't know each other. But I just had to give some sort of indication to someone that I cared."

"You were in school with Carrie, you say?"

"I guess I got to know her best in the Rear Window Society. You know, this film group that got together every week."

If the name meant anything to Rebecca Wayborn, she gave no sign of it. "I wanted her to graduate so badly," she sighed. "Maybe if she had, this—" She stopped herself abruptly. She stared at him, uncertainty for a moment crowding aside any other emotion flickering across her sad features. "I appreciate your coming around. Maybe you'd like a cup of coffee now that you're here."

"I don't want to bother you."

"No bother." She smiled limply. "My social calendar isn't exactly full."

The interior of the house was closed and dark. Heavy drapes had been drawn across the window, cutting off any outside light. The living room with its dull flowered wallpaper was cast in a gloom relieved only by the unsteady light emanating from a television set. On the screen a handsome young man embraced a beautiful woman and swore undying devotion. There was a sagging wing chair drawn up to the televison, and an end table stood beside it with a large cut-glass ashtray overflowing with cigarette butts. Beyond the television set a bricked fireplace dominated the wall with cheerful fakery. The mantelpiece was festooned with pictures of Carrie Wayborn: Carrie as a cute, dark-haired little girl, posing on a front stoop with a smiling father; Carrie in what looked like a high-school production of *Pajama Game*; Carrie graduating from high school; and Carrie the career woman, caught in three-quarter view, slimmer, more glamorous, and if not successful, certainly hiding it very well for the photographer.

For the first time Tom was struck with the reality of her murder and its tragic sadness. The mother meantime puttered in the kitchen just off the living room. There was a threadbare sofa adjacent to the fireplace with a coverlet pushed into a corner. Rebecca Wayborn spent her days smoking, watching television, napping, living with the residue of tragedy. He was overcome with a tremendous despair. This was reality. He wanted out of it. Too late for that, though. Mrs. Wayborn was back, presenting him with a steaming mug of coffee.

"Nothing fancy, I'm afraid."

"That's all right," Tom said kindly. "This is fine."

"I'd offer you something a little stronger with that, except the doctor's had me on sedatives the last few weeks, and I'm not supposed to drink alcohol. So I thought it best to get rid of any temptations." She delivered this with an ironic smirk, as she shambled back into the kitchen. "Have you seen Kelly?" she called.

Should he have seen Kelly? "No," he said. "As I said, I just got back into town."

"It's curious. I thought she would have been at the funeral for sure. She and Carrie were such close friends. They knew each other all their lives." She came back into the living room carrying a lit cigarette. "I'm smoking too damned many of these." She waved the cigarette in the air. "Maybe three packs a day. I don't know. I don't even count any more. Anyway, Kelly never showed up at the funeral. I'm sure it was Kelly who convinced Carrie to quit school. After Carrie's father died—he was killed in a car accident, real sad affair — she never listened to me. Only Kelly. And Kelly, God, she was weird. Even considering it was the sixties she was weird. Wild and weird.

That's what I used to call her. Wild and weird.''

"How about Ashley? Have you heard from him?''

Her face creased. "Ashley? Ashley who?''

"Conlon. Ash Conlon. He was at school at the same time.''

"I never heard her mention anyone named Ashley,'' she said dismissively, as though she had enough to think about without having to deal with this.

"I thought they were pretty good friends, that's all,'' Tom said lamely.

She looked at him, and there was a new shade of suspicion in her face. To escape her eyes, he turned to the mantelpiece and the photographs mounted on it.

"I can't believe anyone would want to hurt her,'' he said, sounding sorrowful. "It's just such a shock. Do the police have any leads? Do they know who did it?''

She shook her head sadly. "If they do, they're not telling me about it. It's very hard to get any information from them.'' She tried to take a drag on the cigarette, but her hand was shaking with such intensity she could not raise it. She saw him watching her and hurriedly doused the cigarette.

"Like I said, I'm smoking too much. This is just so—'' Her voice trailed off. "The police keep asking me who might have done it, and I keep saying I don't know. I don't know who her friends are. Or her enemies. I knew Kelly, of course. But that's about all. You lose your daughter. You think she's yours but then she's an adult, and she's gone. We fought a lot. I mean Derrick was killed in that accident, and that left just the two of us in this little place, and I didn't like the things she was up to. Didn't like her going out. Didn't like her coming home late. Didn't like her makeup, her clothes. Didn't like this. Didn't like that.''

Tears were pouring down her face. "She got her revenge, I guess. She became this person I didn't know.

This stranger. That store. All her idea. I didn't have anything to do with that store. Sex aids. God, I don't know. What kind of upbringing is it that makes a woman go out and start up a store where they sell . . . *sex* aids. In Toronto, for God's sake. But I guess I should be proud. After all, she was very successful. That's all that counts these days. Isn't it? Success?''

Tom didn't know what to say, so he inspected the mantelpiece again. There was another photograph behind the glamor shot of Carrie the professional career woman. He fished it out. It was a small Polaroid picture. Two girls, arm in arm, their heads tipped together, smiling into the camera. It was Carrie and Kelly. They were shot from the waist up, wearing summer clothes. Kelly had inspired *Zoom-Zoom*, Arthur Grinton said. Kelly had starred in the movie. Mrs. Wayborn hadn't heard from Kelly. But Kelly had been looking for Ash Conlon. And now it turned out Kelly and Carrie were more than just members of the same film society a long time ago at school. They were lifelong friends.

He turned to Mrs. Wayborn with the photograph in his hand. "So you don't think Kelly's in town?"

"If she was in town, I would have heard from her."

He held up the photograph. "How long ago was this taken?" he asked.

"About five years," she said. "That was the last time I saw Kelly. She's been living in California. Doing God knows what out there. From what I hear it's her kind of place, though. Wild and weird. Just like Kelly." She looked morosely at the ashtray. "I don't know why she didn't come to the funeral. Just like her, I guess. Miss Mysterious. She loved that. The mystery. Never knew where she'd been, never knew where she was going. That was Kelly. Maybe she doesn't even know Carrie is dead. Maybe that's it."

Tom looked at his coffee. It was now as cold and unappealing as everything else in this room. He had to get out of here.

"Mrs. Wayborn, is there anything, anything at all, I can do for you?"

She turned her head slowly back and forth. "If you see Kelly, you might let her know about this. She'll be devastated, I'm sure." She looked at the ashtray. "Say, you don't have any cigarettes, do you? I'm just about out."

"No, I'm sorry. I'd be glad to run down to a store and get you some."

"It's all right," she said. "I'm smoking too much anyway. There doesn't seem to be a helluva lot to do." She grinned. "Maybe I should join one of those computer dating services. Meet the man of my dreams. He can get my cigarettes for me."

Before he left, Tom placed the Polaroid photo back on the mantelpiece. The two girls grinned permanently out at the room, unaware of the misery in it.

He had an acquaintance at Movie House, the post-production facility that had handled, in one form or another, most of the feature films made in Canada for the past thirty years. An hour and a half later, he was slumped into an easy chair in the tiny screening room at Movie House as *Zoom-Zoom*, in muddy black and white, bounced and stuttered across the screen. The projectionist made some hurried corrections, and the movie settled and came into focus just in time to discover the camera tracking along Yorkville Avenue with a perky dark wisp of a girl. Her hair was like black silk falling to her waist. She looked like a more sensual Ali McGraw, sexy little body poured into a short-short mini, wearing hooped earrings that circus tigers could leap through. The camera zoomed in for a close-up. Kelly Langlois flashed mascara-ringed eyes.

She was Zoom, the youthful Lex Madison's ideal of the 1960s *femme fatale*. Zoom listened to folk music at Yorkville coffeehouses. She smoked dope in a loft, got busted by the cops and ran away from her parents, who, of course, did not understand her. She was, she announced at the beginning of the movie, a Free Spirit. It was the time, Tom noted, when you could still call yourself a Free Spirit and not cause everyone to groan. "I'm all mystery," she told her new boyfriend, Zack. "When I should go right, I zoom left. Zoom-Zoom, that's me." And later, lying in bed together, smoking grass, she promised, "I'll drive you crazy, man. But you'll love every minute of it."

The movie was about how Zoom drove Zack, and just about everyone else, crazy. She was wrong about one thing: nobody liked it. Not even for a minute. When her parents grounded her, she torched the family car. When Zack's father drove her home, she seduced him in the backseat. Then she told Zack about it. She was a nasty, resourceful monster. A monster, Tom conceded, with sex appeal. Her villainy was mesmerizing. The movie itself did not live up to its vaunted reputation. It was something you should hear about and not have to see. It was mostly ridiculous and self-absorbed, a relic from a past already curiously dated. It was not helped by the Peter, Paul and Mary songs, a love-in, a bad film reproduction of an LSD trip.

But Madison did manage to catch Zoom's essential soullessness. The soullessness reached a climax of sorts when Zoom maneuvered Zack into bed with one of her girlfriends. The incident—ugly, sordid, and surprisingly erotic,—caused Zack once and for all to confront his feelings about a young woman who could feel nothing. He decided that, for his own good, he wanted nothing more to do with her. Zoom, however, never conceded anything to anyone. "I'm a witch," she said to Zack. "I'll never let you go. I'll come for you." Tom wondered how much of this was fiction, how much was autobiography. The final bed scene was particularly haunting. Zoom naked, her face painted into a primitive mask of color, stripped of all civilized restraints, reduced to animal passion, squirming against an equally naked girl, demanding, and finally getting, a long, lingering kiss.

As their passion mounted, and Zack looked on with horror, the girl fell back on the bed to allow Zoom to kiss her breasts. The shot was a momentary one, but the girl in bed with Kelly Langlois was Carrie Wayborn.

Munro's was a private club on Cumberland Avenue in the Yorkville district. Where once hippies had walked in sandals with flowers in their hair and dreamed of a world full of peace, love, and Paul McCartney, there now traveled Yuppie trendies in Gucci loafers with fifty-dollar haircuts. Their dreams were of the delicious little Geoffrey Beene number in the window of that au-courant boutique that just opened. Paul McCartney sang silly little love songs. These people bought Bruce Springsteen records. The world had changed at great speed since the naiveté of *Zoom-Zoom*.

Just to make sure no sixties hippies were still hanging around, the management at Munro's inspected you through a peephole before allowing you in the door. For insurance purposes, there were always two or three beefy gentlemen hanging around the anteroom just beyond the door. They wore evening clothes and looked as though they needed to shave a couple of times a day. They also looked as though they would just as soon be out in the alley beating up patrons as letting them into the club.

There was no Munro at Munro's, only Freddie Agostini. He wore a Borsalino hat just like the one he had seen his hero Alain Delon, wearing in a movie. He loved to encourage rumors that Munro's was operated by organized crime, which somehow lent to the place an irresistibly cheap glamor. The glamor was particularly appreciated by the professional hockey players who hung out there, picking up the languid beauties the club featured, and trying to figure out which fork to use.

When Tom came in with Lea Madison, even the goofs on the door allowed themselves to look impressed. She was dressed simply: Anne Klein necklace; white silk shirt opened to reveal a black lace camisole with breathtaking cleavage; narrow black Jasco slacks. Her chin curved flawlessly past the boys on the door, and they got out of the way with deferential bows.

"My God," said Tom, marveling at it all. "I must come in here with you more often. The last time I saw a smile on those guys Jimmy Hoffa had just disappeared."

The maitre d' was Mario. He wasn't really Mario, but Freddy insisted that, in a place like this, the maitre d' must be called Mario. This Mario was a fat man with a red face. The toupee he wore was terrible, like a little sailor's hat perched uncertainly on his head. He made loud smacking sounds when he saw Lea.

"Good evening, Meester Tommy," he said. "So goot to have you back in town. And such a *boot-i-ful* lady you bring wit you." Because she was such a *boot-i-ful* lady, Mario now looked upon Tom as a long-lost relative newly arrived from Calabria.

"Hello, Mario," Tom said, slipping him the usual twenty-dollar bill. "Add that to the Italian earthquake fund."

The white-coated waiters moved in with the disciplined co-ordination of an Israeli commando unit. Water was poured, napkins unfurled, all in the name of getting a good look at Lea. "This is very impressive," Lea said. "They know you here."

"I phoned ahead. Told them to pretend."

She glanced around the warmly lit room. "So tell me who you know."

"A few years ago, I could have introduced you to everyone in the place. That was when the movie boom was on. Now," he shrugged, "there is no movie boom. And I don't know a soul."

"So what brings you to Toronto?"

Tom looked at her. "I told you. I'm doing a story on Lex Madison."

"The real story?"

He laughed. "No, no. Just a story. I gave up trying to do real stories. I stick with the fantasy. It's much easier."

Mario put on a great show of lighting the candles on the table. The candlelight caught Lea's features. They ordered double martinis.

"Pru says you came back to town because of your ex-girlfriend."

"Is that what she said?"

"She said the two of you broke up because you couldn't settle down. Now she's going to marry someone else, and you're heartbroken."

"Come on. She told you all that?"

"And more."

"More? What else did she tell you?"

"She thinks you are cute and wonderful. But unreliable."

"I'm sorry to hear that."

"I'm not. I'm looking for cute, wonderful, and unreliable."

"Is that so? What about Lex? When I was supposed to see him in California, he closed down the set for a week and flew back here. The story was that he was trying for a reconciliation with you."

"Well, if you call a lot of yelling and screaming trying for a reconciliation, yes, he was trying for a reconciliation. Are you taking notes?"

The waiter placed martini glasses in front of them. "I never take notes when I'm drinking." Tom lifted the glass. "Cheers."

She touched her glass to his. "Cheers." She sipped her

drink. The waiter presented menus. "I'm not at all hungry," she said. "Are we in a hurry?"

"Of course not. Tell me all about yourself."

"And you're not taking notes?"

"I swear," he said. "What did you do before you married Lex?"

"I married other men. Some of my friends became TV script girls. I married the rich and the famous. We all have to keep busy. Let's see now. Husband number one. British actor. Boy wonder of the British cinema in the 1960s. You know, Carnaby Street. England Swings. The Beatles, Michael Caine, that sort of thing. An Italian director made him a star in a movie about English decadence. After the Italian director went back to Italy, he made a lot of spy thrillers. He made so many spy thrillers that he became a tax exile. Summers in Monte Carlo. Winters in Vevey in Switzerland. I was into my photography stage at that point, snapping pictures that no one ever bought on locations no one could ever remember. Then there was the Moroccan."

"You married a Moroccan?"

"He looked like Omar Sharif." She giggled. "Acted like the Ayatollah Khomani. We spent three months a year at the Mena House outside Cairo, three months in London, and a couple of months a year in New York. He was an international financier. Very mysterious. Men with suitcases bulging with money arriving late at night. That sort of thing. Anyway, he decided it might be fun to finance films. He put the money up for one of Lex's horror pictures, and it made a mint. No one could believe the amount of money. My husband was very pleased. Or that is, he was pleased until he discovered Lex and I were having an affair."

"And what about Lex?"

"A lot of locations. A few months at the place in Malibu. A couple of weeks a year here while Lex gave interviews about how much he enjoyed being a Canadian, and how disinterested he was in ever living in Hollywood."

"What attracted you to Lex?"

"Hard to say, now. I mean it all turned so nasty. I suppose he had a certain mesmerizing power that attracted me. Most men don't understand that aspect of themselves as far as women are concerned. Those that do are tremendously successful with women, no matter what they look like. Money and power. They're great aphrodisiacs. I should know."

"So what now? Are you looking for another rich husband?"

The eyebrow went up again. "Not on your life. Too much wear and tear."

"Now you've got to elaborate on that statement," Tom said.

"Let me think." She pursed her lips. "The actor didn't require much, although he had a hell of a time getting it up, and he occasionally preferred fresh young boys. The Moroccan was a capitalist through and through. He wanted me to sleep with the odd business associate. Strictly business, of course."

"Of course," Tom said. "Did you?"

"Would it shock you if I told you I did?"

"No."

"And Lex," she continued, the acid dripping off the rose-covered accent. "Let's not forget dear, wonderful Lex."

"He made you dress up like Shirley Temple and beat you with a hula hoop."

"Nothing that complicated. Lex just liked to watch me fuck other men. That's all."

Tom cleared his throat. "I love these first-date conversations."

She sat back. "I'd like another drink."

He lifted his arm to motion to the waiter and saw Lex

Madison come in the door. He looked gaunt in a suede jacket and turtleneck sweater. He glanced casually around the room. At least, he glanced casually until he saw Lea. Then he stiffened noticeably.

"I think we're both going to need another drink," Tom said. "Lex is here."

Lea rapped long nails against the linen of the tablecloth. "Shit," she said softly. "I don't want a scene."

Lex began threading his way through the tables, headed for where they were seated.

"We may not have any choice," Tom said.

A moment later he arrived at their table. He was wearing the sort of grin usually found on skulls.

"Hello, Lea," he said with a brittle politeness that was liable to snap at any moment. Tom looked at his eyes. They were threatening black pinpoints. Lex Madison was wired for sound.

Lea turned to him. "Lex, can we talk later? Please?"

"I just got back to town," Lex said. He shoved a hand into his jacket pocket in order to demonstrate casualness. It didn't work. "I telephoned you a couple of times. But I couldn't get through." The black pinpoints drifted like sonar blimps over to where Tom sat. They did not register recognition.

"Hello there, I'm Lex Madison." The hand came out of the jacket and was offered to Tom. He shook it. "You do realize you're sitting here with my wife," he said. "I don't know whether you realize it or not."

"Lex, please," Lea Madison said.

"No, no, this is important." Lex put his hands on the table and leaned forward. "I want to know if this gentleman here realizes that he is sitting with my wife." His voice was beginning to get louder.

"I'm not your wife," Lea Madison said.

"Let's not get into an argument over semantics," Tom said.

Lex's taut brown face was very close to his. The glare would have stopped a charging water buffalo. Lex slammed his hand down on the table. A water glass tumbled over.

"Do you know that" — he measured out every word — "*this is my wife!*"

"Every time we meet, Lex, you always start yelling," Tom said to him. "Why is that?"

The eyes narrowed. "Who the hell are you?"

"Tom Coward," Tom said. "I spent a delightful evening with you and the lovely Tina at your beautiful place in Malibu. You and that young lady are just delightful hosts."

Lex swung a fist. Tom jerked back and it went sailing by the end of his nose. By that time Mario and a couple of the goons from downstairs were grabbing Lex around the neck, holding his arms. Tom was on his feet.

"Take it easy with him, boys. Otherwise, we'll all be in the papers."

The goons looked disappointed, the visions of happily beating the shit out of a troublemaker quickly disappearing. Lex didn't pose much of a problem, but he made a show of not giving up easily.

"I'll get you. I'll get you for this," he yelled at Tom.

The goons, with Mario alongside sadly shaking his head, hauled Lex kicking and screaming out of the room. Mario scooted back a moment later.

"Mr. Madison is very well known, Mario," Tom said.

"Don't worry about nothing, Meester Tommy. We have long, long experience in these matters." He turned to Lea. She was as white as the tablecloth the busboys were hurriedly changing. "My sincere apologies for thees interruption, signorina. There will, of course, be a bottle of champagne ona thees house. Meester Tommy's favorite, the champagne. No charge. Meester Tommy's favorite words."

Mario hurried away. Tom leaned forward and took Lea's hand. It was trembling.

"You okay?"

She nodded.

"Let me tell you, Lea. You are one hell of a first date."

She looked at him, her eyes full of tears. Then she dissolved into laughter.

They polished off the bottle of champagne. By that time neither one of them felt much like eating. She suggested a walk, and when they were outside, she took his arm. He expected Lex Madison to leap out of the bushes and murder them.

"Don't tell me you're scared," she teased.

"Of course not. I'm as tough as they come."

She regarded him seriously for a moment. "Actually, you look as though you could be as tough as they come. Maybe you fool everyone."

"Maybe I do," he said.

"Why don't you buy me a nightcap somewhere?"

"Christ, you're an expensive date."

"Expensive? You didn't have to buy dinner, and I got us a free bottle of champagne."

"All right," he said. "You talked me into it."

They went into the Bellair and sat upstairs where it was almost empty and no one would see them. Except Alvin Jarvis. He was sitting alone at the bar, nursing a magnum of Dom Perignon.

"What's the matter, Alvin," Tom called. "I bet you didn't make the payroll this week and now no one will drink with you."

Alvin looked surprised to see Lea and Tom together. But he did not say no when they invited him to join them.

"How is the movie business, Alvin?" Lea said.

"God, don't ask," Alvin groaned.

"The last time I saw Alvin," Tom said, "he was trying to gun down his director."

Alvin looked sullen. "I got a little carried away. No question about that. However, it's not a bad idea. I should probably get someone else to do it, though. You know, a hired killer or something." He looked at Lea. "You've been around a bit, Lea. Any idea where I could get my hands on a professional killer who would be interested in knocking off the director of *Buns*? It would make the world a better place."

Lea shook her head. "When are you going to stop making crummy movies, Alvin?"

Alvin was incensed. "Who says I make crummy movies?"

"Alvin," Lea said.

"They're commercial, that's all."

Lea put her arm around his shoulder, and kissed him on the cheek. "I like you, Alvin," she said. "You could do so much better. That's all."

He studied those deep green eyes of hers, and said, "Do you really think so?"

"You undervalue yourself, Alvin," she said. "You really do."

Alvin sighed. "Maybe I do," he said. "Maybe Tom should have let me shoot Bobby Putnam. He still wants giant rats in this picture. Jesus. Rats at a boys' camp. It's ridiculous."

Lea moved against Tom. "Let me take you home," she murmured into his ear.

He looked at Alvin Jarvis. "Let's take him along with us."

She ran a finger around the corner of his mouth. "Don't disappoint me, Tom. Don't be like everyone else."

"I won't be like everyone else. Don't worry."

She looked speculatively at Alvin for a moment. "Come along," she ordered.

Alvin looked pleased with the invitation. "I don't want to interfere with anything," he said.

"Don't worry about it, darling," Lea Madison said, starting to get up.

Lea's house was a low one-story affair, the entire south side done in glass that looked out through a Jacuzzi onto a beautifully lit swimming pool. It was small and cozy, a woman's house, with quilted cotton sofas and lots of art pieces. Alvin Jarvis promptly produced the coke Tom somehow suspected he would be able to produce.

Lea swept into the living room carrying a silver tray laden with Grand Marnier and coffee. She did two lines, followed by Tom, followed by Alvin Jarvis. Everyone was ripped and roaring. She ran her hands over Tom's face and looked at him imploringly, but the booze and the dope had effectively banked sensitivity. He liked her but didn't want her; or wanted her and didn't like her — he could not decide which. Instead, he thought of Stormy.

Somehow, they all floated into the bedroom. There was a massive four-poster bed, the posts lacquered and brass-capped. Lea Madison removed her silk shirt. Alvin pushed the straps of the lace camisole down along her arms and lifted out her breasts. Tom collapsed on a nearby couch.

"Come on," she said to Tom. But he clung to his drink and a sense of puritanism, knowing his true love was waiting for him out there in the darkness of the night, and expecting him to be faithful.

Lea swayed over to him, her high breasts naked. "Help me," she said. But he would not help, and Alvin undid the slacks for her. "Come on, darling," she said huskily to Tom, as Alvin groped over her. "Don't be a spoilsport. You wanted this."

He wanted Stormy, he cried out. Only the words refused to tumble. He was mute in his abstinence from Lea's hotly obvious charms. Alvin, for his part, was displaying unaccustomed nimbleness getting out of his clothes.

He was behind her caressing her breasts, and she was sinking back against him, naked except for the wisp of lacy camisole crumpled around her waist.

"See?" she moaned staring at Tom with heavy eyes. "See? See?"

His spirit remained unpossessed as he watched the two of them grapple on the carpet in front of him, the bed, a few feet away, for the moment neglected. That spirit, pure as driven snow, refused stubbornly to allow him to wallow in the gymnastics, although he certainly could not deny the temptation that was being presented to him. Lea rolled onto her stomach and was making certain loud demands.

"Give it to me from behind," she ordered breathlessly. "Fuck me from behind. I love it that way."

The independent producer of *Death Elevator, Buns,* and other hits complied with a veteran's smoothness and attention to detail. If Alvin did not look like much, he could at least be the sensitive lover. Lea, her dark hair thrown forward, her breasts quivering, her body slamming back against his, was quick to acknowledge expertise.

"There, there, that's it," she announced. Her hands clawed at the carpeting as again and again she was pleasurably wounded.

Curiously, though, when she came, she screamed out, "Tom!" Her face was turned toward him, sensually anguished, in the throes of climax, yet somehow trying to share it with him. When Alvin Jarvis, finally spent, fell away from her, panting hard, she crawled to Tom on the couch and kissed him deeply. When she pulled away, her face was brightly flushed, and there were tears in her eyes. She put her arms around his neck. Her body was damp with sweat. She smiled weakly.

"There, there," she said. "That wasn't so bad. Was it?"

11

K elly Langlois had set her new digital alarm clock for
8 A.M. As soon as it went off, she sat up in her small
bed in the little apartment that she had spent the last three
days cleaning up. She stood under the miserable trickle
of water that managed to extract itself from the shower
nozzle, then dressed in jeans, sweatshirt, the Mexican
cowboy boots, and went out into the cloudless day. She
walked to the telephone booth at the corner, picked up
the receiver, dropped in a quarter, and dialed. The phone
rang four times before he picked it up, sounding groggy.

"Sorry to wake you up so early, hon," she said to Ashley Conlon. "But you're very hard to get hold of, particularly since you seem to have left your place of
employment. Tsk. Tsk. Jobs aren't that easy to come by,
hon. You should be more careful. But then maybe it'll
work out for the best. Now you have more time to help
me solve the Case of the Murdered Dyke. In fact, babes,
I think I'm mighty close to solving that case. It remains
only for me to bring the principals together for the final
climactic confrontation. You know, just like a *Columbo* episode. I'm even gonna buy myself a wrinkled raincoat for
the occasion. Won't that be nice?"

She paused and listened to him for a moment. "Now,
be nice to me, hon. I don't imagine you're particularly
anxious for me to meet your new lady friend. I'd have so
much to tell her. What do you mean, where am I? I'm
standing here in a telephone booth. If you mean where
am I staying, well, I've got this nifty little apartment

133

tucked away inside the Lakelot Studios. I'm gonna have you and Lex around for dinner soon. We'll have coq au vin or some such thing. Candlelight and wine. After-dinner revelations. It'll be great fun. I'll be back to you soon, hon, with the details. Ta, ta.''

She hung up, waited a moment, then dialed another number. Lex Madison answered.

''Goodness gracious me,'' Kelly said. ''Everyone is sleeping in this morning, C'mon, Lexy, rise and shine. It's your best girl. Sounds like you had a bad night. Listen, hon, I was just talking to Ash. Damn, if he's not convinced that you're the killer. He wants to go to the police right away. Tell them that Carrie was trying to blackmail you. Of course, I worry about the scandal involved in that sort of move. I think we should get this whole situation straightened out, though. Don't you? What we have to do, the three of us, is get together for a little chat. Now I'm trying to work something out that fits into everyone's schedule. I know how busy you all are. So stay tuned, darlin'. I'll get back to you.''

Kelly hung up and stepped out of the phone booth, delighted that so early in the day she had accomplished so much.

He was far down into a darkness. For a moment he could not tell whether this was the nightmare or the horror movie. He moved along, groping blindly. Something shifted in the distance, outlined in vague light. This was the answer, he was sure, and he hurried for it. Someone turned as he approached. There was a knife in the stranger's hand. He tried hard to make out the stranger's features, but they were never quite discernible. Whoever it was had a knife, and so it must be the horror movie. *Death Elevator*, perhaps. Produced by that master of macabre entertainment, Alvin Jarvis.

But then Stormy appeared, naked and frightened, and

the stranger with the knife grabbed her by her hair,
dragged her back against him. Stormy screamed, and he
knew it was the nightmare, not the goddamn horror
movie, and he could no longer sit there and watch. He
had to do something. The stranger raised the knife. But
he could not move. He tried to get to where Stormy wrestled frantically with her assailant, but he could not move.
The knife slashed across Stormy's throat, making a neat,
decisive incision. The skin parted into an angry red mouth;
blood suddenly erupted everywhere. It looked to him like
maple syrup as it spread down her throat and over her
naked breasts. It was the cheap, fake blood of a dozen
bad movies, only this was not a bad movie. This was
Stormy dying, and he could only watch, as the stranger
with the knife finally became recognizable. It was Ashley Conlon.

"Shhh, baby," someone called to him from far away.

He was rising quickly out of the blackness, as if emerging from some deep pool. He broke the surface and there,
shaking him, her face etched with concern, was Lea
Madison.

"Oh," Tom Coward said. "Oh, brother."

She held him. "Are you all right?"

"Bad dream," he said.

The sunlight streamed in through the windows, falling past where he lay sprawled on one of the quilted cotton sofas. There was a blanket tossed across him. In front
of him, through the windows, the swimming pool was
smooth and placid. Lea brushed a hand across his
forehead.

"You're all sweaty."

"I'm all right." He tried to sit up.

"Darling Tom, you are many things, but you are not
all right."

For the first time he realized she was naked. She had
rushed from the bedroom as soon as he called out. She

said, "Why don't you get out of those clothes? Take a shower."

"Okay, yeah," he said.

She got his clothes off, then helped him under a hot shower. She reappeared with a large fluffy bath towel and insisted on helping him dry when he finally stepped out from the stall onto a bath mat.

"What happened to Alvin?" he asked.

"He's gone. Early day on the set, he said. He apologized for last night."

"Was an apology in order?"

She shrugged. "Let's just say we all got carried away. He wants to see me again. At least that's what he says."

"Do you want to see him?"

Another shrug. "I'm not sure." She tossed the towel to one side. "Stay put. I'll bring your clothes. I ran an iron over them while you were in the shower. Do you want to shave?"

"Do you have a razor?"

"Of course," she said. "It's in the cabinet over the sink. New blades. Shaving lotion is right beside it."

"For overnight guests?"

"A little sardonic this morning, are we?" The eyebrow was up, and she had a manner of looking straight through him that he found disconcerting. Not to mention her unassuming nakedness.

"My head hurts," he said.

When she returned with his clothes, she had slipped into a white caftan, very much like the one Tom has seen on her husband in Malibu. He was at the mirror with the razor, trying not to cut off the end of his chin. He turned when he saw her.

"You look like the virgin sacrifice to the gods."

"I feel like the virgin sacrifice to the gods," she said.

She left the bathroom. When he came out, shaved and dressed and feeling a little better, he found her in the kitchen making coffee.

"What do you know about someone named Kelly Langlois?" he asked.

She looked up from the percolator. "You have the most peculiar line of conversation in the morning."

"Do I get an answer?"

"You can have it with your coffee," she said.

Outside on the patio, at a table adjacent to the pool, she served coffee, fresh orange juice, melba toast, cheese, and fruit.

"You're going to make me fat," he said.

"I detest eggs and bacon in the morning. This is much better for your hangover."

He drained a glass of orange juice. "Nothing is any good for my hangover."

She sat down across from him so that her face, somehow tiny and fresh this morning, was exposed to the sun.

"Anyway," she said, "why do you want to know about Kelly Langlois?"

"A couple of weeks ago I was in Los Angeles to do a story on your husband," Tom said. "I telephoned Stormy Willis. She's the woman I used to live with."

"She's the woman you're still mad over," Lea said. "The one you have nightmares about."

"It wasn't a nightmare."

"What was it then?"

"A bad dream."

"Okay. You were in Los Angeles. You talked to your ex-girlfriend, this girl named Stormy."

"Her next door neighbor had been murdered. Her name was Carrie Wayborn. Stormy found her body."

"This woman was a friend of Stormy's?"

"Not exactly. Stormy knew her, but only slightly."

"Still, it must have been a terrible experience for her."

"Anyhow, the murdered woman, Carrie Wayborn, was in the Rear Window Society at the University of Toronto. With Kelly."

"And with Lex," Lea interrupted.

"Yes, with Lex. In fact she's in *Zoom-Zoom* briefly. Carrie used to go out with a guy named Ashley Conlon. Ashley also belonged to the Rear Window. Do you know him?"

She looked at him for a moment before answering. "No," she said. "Why should I?"

"No reason," Tom said. "It's just that Ash Conlon is the guy Stormy is involved with."

Lea sat back. "Ah, I see."

"No, you don't. I think Ash Conlon may have murdered Carrie Wayborn."

"But why?"

"I'm not sure about that. But he fits the description of the killer."

"Why are you telling me all this?"

"Everything seems somehow to be linked to the Rear Window. Something may have happened back then that caused Ashley to murder Carrie years later. Kelly never turned up at Carrie's funeral. Maybe she was too scared."

"Of what?"

"Maybe of Ashley."

"It seems to me you're jumping to a lot of conclusions." She poured herself more coffee. "Want some?"

"No thanks," he said. "Anyhow, I need more answers before I can go further. And at the moment, there's only one person who can provide me with the information I need."

"And who's that?"

"Your husband. Lex Madison."

"Oh, great," she said.

"I'd like to talk to him. But I don't think he'll talk to me."

"And you think he'll speak to me? After last night?"

"He'll talk to you. He's still crazy about you. I know the feeling. Believe me."

"You're quite the user, aren't you?"

"If Ash Conlon is a killer, Stormy could be in a lot of trouble," Tom said.

"Okay, okay," she said. "I'm not promising anything, though. I don't have much sympathy for men who suddenly decide they want their women back. I have some knowledge of how they lost them in the first place."

"Thanks," Tom said. He looked at his watch. "I'd better be going."

She nodded. "Yes. It's a long way, and you've got a big torch to carry."

12

Ashley Conlon lived in an elegant turn-of-the-century brick house on the corner of a quiet street in the wealthy Rosedale section of Toronto. The house was on a wide, pleasant thoroughfare, and it backed onto a tree-clogged ravine. The lawn in front was flat and carefully manicured. Oak and elm trees shaded the large bay windows and flanked a wide stone walk that cut through a wrought-iron fence almost hidden by thick hedges, and made its way to an enameled door, framed by coach lamps.

"Mr. Coward, I don't think I'm supposed to be doing this," Louis whined.

Tom could hardly hear him over the sound of the Van Halen tape Louis had shoved into the tape deck. Tom had made the chauffeur park the car just around the corner on a narrow winding street that ran at right angles to Conlon's house. From here, he had a good view of the front entrance and the garage adjacent to the house. Unless Ash Conlon decided to walk out through the ravine, there was no way he could leave the house without Tom spotting him.

"What do you mean, you're not supposed to do this? You're supposed to drive me. Will you turn the volume down a bit? It's driving me crazy."

"But I'm not supposed to follow people."

"You're not following people. I am. You're just driving."

"But how can you follow someone in a limo, for Christ's sake?"

"Easy," Tom answered. "Who would ever expect to be tailed by a limo? It's a great cover. Trust me."

Tom looked at his watch. It was nine o'clock in the morning. At nine-thirty, the automatic garage door opened and a taupe-colored Porsche drove out. Ash Conlon was behind the wheel.

"Okay," Tom said. "Here we go."

"Jesus Christ, Mr. Coward, he's gonna see us. Sure as anything."

"No, he's not. Come on, Lou. Let's go."

The Porsche turned south onto Mount Pleasant. By now Louis had replaced Van Halen with Billy Idol, who was cranking out "Rebel Yell" as Louis swung the big car onto Mount Pleasant. Louis was bobbing his head to the music, chewing frantically on a piece of gum as he drove.

"This is fucking crazy," he said. "Wait'll I tell my old lady I was in a limo following a guy."

Ash drove straight south, staying well within the speed limit. When Mount Pleasant spilled into Jarvis Street, Conlon stayed on Jarvis, still heading south. At the bottom of Jarvis, he swung west on Lakeshore Boulevard. He continued to cruise along at an unhurried rate of speed.

"Jesus," Louis said. "This isn't exactly *The French Connection*, Mr. Coward. This guy is taking it slow and easy. Out for a Sunday drive, I'd say."

"Just stay on him, Lou," Tom said.

"Why we following this guy, anyhow?"

"Because I want to see where he goes, and what he does," Tom said.

"That's reasonable," Lou agreed.

Ashley Conlon continued west, past the Canadian National Exhibition grounds. He drove past flat industrial buildings and seedy-looking motels until he reached a yellow brick warehouse. It sat at one end of a vast and vacant parking area.

"Now what the hell is he doing here?" Tom wondered aloud.

"Where are we?" Lou asked.

"It's the old Lakelot Studio. But no one's used it for years."

"We sure as hell can't go driving in there," Lou said. He pulled over to the curb, beyond the building. Tom leaped out and ran back to watch Ashley. He was parking his car in the lot next to the studio. He climbed out and stood, his hands on his hips, and stared at the building. He wore a linen suit with a herringbone weave that made him look as though he had just walked out of a magazine advertisement.

He stood motionless for a moment, then Tom watched him as he walked around to the side of the warehouse, and up a small flight of stairs to a thick metal door set flush to the wall. He tried the latch and found it locked tight. He stepped back and studied the door. Then he pounded on the metal surface and waited. No one answered. He pounded again, then walked back down the steps and headed back to his car.

Tom hurriedly put on his cheap plastic sunglasses and moved out from his vantage point behind a clump of shrubbery, walking toward Ashley Conlon.

"Excuse me," Tom called out to him.

Conlon was about to slide a key into the door of the Porsche. He looked up at Tom, and his face creased with annoyance. As he got close to him, Tom caught a whiff of Pierre Cardin cologne. The wind caught at a curl of his hair, tossing it across his smooth brown forehead. He quickly patted the errant strand back in place and looked more irritated.

"Excuse me," Tom repeated. "Is this 706 here? Seven-o-six Lakeshore. That's what I'm after."

"I have no idea," Ashley said.

"You work around here or what?"

"No," Ashley said. "I'm in a hurry, though."

"Hey, sorry, man. Just trying to find 706. You sure this isn't it?"

"I have no idea."

"Hey," Tom said. "Anyone ever tell you, you look like that gigolo guy? What's his name. That guy."

"I don't know what you're talking about," Ash said brusquely. He went to step past Tom.

"You know that guy. Dude that shows his pecker in all his pictures. Richard Gere. That's it. You look just like him, man. *American Gigolo*. That's the guy."

"Oh, come on now," Ash Conlon said. He suddenly did not look so irritated.

"I ain't shittin' you, man. Richard Gere. Spittin' image."

"I still don't know where 706 is," Conlon said. "Sorry about that."

"Hey, that's okay man," Tom said as Ash got into his car. "Richard Gere in *American Gigolo*. That's you, all right."

The Porsche wheeled out of the parking lot.

"How come you were talking to that guy?" Louis wanted to know when Tom got back to the limo. "We're following this guy, and you go up and talk to him?"

"I wanted to hear what he had to say," Tom said. "Okay, come on, he's still headed west."

"You wanna follow a guy, you don't run up and talk to him. You follow him." Louis eased the limo out into the traffic. "You know that guy or what?"

"I know him," Tom said. "He doesn't know me."

Now Louis had Bruce Springsteen on the tape deck. As the Boss sang about glory days, Ash Conlon turned onto the Queen Elizabeth Way.

"He's heading for the airport, bet you anything," said Louis.

"Why would he go to the airport?" Tom said.

"You shoulda asked him that when you were talking to him, Mr. Coward."

Conlon turned north on Highway 427, and from there

turned onto the airport expressway. "He's going into Terminal One," Louis announced.

Ash Conlon parked his car in the garage adjacent to the terminal. Tom made Louis draw the limo over to the curb. Tom hopped out and ran inside the terminal. The lines at the check-in counters were long, interrupted by piles of luggage and concerned relatives.

Tom spotted Ashley Conlon at the American Airlines counter. Conlon carried a small overnight bag, and he smiled disarmingly at the pert auburn-haired agent as he handed her his ticket. She gave him a dazzling smile back. Tom watched as Ashley moved back behind the ticket counter toward customs inspection. He joined the auburn-haired agent's line. It took him ten minutes to reach her.

"Could I have your ticket please?" She wore a professional smile.

"This is silly," Tom said. "But a friend of mine is leaving the country today. Ashley Conlon. Tall, dark, good-looking guy. Lovely dresser. He's wearing a linen suit with a herringbone weave. Beautiful piece of cloth. We had a bit of a falling out the other day over a business deal. I've just discovered it's my fault. I don't want him getting on the plane without him knowing that."

"Of course. Mr. Conlon. We know him very well around here. He's going to New York. Mr. Conlon is always going to New York."

"Is that so?" Tom said. "He goes to New York that often?"

"Three or four times a week, I'd say. He's one of our regulars. An Advantage passenger, I'm glad to say. I signed him up myself. But you'd better hurry. You have to catch him before he goes through security at the end of the concourse."

"Thanks ever so much for your help," Tom said.

He went back out to the limo.

"Let's go," Tom said to Louis as he climbed in the backseat.

"So what happened to your buddy?"

"He went to New York," Tom said. What's in New York? Tom wondered. Business? But Ash had quit his job. Maybe he had a new job. A new job that took him to New York three or four times a week? It did not seem likely.

Tom was asleep when the knock came at his door at midnight. He pulled himself out of bed, thinking vaguely that it might be Alvin, bored with the company downstairs at the Twenty-Two and looking for a nightcap. But it wasn't Alvin. When he opened the door, he was confronted by a tall, muscular man, dressed in a brown-leather bomber jacket, his hair slicked straight back. A small scar dug a trench along his left cheekbone. He carried a small gym back with NIKE stitched across the side.

"Mr. Tom Coward?" the man inquired politely.

"Yes," Tom said.

The man hit him in the solar plexus, then stepped past him into the room as Tom sagged to the carpet. He was down on all fours, trying vainly to catch his breath, as the man closed the door.

"My name is Malik," he said. "Lincoln S. Malik. That's not my real name, naturally. I always refer to myself as Lincoln S. Malik. I think it adds a little something to the name. A little polish. I added the *S.* myself. The *S.* doesn't stand for anything. It just adds something." As he spoke he placed the gym bag on the carpet, opened it, and drew out a short black crowbar.

"I like your name, Mr. Coward. I like the sound of it, although if I were you, I would refer to myself as Thomas, rather than the diminutive Tom. Tom makes you sound rather young and immature. I am sure, though, that you are quite mature. Therefore, I'm going to refer to you as Thomas, if you don't mind." He bent over Tom. "Anyhow, Thomas, I'm going to be counting on your maturity to see you through this. As you may already have guessed, I'm in the enforcement business."

"You must be going great guns," Tom managed to gasp.

"You might say that, Thomas. You might say that." He tapped the end of the crowbar against his shoulder. Then Lincoln S. Malik straightened and went over to the television set. He slammed the crowbar through the screen. The cathode-ray tube shattered. Glass flew everywhere.

The movement was so violent, so unexpected, that it made Tom gasp.

"Jesus Christ," he said. He struggled to his feet, still holding his stomach. "What the hell are you doing?"

"Apparently you have angered a person or persons, Thomas. You seem like a nice enough fella. I don't know what you did to get people this mad. But they are angry enough to insist that you get out of town. They have sent me around to make sure their wishes are carried out."

He went over to the dresser and smashed the crowbar into the mirror, shattering it. Shards of glass hung momentarily, then fell forward on top of the dresser. Malik walked to the closet door and slammed the crowbar into the mirror that ran its length.

"Just stay put, Thomas. This won't take long. Believe me."

He continued around the room, using the crowbar with a methodical brutality on anything that caught his eye: wall hangings, Tom's portable stereo, the bedside alarm clock. Tom leaned against the wall, his stomach still aching.

Lincoln S. Malik was now in the bathroom, going at the mirrors around the sink, gouging holes in the plaster, slamming away at the faucets, ripping the shower nozzle out of the tile. Tom watched as Malik walked back into the bedroom again. He was calm and professional, a good workman going about his business. He went to his gym bag and extracted a bottle of cheap Scotch.

'There's no use using the expensive stuff," Malik said,

unscrewing the cap. "It's a waste to use the expensive stuff."

He walked over to the bed and poured whiskey over the rumpled bedsheets. Then he went to Tom's open suitcase and tipped the bottle into it.

"Come on," Tom said. "For Christ's sake."

"Just stay calm, Thomas. Remember, I'm counting on that maturity we discussed. Your getting out of this with nothing more than a stomach ache depends on your maturity."

He doused portions of the carpet with the Scotch, poured it along the top of the bureau, over a pile of newspapers and magazines. The harsh smell of the booze began to fill the room. As Malik moved around, his feet crunched continually on the broken glass. When he finished with the bottle, he threw it against the far wall. It bounced off the surface, then hit the floor and spun against a table leg.

"There we go, Thomas," Malik said, coming over to him. "All finished. Now here's what's going to happen. The management will see this, and unless you are one hell of a convincing talker, they're not going to believe you when you tell them that some guy you never saw before came in here, busted the place up, then dumped whiskey everywhere. They're going to think you got pissed and went loco. They're going to think that, and you're going to get your ass thrown out of this hotel. It's a nice hotel. I've never been in here before. But it's real nice, and I don't suppose they tolerate this kind of behavior at all." He moved back, bent down, picked up the gym bag and carefully placed the crowbar inside, then zipped it shut.

"This is what we call the warning phase. In about 99 percent of cases, the warning is enough to get action. If it isn't, I come back, and we begin phase two. Phase two involves actual physical harm to the subject. In other words Thomas, we take you somewhere and we beat the piss out of you. I'm sure phase two won't be necessary.'' He picked up the gym bag. ''I'm gonna get out of here now. Let you deal with this mess. Once you've dealt with it, Thomas, pull up stakes. Now I don't know much about you, but I do know that you're from out of town. So it's not like you're leaving a lot behind. Just get to where you're going, and get there fast. Or I'll come back. Oh. And one other thing. I wouldn't bother calling the police. I doubt it would do any good. Good night.''

Lincoln Malik opened the door and stepped out into the hall. He closed the door behind him with, Tom observed, unexpected gentleness. It was as though he didn't want to wake guests in the other rooms this late at night.

13

J oe Allen's restaurant was, as usual, packed at noon hour. The narrow brick-walled room was festooned with theater posters and celebrity photographs to remind the locals of what they were missing by not being in New York, where the original Joe Allen's was located. The menu was on a blackboard, so patrons could inspect each other without being too obvious about it.

Alvin Jarvis already was digging into a cheeseburger at a table with a red-checked tablecloth when Tom got there. The table was positioned just inside the door against the brick wall at the front of the restaurant. If Max, the manager, had banished Alvin downstairs to the center of the room, then he would have been nobody. Today, however, Alvin was a somebody. He washed the hamburger down with a Bloody Mary.

"Where have you been?" Alvin said between mouthfuls as Tom sat down and ordered a glass of white wine.

"I've been out getting into trouble," Tom said.

"Trouble," Alvin said between mouthfuls. "Trouble is my fucking middle name. Bobby Putnam, that renowned auteur who always manages to keep the boys at Cahiers du Cinema guessing, is running five days behind schedule, and three hundred thousand dollars over budget. If we stay over, the completion guarantors are making noises like they won't pay. Or if they have to pay they'll take the picture away from me. There's hardly been a cloud in the sky since we started shooting; I don't think they're about to buy my excuses about bad weather. Now what's your trouble?"

"I got thrown out of the Windsor Arms this morning."

"They did warn you, Tom. Any more trouble, and they said they would give you the old heave ho."

"Some guy knocked on my door last night, came into the room, and hit me in the stomach. Then he used a crowbar, busted up the place and poured Scotch over everything. He told me to get out of town, and he left."

Alvin looked at him, his mouth bulging with hamburger. He shook his head. "Come on, Tom. Cut the crap. This is uncle Alvin you're talking to. Your partner in sex."

"Yeah, well, the management at the hotel didn't believe me, either."

"You wanna move in with me for the time being? There's plenty of room at my place. The house I'm in is driving me crazy. No room service. No bar off the lobby. Who wants to live in a place like that?"

"It's okay. I'm at the Four Seasons around the corner. At least what's left of me is. All my clothes are out getting cleaned. Can you get the smell of Scotch out of jeans?"

"I've spilled enough of it on mine. I guess you can, sure."

Lea Madison walked in, looking dazzling in white. She was with a man who wore glasses and a pinstriped suit. She stopped at the table and arched the telltale eyebrow at Tom.

"I called you this morning. They said you checked out. I thought maybe you left town."

"I think someone wants me to leave town," Tom said. "But I'm resisting temptation. I'm at the Four Seasons."

Alvin looked like a small boy, avidly waiting for attention. "How are you, Lea?" he said.

She blessed him with a radiant smile. "I got your message, Alvin. I was going to call you this afternoon."

"No hurry," Alvin said. "We can talk later."

Lea turned to Tom. "But we have to talk now. Have you got a moment?"

They went out into the stairwell. "I had a long talk with Lex," Lea said. "He's feeling pretty silly about the other night. I told him all about you. He's intrigued."

"Does that mean he'll talk to me?"

"That means if you drop around to the editing studio where he's working about lunchtime tomorrow, the two of you can probably get together and lick each other's wounds."

"Thanks, Lea," Tom said. "I appreciate this. Really."

"Don't mention it," Lea said. "Call me sometime. It gets lonely out there in the trenches."

"What about Alvin?"

"I am still considering Alvin," Lea said.

They went back into the restaurant and Alvin perked up. He motioned toward the man in the pinstripe suit, who was now seated against the wall in the restaurant's lower level.

"Who's your friend?"

"He's a lawyer," Lea said. "He wants to make movies."

"Good God," Alvin said. "Somebody should warn him."

She looked fondly at Tom. "Call. Okay?"

He nodded, and she was gone.

"What was that all about?" Alvin asked.

"Jealous?"

"No, of course not," Alvin said. "I just don't want to call her if the two of you are an item. That's all."

"I'm in love with Stormy, remember?"

"That never stopped you before," Alvin said.

"Let's change the subject," Tom suggested. "When do you start to shoot inside the Lakelot Studios?"

"Couple of weeks. We're trying to get the exteriors while the weather is good. Although at the rate Bobby is shooting this fucking thing, we'll be shooting broads in bikinis in a snowbank."

"Let's take a drive out there," Tom said.

"Out where? To the Lakelot? What the hell do you want to go out there for?"

"I want to see it," Tom said. "Indulge me, will you? I want to see the scene of your greatest triumph. The place where you actually shot *Death Elevator*."

Ten years later, the elevator that starred in *Death Elevator* was still there, a huge gantry, its latticework of girders hung now with cobwebs and covered with dust and grime. Once his eyes were used to the darkness of the cavernous studio, Tom could see where the set came to an end about eight feet below a catwalk that ran along the east wall of the sound stage.

At the base of the gantry, there was a mock-up of a hotel lobby. Alvin Jarvis stood in it, amazed it all was still here.

"Movie magic," he cried. His voice reverberated through the musty gloom. He hurried over to a control panel that was shrouded with a tarpaulin. He pulled off the tarp and began throwing switches. There was an electrical whir as the motor operating the drive pulley went into action. The elevator car on the ground floor shuddered, then the steel hoisting cables began pulling it up along the guide rails — much to Alvin's delight.

"It still works," he called out to Tom. "Can you believe it? This baby cost me one hundred thousand dollars at the time. I didn't spend that much on my first movie. Special effects. I felt just like Steven Spielberg."

"Hey, what's going on?"

Tom looked up. Above, on the catwalk, a woman in jeans was leaning against the railing, glaring down at them. Behind her was an open door.

"Who are you?" the woman called out. Tom could not

see her very well. From this distance, she looked small, brown, and tough.

"Who am I?" Alvin looked up at her shielding his eyes. "I'm the goddamn producer who is paying five thousand dollars a week to rent this place. Who are you?"

"Sorry, hon, I thought maybe you had broken in here, that's all. I'm a friend of Dude's." She shifted somewhat. Under the light from one of the hanging fixtures, her face became more clearly defined. She was older and time had hardened her around the edges, but there was no doubt about it. That was Kelly Langlois standing up there.

"Sorry to bother you guys," she said. "Dude's got me here to make sure no one breaks into the place." She turned and sauntered back through the doorway.

"Come on," Alvin said. "Let's get the fuck out of here. I've gotta get to the set. I'm beginning to worry that Bobby hasn't got the first setup in the can yet."

Tom wondered later if he shouldn't have said something to her. But what? Hi there. Ashley Conlon murdered Carrie Wayborn. Now he's snooping around here, and I think it's because he is planning to murder you. Furthermore, I think he's already sent a goon around to persuade me to leave town. Most of this is difficult, if not impossible, to prove. But what the hell. I just thought you should know. He hardly believed any of it himself. How could he expect anyone else to?

So he said nothing. Louis drove them back into town and wisely kept his mouth shut in front of Alvin about being at the studio the other day. Alvin, for his part, prattled on about the rotten state of *Buns* in particular, and about independent filmmaking in general. He already had forgotten the girl on the catwalk.

Lex Madison, wearing an open-necked denim shirt and a grim expression, stood over a small man who sat with his shoulders hunched toward a Steenbeck editing machine attached to a television-sized monitor. On the screen, a distant voice could be heard intoning, ''Scene ten, take five.'' A clapper board snapped and was removed from in front of the camera. Tina Deni, the actress, emerged from a bedroom wearing only a black-lace bra, panties, and high-heeled shoes. She stopped in mid-frame as though hearing something. Her face rearranged itself in a fairly close approximation of worry. The little man hunched over the machine stopped the film at this point, rewound it, and played it again. He wore white gloves, and they made his hand movements almost prissy.

''That's not going to cut in very well,'' the little man said. ''And I don't like the expression on her face.''

''They say Billy Wilder shot up to forty takes to get a moment out of Marilyn Monroe,'' Lex said. ''But, Jesus, I don't know. I don't think fifty takes would get it out of her.''

''Take three would cut in better,'' the little man said.

''Okay,'' Lex sighed. ''Let's try take three.''

Tom Coward stepped farther into the dimly lit cinder-block editing room. Lex Madison caught the movement and swung around. Tom saw that his eyes were red-rimmed, his face drawn. He nodded at Tom, then turned to the hunch-shouldered man.

''Felix, why don't you and your people take a lunch break. We've been going at it pretty hard all morning.''

''No argument there.'' Felix sounded tired. ''Okay,'' he called to his two assistants sitting nearby at movieolas. ''Let's get some lunch.''

''I'm afraid we're all a little whacked out,'' Lex said to Tom. He indicated the cramped cinder-block room. ''What do you know about this?''

''Probably not as much as I should,'' Tom conceded. He inspected the half-dozen barrels along one side of the room with lengths of celluloid dangling into them from a rod running along the low ceiling. Pieces of film were scattered across the floor, momentary droppings in the painstaking search for the movie that lay somewhere within the miles of celluloid Lex Madison had shot.

"Some directors love this part of the process," Lex said. "It's where they get to mold the film. When they can take their time, away from the pressures of the set. But for me this is the tough part. This is when you find out you should have gotten that extra angle or made an actor do one more take. This is when you realize you're a bit of a fuck-up, and you thank Christ there's such a thing as a film editor who just might be able to save your ass a half a dozen times a day."

The Lex Madison on display this morning lacked the haughty arrogance of the Malibu Gandhi in his white caftan, and craziness of the husband who found his wife eating dinner with another man. This Lex Madison was calm and subdued. Tom wondered if it was just another act in the unceasing performance of being Lex Madison.

Tom leaned against one of the editing tables as Felix and his assistants departed. It was quiet in the room; the whirl of machines, the blast of voices emitting from tape heads was for the moment stilled. Madison stared at the floor.

"I think I owe you an apology, Tom," Madison said. "I have a reputation for being hotheaded, impulsive, and just plain crazy. At times, I think it's deserved."

"You don't owe me anything," Tom said. "You might be able to help me, though."

"How can I help?"

"I saw Kelly yesterday," Tom said.

Lex looked at him sharply. "Kelly Langlois? Where?"

"At the Lakelot Studio. It looks as though she's staying there."

"I didn't know that."

"Apparently Ash Conlon does. The other day I followed him out there."

"Did he talk to Kelly?"

"No. He pounded on the door a couple of times, and then left."

"She thinks one of us killed Carrie Wayborn." He emitted a snort of laughter. "Correction. She thinks I killed Carrie."

"Why you?"

"Carrie was in bad financial shape. She made a lot of money at one time, but she spent more. She was threatening to sell a story about the two of us. She wanted me to invest in her business. That way she would keep quiet. It was blackmail, although we were too polite to call it that."

"Did you see Carrie?"

"I saw Carrie, sure. She was trying to gouge money out of me. But I didn't kill her."

Tom then told him what he knew about Ashley, his involvement with Stormy, the description provided by Laura Crawford Dougall of the darkly handsome young man who argued violently with Carrie Wayborn. He suggested that the young man could be Ashley Conlon. If it was, then he could be her killer, and Stormy was in a lot of trouble. Certainly there was an awful lot about Ashley she didn't know.

"Ashley Conlon," Madison sneered. "A misleading advertisement for himself. But then I guess Ashley's not responsible for that."

"Who is?" Tom asked.

"Kelly. She made him what he is. He was nuts about her. We were all a little nuts about her. Do you remember the Alfred Hitchcock movie *Vertigo*? Jimmy Stewart remade Kim Novak into the image of his dead lover. Kelly did much the same thing with Ashley. Only she reversed the roles. She was the dominant partner. He was shy and scared and a bit of a nerd. She made him into this gorgeous matinee idol that every girl dreams about. She called him her creation, and did everything but put him on display. And when she had created him to her satisfaction, she tried to destroy him.''

''How did she do that?''

''She tried to kill him,'' Lex Madison said.

The story, as Lex Madison told it, actually began with Carrie. Madison met her first, at a fraternity dance on campus. She was heavier in those days, but very attractive. He was timid and ineffective with women, having spent most of his life huddled inside darkened movie theaters. He was slightly neurotic, consumed by movies, and afraid of the real world. Carrie was neither timid nor ineffective where men were concerned. She was what was known in those days as a loose woman. She ''did it.'' That first night she did it with Lex in a tiny two-room apartment, with Roy Orbison playing in the background.

After she finished demolishing his virginity, they talked. She shared the apartment with a friend. The friend turned out to be Kelly Marie Langlois. She came in late that night, high, interrupting them in bed together, replacing Roy Orbison with Little Richard. Kelly smoked a joint, talked nonstop about rock'n'roll and the musicians she knew, the guys who hung out on the Yonge Street strip and in Yorkville coffeehouses, guitarists who were into smack, singers who recited Allen Ginsberg poetry. She sounded very worldly to a distinctly unworldly Lex. By the time the sun began to seep into the apartment, he had smoked his first joint and slept not only with Carrie but with Kelly as well, acting mostly as uneasy but fascinated spectator while the two women went at it.

By the end of the second week, he was head-over-heels in love with Kelly. There was a wild energy about her that was irresistible, and, perhaps more intriguingly, also a darkness. She called that part of herself the Dark Side, and she explored it in the Lenny Bruce records she listened to, the poetry by William Burroughs she read, as well as the dog-eared paperback editions of Herbert Selby's *Last Exit To Brooklyn*, and Conrad's *Heart of Darkness*. The offbeat and the grotesque excited her. She despised what she considered to be the dullness of the middle class. She was easily bored and desperate for excitement.

There were rumors about her past, that her father was an alcoholic former member of Parliament, that her mother long ago had an affair with Louis Mountbatten. There supposedly was a sister living in Nepal, a brother who committed suicide.

But then there was also speculation that her father was a doctor from Peterborough, and that her mother was a mere housewife with an apron on and bread in the oven. Mystery swirled around her, a living thing. Mood and whim carried her forward. She was totally unreliable. If she said she could not possibly under any circumstances make it, then she would probably show up. If she swore on all that was holy that she would be there, then she was sure to be missing.

By this time Madison had founded the Rear Window Society. He considered himself Kelly's "steady," although there was nothing steady about their relationship. For one thing, Carrie kept getting in the way. She was Kelly's friend, lover, slave. For another, Kelly had begun to experiment with LSD, riding out on long, edgy, shrieking acid trips to the nether regions of her soul, and coming back again quite profoundly shaken and anxious for a return journey. She began to see herself as a witch, able to alter those around her. She lacked only the right victim.

When Ashley Conlon appeared, she had her victim. She brought him along one evening to a showing of *La Dolce Vita*, a movie she loved. She wanted to live in Rome and, like Marcello Mastroianni, experience decadence from the back of a convertible sports car driving along the Via Veneto.

She said she was attracted to Ash Conlon because he had been present while the ultimate mystery was played out. Ash, she said, had watched his mother kill his father. The thought of it made her positively shudder. She was now fascinated with the possibilities of Ashley Conlon. Lex remembered Ash as a weak and sniveling imbecile, following Kelly around like a lost dog, constantly running back to his wealthy mother, who bankrolled his good time at university.

But Kelly got to him. And even Lex, watching jealous and hurt from the sidelines, had to concede the change was quite remarkable. It was like watching an artist create life on a white sheet of paper with a couple of strokes of charcoal.

Tom and Lex had retreated to one of those ersatz British pubs where there is Guinness and a dart board, and a lot of brawny young men who look as though they play soccer. Lex Madison made a face and ordered a Molson's Golden.

"How?" Tom asked. "How did he change?"

"He took on what appeared to be a new confidence. And in turn that enabled him to develop this . . . presence. There was something, well, quite sexy about him. Sensual. We all could see it. We didn't like to admit it, but we could see it."

"And Kelly was responsible for the transformation."

"Yes, but you see it was all very facile," Lex said. "Like teaching an actor the correct fingering for a saxophone. You're not teaching him to play the saxophone. You're teaching him to *look* as though he can play the instrument.

"There is a big difference. Ash acted as though the world was one big movie set, and he was constantly on camera. You see that in some movie actors, and it works well for them. They become the character they portray. In a way that happened to Ash. Life became his movie screen. Once that happened, he didn't need Kelly any more. I don't think Ash ever really cared about Kelly. Not the way I did. But then I don't think Ash ever really cared about any woman. For Kelly it was all a game, anyway, and she started to get tired of it.''

''Kelly became bored?''

''I think so. Besides, she wanted to push at the frontiers. She didn't care who got hurt. I don't think she considered the possibility of anyone getting hurt. That was the way she played things on the Dark Side.''

''So she decided to kill Ash?''

Madison pushed his beer mug to one side. ''I think so. I don't mean to say I could see it coming. On the contrary. I thought she was crazy about him, and I was crazy because of it. I was following the two of them around at night, spying on them outside her apartment. I guess you don't learn all that much as you grow older. I'm carrying on in the same juvenile sort of way with Lea. What is it about us men, anyhow? We don't want what we've got. We only want what we can't have.''

Tom gently prodded him. ''Tell me about Kelly and Ash.''

''You must remember they were all taking a lot of drugs: Kelly, Carrie, and Ash. So don't ask me how much rational thought went into this, how much premeditation. I doubt there was any. In any event, it was summer, and Kelly and I had broken up, and I was feeling pretty shitty. I knew Carrie had rented a cottage down by the lake in the west end. It was a pretty ramshackle place, but it was okay for partying. I wasn't involved, because I couldn't stand to see Kelly with anyone else. Except I was involved. I was hanging around the fringes every night, working myself into a real state. One night, I sat outside the cottage, out there in the darkness most of the night, drinking cheap red wine, knowing the three of them were inside, knowing what was probably going on.''

His voice was a monotone now. He was staring off into a distance that held the past. From behind him, Tom could hear the banter of the soccer jocks.

"I got pretty hammered up. I was driving this old De Soto at the time, and it was parked on a dirt road, just above the cottage. I fell asleep. The Del Vikings were on the radio, I remember, and this half-empty bottle of cheap red wine in my hand. I woke up with a start. I guess it was about three hours later. Just before dawn. I was pretty groggy, and I wondered what it was that woke me. Then I heard it again. This long, woeful scream. For some reason, I thought maybe it was Kelly in trouble. The scream was high-pitched. A woman's scream.

"I got out of the car, and I raced to the cottage. There was a screen door, I recall, and the screen was torn. Crazy what you think of at those moments. I thought the screen was pretty useless. Flies could get into the cottage with the screen torn like that. I opened that screen door — it wasn't locked — and I went inside. There was a table. There was an oilskin cloth with a plaid pattern thrown on the table. There was one of those old-fashioned toasters, you know, the ones where the coils heat up. There was a calendar on the wall that showed a girl with very long legs and short shorts. She was bending over the hood of a Mercury sedan, about to apply some polish, or something. I remember all that stuff, all those details very clearly.

"They were in the bedroom off the sitting room. There was a curtain on a rod, pulled across the door. I yanked the curtain back, and there was a plain iron bedstead. I don't remember any other furniture. Just the iron bedstead."

Madison paused for a moment. He shifted slightly in his hard-backed chair. He drew in a deep breath.

"They were on the bed. The three of them. Naked. I expected that. The rest of it, well, the rest of it was a shock. Ash was on his back, spread-eagled. They had taped his hands and legs to the bedposts. They had a straight razor, a really deadly looking thing, and they had used it to nick his body, to cut him in hundreds of little places. Not a lot of blood in one cut. But there were hundreds of cuts, and there was a lot of blood. It was as though they were trying to destroy the perfection of him with a thousand small wounds. It was very ugly.

"They were all pretty well out of it. On acid. Ash was moaning and sobbing. Carrie was leaning back against the wall, glassy-eyed. Kelly was down between Ash's legs. She had painted her face with Ash's blood, just like the final scene in *Zoom-Zoom*. She looked like a small, dark animal crouched there. She had the razor in her hand. It was covered in blood. She was about to go at him again when I burst into the room. She looked up at me. Her eyes were glazed and wild. I went over and took the razor out of her hand, and I thought for a moment that I might use it on her. She knew it, too. As far gone as she was, she *knew* I might use it. And she just crouched there, looking up at me."

He heaved a sigh. "But I didn't touch her. I used the razor to cut the tape at Ash's wrists and ankles. I got him into the shower, got him cleaned up as best I could. I had a friend who was a third-year medical student. I drove Ash over to his place. He'd gone into shock by then, and I was pretty worried about him. But the med student took care of it. Ash was more whacked out on acid than anything else. It took him three days to come down off that trip."

He ran a finger around the edge of the glass. "There you have it. The whole sordid story."

"But it didn't end there, two decades ago."

"Not really. At least not for Kelly and me. We went on, in a manner of speaking. I remained fascinated by her. Appalled. But fascinated. It was like Scott Fitzgerald with Zelda. I couldn't live with her, but I could use her. If nothing else, she was a marvelous character."

"So you wrote *Zoom-Zoom* with her in mind."

"That's right. A story of destructive manipulativeness. Then, I thought, why not use the real thing? Nobody was a better actor than Kelly. Nobody, that is, except Ashley Conlon.''

''Were you involved with Kelly when you shot the movie?''

''No, not involved. A little infatuated, maybe. But not involved. She was in pretty bad shape by that time. She was doing cocaine and even heroin. She was running with a pretty fast rock crowd. I heard she drifted down to Mexico, then back up to L.A. I heard about her from time to time when I was out there. She was part of the Sunset Strip drug scene, dealing dope for record producers and second-echelon rock stars. Nothing serious, I don't think. Just enough to make ends meet. The first time I actually heard from her since *Zoom-Zoom* was just after Carrie was killed. She started calling in the middle of the night, obscene phone calls, scaring the shit out of Tina. Then she started calling me and accusing me of killing Carrie. She never identified herself, but I knew it was her. You don't miss that raspy voice of hers anywhere.''

''She called the night I came to your place.''

''Yeah. That's right. Tina couldn't take it any more. It really frayed her nerves. She didn't understand what was going on. Neither did I, until I got to Toronto. I walked into the house I rented, and she was there with a gun. She said she was back to find out who killed Carrie.''

''When did Carrie get in touch with you?''

''Maybe three months ago. Lea and I were just breaking up. I suspected Lea was seeing someone else. Correction. I *knew* she was seeing someone else. I was angry. Jealous. Carrie telephoned. We got together for a drink. We ended up back at her apartment. One thing led to another. Just for old times' sake. All that stuff. It was fine, too, except afterward. She got nasty. She'd already told me about her financial problems. She wanted to make me an investor in this place of hers, this Intimate Moments. I said no. She got angry, and I left.

''I thought that was the end of it. An inappropriate one-night stand. But then she telephoned a week later and said she had decided to sell 'our story.' That's the way she described it. 'Our story.' That's all I needed. I'm trying to shoot a movie, and I'm trying to reconcile with my wife, and Carrie is going to tell 'our story.' Jesus Christ.''

"But you didn't kill her.''

"It didn't even cross my mind.''

"Could Ash have killed her?''

Madison ran a hand around the edge of his face. "I don't know. I really don't. Maybe Carrie planned to blab to your ex-girl friend if he didn't pay her. Maybe he got pissed off and couldn't control himself. I've made a lot of movies about murder, but I still don't know anything much about the subject. To me it's a fictional device.''

"What do you think about going to the police?'' Tom asked.

"I don't think very much of that idea at all. I get involved in a scandal, and for what? There's no evidence of anything. There's a half-nuts druggie rumbling around, trying to discover who killed her ex-lover. For the moment, I'm trying to keep the lid on it. If I don't I'm involved in a murder. And right now, I don't need that, thanks very much.''

"Do you think she'll contact you again?''

"She called the other day, in fact.''

"What did she say?''

"She said she wanted to get together with me and Ash. She said she wanted to resolve this thing once and for all.''

"Did she say where you would meet?''

"No. But now that I know she's holed up at the Lakelot Studio, I suppose that's a possibility.''

"Will you let me know if she calls again?''

"Listen, did you ever think of this: maybe Carrie just brought home the wrong guy on the wrong night? There are plenty of tall, dark and handsome men around. That's how Carrie liked them, male or female. Tall, dark and handsome.''

"I think it was Ash."

"But then you want your girl back, Coward. So you allow yourself to think whatever is convenient." He got up from the table. "I've got to get back to work." He threw some money down on the table.

"Let me get it," Tom protested.

"It's all right," Lex said. He looked down at Tom. "I want you to stay out of this. I'm playing along with Kelly because she's crazy and I don't want to upset her. At least not right now. If I bring you into it, chances are she's going to do something very stupid. I don't want my name in the papers. Not because of her. Not because of you."

"Does that mean you wish I would leave town?"

"It means I wish you would stay out of this."

"You didn't by any chance send someone around to my hotel the other night to encourage me to get out of the city?"

Lex Madison looked dumbfounded. "Are you joking?"

"Someone did," Tom Coward said. "Someone doesn't want me snooping around."

"Oh, Jesus, Coward," Lex groaned. "They told me in Los Angeles not to talk to you. They said you were more trouble than you were worth."

"I know," Tom sighed. "You just can't trust the press."

14

The night before, in the muted light of an intimate French restaurant both of them had grown to love, Ashley Conlon asked Stormy Willis to marry him. To become his lawful wedded wife.

That, Stormy thought, was the way she would start the novel of her life. That would be the first sentence. She was on the set of a deodorant commercial, wearing a bright red Danskin, headband, and leg warmers.

He took her slim, delicate hand in his, and a moment later he was sliding an engagement ring — diamonds inlaid in gold — on her finger. She gasped her surprise. He gently told her how much he loved her.

Those would be the second, third, and fourth sentences. It had been that romantic. Like something out of a movie. An old and corny movie, perhaps, but a movie nontheless. It gave her goosebumps just thinking about it.

She was standing in the middle of a gym surrounded by Nautilus equipment. A prop man handed her a can of deodorant. The director, a man with a bald head and a Santa Claus white beard, stepped over.

"Now darling," he said in a softly sincere voice, "you've been sweating through a workout, and you're going to meet the man of your dreams afterward."

"Entirely possible," Stormy said.

"Just what we need," the director said. "A method actress." He paused for the laughter from Stormy and the crew. "Anyhow, you're worried that you're going to stink to high heaven when you meet the gentleman of your dreams. However, your social life is saved when you discover in your gym bag a can of Good Life — 'the deodorant for people who *really* enjoy living.' You're happy as a pig in dirt. In other words, darling, this is a slice of life. Who among us has not reacted with joy and relief at having discovered a can of deodorant?"

"Who indeed" Stormy nodded. She flared up her best joyous smile and held high the aerosol can of Good Life.

The director rearranged her hand on the can. "There. That's it. A little higher so we can see the product. Good." He turned to the crew. "Okay. We all set, chaps?"

The lighting director stepped forward. "There's a shadow on the label." He turned to an assistant. "We're gonna have to change that scrim. About five minutes," he said to the director.

"Oh, shit," the director said. "Okay, Stormy, relax for a couple of minutes."

When she walked out past the lights, she spotted Tom Coward leaning against a pommel horse, the brim of the fedora pulled down low over his eyes.

"Tom," she said in a voice that barely hid her irritation. "I don't think you should be following me around."

He looked entirely innocent. "Your agency said you were here. And I'm not following you around." His voice was indignant. "I just happened to be in the neighborhood, that's all. Besides, I thought we could be friends."

"I could. I wonder about you."

"You look gorgeous."

She laughed. "I'm supposed to look as though I need deodorant."

"On television nobody looks as though they need deodorant."

Then he saw the engagement ring, and the shock made his face go flat and blank.

"I was going to phone you," she said. "It just happened last night."

"Christ, Stormy," he said. "This is serious stuff."

"I tried to tell you that, Tom. Please be happy for me." She put her hand on his arm. It was the way she used to put her hand on his arm when she wasn't engaged to someone else. "Please?"

"I don't think you should do this, Stormy."

"Tom," she said, her voice getting tough, "I don't want to know what you think."

"All right. I understand that. Do me a favor, will you? Let's go to a phone right now, and we'll phone Ash at work, and I'll talk to him. I want to offer him my congratulations. No hard feelings. The best man won. That sort of thing."

"Tom, what are you talking about?"

"I want you to telephone him, that's all. Simple thing."

"I can't."

"Why not?"

She was becoming impatient again. "They don't like him taking personal calls at work, that's all. It's a thing they have. I just don't phone him at the office. It's no big deal."

"Have you told him about me? That I'm in town?"

"Yes."

"What's he say?"

"He says I shouldn't be talking to you."

An assistant director called over. "Stormy. We're ready for you."

She looked relieved. "Tom, I have to go."

"Stormy. I must talk to you. There is something very wrong here. Believe me."

"Tom, I'm sorry." Her face pitied him for an instant, then she ran back to the Nautilus equipment and the director with the Santa Claus beard.

Alvin Jarvis was sitting very close to Lea Madison when

Tom stumbled into the downstairs bar at Munro's late that night. He did not look at all pleased as Tom slumped down in a chair beside Lea.

She looked properly concerned. "Are you all right?"

"I am peachy keen, just," Tom said. "Have you seen my chauffeur? I have lost my goddamn chauffeur."

Alvin poured him a glass of champagne. "Have a drink. You don't need one. But have a drink."

"My God, Alvin," Tom said. "Quit frowning."

"I'm not frowning," Alvin said.

"You are not glad to see me," Tom said.

"I'm delighted to see you."

"Oh, no, Alvin. You're thinking to yourself, that son of a bitch is gonna wanna come back and watch us do it again. Well, don't worry, Alvin. Once is enough."

Lea said, "Did anyone tell you that you've had too much to drink?"

"Tom," Alvin said. There was a warning look in those small eyes. "We're having a business meeting, here."

"Oh! A business meeting. I thought you wanted to get laid, Alvin. And here you are having a business meeting."

"Look, I know you're drunk. But don't push it too god-damn far."

Tom looked at him in feigned shock. "Is that a threat, sir?"

"What's wrong with you, anyway?"

"Stormy," Tom announced, "is getting married."

"Big fucking deal," Alvin said.

"Alvin," Lea Madison said. "Come on. Go easy."

"No, to hell with this. I was in the Twenty-Two bar the other day. I ran into the manager of the Windsor Arms. You fucking wrecked your room. Absolutely smashed it to smithereens. They just about called the police on you."

"I did not do that." Tom hiccuped.

"Yeah? Who did?"

"A gentleman named Lincoln S. Malik. That *S.* is very

important. He told me so. He had this crowbar. He went smash. *Smash.*'' Tom waved his hand about grandly. ''All over the place. Destroyed *everything.*''

''Sure, sure,'' Alvin said. ''And Santa Claus will be here Christmas Eve to buy us all a drink.''

''Alvin's interested in my script,'' Lea said, her voice full of false cheer.

''I thought the script wasn't commercial,'' Tom said.

''But it's good,'' Alvin said.

''Jesus. Quality comes to the creator of *Death Elevator.*''

''Fuck you,'' Alvin said.

''Sounds to me like you're more interested in the fucking,'' Tom said to Alvin. He looked at Lea Madison and raised his eyebrows up and down.

She slapped him across the face. Hard.

''I don't like drunks,'' she said.

''I'll inform the management,'' Tom said. Then he stood up and lurched out of the bar.

''Ah, let him go,'' Alvin said. ''He'll be okay. He's trouble. He gets all wrapped up in his own problems, drags the rest of us along with him. The next thing you know, he'll have flown off to Rome and be chasing some chick around Harry's American Bar, and he'll have forgotten what it was that was bothering him. He's like that. He's not reliable.''

Lea got up from the table. ''Thanks for the drink, Alvin. I'll talk to you later.''

Alvin shook his head. ''You're wasting your time with him.''

''I know,'' she said grimly. ''It's my mission in life. Wasting my time with the wrong men.''

''I am not necessarily the wrong man,'' Alvin said.

She smiled at him. ''No, Alvin. You are not necessarily the wrong man at all.''

She went outside and found Tom in the parking lot, throwing up over the grillwork of a black Ferrari.

"Your aim is lousy," she said, steering him gently away from the car.

"I'm coming up in the world," he gasped. "I used to throw up on Buicks."

She got a wad of Kleenex out of her purse and handed it to him. "Why not can the glib patter for a while, just until you get yourself straightened around?"

"I am straightened around," he said, wiping his mouth. He straightened up, stumbled. She held his elbow. "Oh, boy," he said. "I'm not doing this very well, am I?"

"Come on, let me take you home," she said.

"No. Not home." His face took on a dumb resoluteness. "Gotta get to Ash Conlon. Gotta keep an eye on the son of a bitch. He's a goddamn murderer, you know."

"Ash Conlon is a murderer. Right. And you've got to get some sleep. Now come along."

"You don't understand," he mumbled as she began to direct him toward her car.

"What don't I understand?"

"We're talking about death here. The end of it. Lights out. This is the real thing, for Christ's sake. It's not like the movies."

"Poor Tom," Lea Madison said, as she got him to the car. "Didn't anyone ever tell you? Nothing is like the movies."

A few minutes after midnight, Kelly Langlois, loudly humming the theme from *The Twilight Zone* television series, walked to the pay phone at the corner.

"You unlock this door with the key of imagination," she said when Ashley Conlon answered the phone. "Beyond it is another dimension." She paused. "Of course, it's me, hon. I'm reviving the old *Twilight Zone* series. Rod Serling unfortunately can't be here, so I'm going to host the show. We start to shoot the first episode tomorrow night at the Lakelot Studio. Lex Madison is the star, although he doesn't quite know it yet. It's the story of a famous director who fucks around with a beautiful cokehead from the greater Los Angeles area and lives to regret it. I need your help with the script, though, hon. I think it's going to be a hell of an episode, full of sex and death, the things that make television, not to mention life, so great.''

Tom Coward awoke in Lea Madison's huge bed with its lacquered posts and brass caps. He was naked under the cool linen sheets, and he felt dreadful. Absolutely dreadful. He sat up slowly, and the dull dry ache of the morning after lunged through his body.

Lea Madison leaned against the bedroom door frame, watching him. She wore a champagne lace bra and panty briefs, and she cradled a cup of coffee in her hands.

"Good morning," she said.

"Oh, brother," Tom groaned. He lay back on the pillows. "What time is it?"

"About seven-thirty."

"Give me the damage report."

"Minor. But notable. You insulted Alvin. Everyone became angry. I slapped you across the face. You went out into the parking lot and threw up. I took pity on you, and brought you back here."

"Now why did I get so nasty?"

"Because your beloved Stormy is going to marry another man. At least that's what you told us."

"Ah, I remember. Shit, Lea. What am I going to do?"

She made a face. "Maybe you should stop fretting so much."

"For Christ's sake, she can't marry him."

"Because you're in love with her? Are you in love with her, Tom? Really in love with her?" She placed the coffee cup on a bureau. "I could help you forget her, Tom."

"Come on, Lea," he said. "This is serious."

"I am serious. I've never been more serious. I like you."
She reached around and undid the bra, allowed it to slide
down her arms. "I'm not sure exactly why I like you.
You probably don't have a charge card for one single store
on Rodeo Drive." She stroked her high, conical breasts
as she moved toward him. "Come on, Tom. Forget
Stormy for a few minutes. Love me."

"Lea," he said. "Don't."

But she was on the bed now, advancing toward him,
dark hair thrown foward, those full lips parted. She pulled
at the sheet, exposing him. There was the booze of course,
and the hangover, the fuzzy lethargy it induced. There
was no energy for the objections, and she wasn't listening to them, anyway. She had only to look at the physical evidence currently rising up before her to know that
he did not mean them.

Those lips, they now kissed hungrily at him, and he
was touching the warm smoothness of her breasts, back,
trailing down to her buttocks, helping her with the panty
briefs, touching at the naked mound of an ass, listening
to her breathing, the intermittent groans, and, shit, he
was gone, lost in the valley of lust. Her hands, then her
breasts, swept across his rampant penis. His fingers were
between her legs.

"Baby," she said. "You want it. Fuck me."

He pushed her away. She gave him a Cheshire smile
and was right back on him. He was stretched out. She
straddled him, her breasts dangling off his face. He licked
at the long straight nipples with his tongue, noted the
sheen and ripple of her arm muscles as she balanced, her
incredible ass going up, then beginning its descent toward him. "Baby, baby," she breathed. She was poised
just off the end of his cock, her dark moist parts set to
plunge downward, and Jesus, he was pulling her down
now.

"Come on," he demanded.

Then, nothing. She was gone. Magician's move. A great disappearing act. Next thing she was standing naked at the end of the bed, breathing hard, looking satisfied.

"True blue, eh, Tom?" she said nastily. "Look at you. You want it so badly you can taste it. Where's Stormy now, Tom? She's not exactly the great lost love at the moment, is she? And I'm willing to bet Ash Conlon isn't quite the killer you thought he was last night."

"You're wrong," Tom said. He sat up in bed, shaking with want.

"You're playing games with everyone, Tom. You're fucking everyone's mind around, and for what? Because you think you want this Stormy Willis. I don't think you have the slightest idea what you want." She swooped down for her bra. "There's coffee on the bureau here. Your chauffeur's outside. Good luck, Tom." She left the bedroom.

15

H is head was throbbing, his mouth was dry, and Louis was giving him problems.

"Listen, Mr. Coward," Louis said as he drove the limo away from Lea Madison's house, "I talked to my supervisor re this entire situation, and he's not very happy. He doesn't like me following people around, you know? That's not part of the job."

"You mean you told your supervisor? Jesus Christ, Lou. I thought you were on my side."

"I'm a company man," Louis said. "Well, basically, I'm a company man. There is also the little matter of the bill. They haven't received payment for last week, as yet."

"Jesus, Lou," Tom said. "The check is in the mail."

"Maybe it is," Lou said. "But my supervisor, he wants a little something on account. You know, maybe you could give me a check or something."

Tom was holding his head between his hands. He was sure he was going to be sick. "Listen, Lou. I'm tired. I'm hung over, and I'm in no mood for arguing with chauffeurs. Will you please just drive?"

"Where are we headed?"

"I want you to drive over to Mr. Conlon's place."

"Aw, come on, Mr. Coward. Gimme a break. I can't do that. It's ridiculous, I tell you. Following this guy around in a limo. It's ridiculous."

Tom held his head more tightly. He tried to drown out everything. It didn't work. The insinuating sound of Lea Madison's voice kept replaying in his mind. *You don't know what you want*. Of course, he did not know what he wanted. It was the way of the world. He tried not to think about it.

Ash Conlon left his house precisely at nine-thirty. He was carrying a vinyl suit bag, and he was dressed in white shorts and a bright red Armani T-shirt. He wore Ray-Ban sunglasses that glinted in the sunlight. He walked to the garage, and a few moments later the door raised and the taupe Porsche once again emerged, turned onto Mount Pleasant, and began heading south. This time Louis played Iggy Pop singing the theme song from *Repo Man*. The chauffeur's body shook in time with the music as he drove. It made Tom's head hurt that much more. He did not dare say anything.

Conlon left his car in the east end of the city in a parking lot situated between the Greenwood racetrack and Lake Ontario. Tom watched him saunter toward the water, a large towel thrown over his shoulder.

"He's going to the fucking beach," Lou said disgustedly.

"Stay here," Tom said. He put on his sunglasses and got out of the car, waited for a break in the traffic, and dodged across the road to Conlon's car. The suit bag was hanging in the back. He tried the door handles. Locked.

Conlon stood on a grassy knoll just above the boardwalk. Beyond the boardwalk was a wide stretch of sand. He squinted up at the sun, then moved to a secluded spot away from other bathers, but close to the water. Tom watched him, standing beside a sign that advised visitors with dogs to stoop and scoop. Someone wasn't paying any attention to signs. When Tom moved off, he stepped directly into a pile of dog shit baking in the morning sunshine. He hobbled around frantically on one foot, while Ash Conlon carefully spread out his bath towel on the sand.

Tom reached a nearby picnic table, scuffing his shoe in

the long grass, trying to get rid of the crap. "Goddamn," he muttered. A small boy with a large beach ball wandered past, and looked at him. Tom sat down at the picnic table.

On the beach, Ash Conlon removed his shirt. His torso was chocolate smooth, and hairless. The stomach was flat. The muscles rippled in his arms and along his shoulders. Tom watched as Ashley applied suntan lotion to his arms and stomach, then stretched out on the towel. He lay with his face buried in the crook of his arm, and seemed to doze off. After twenty minutes, he rolled over and lay on his back. Twenty minutes later he was on his stomach again. And twenty minutes after that, he abruptly rose to his feet, pulled on his top, grabbed the towel, and strolled quickly to his car.

He retrieved the suit bag and went into nearby changing rooms. Ten minutes later, he emerged dressed in a superbly tailored glen-plaid double-breasted suit, and went to his car. Tom raced back to Louis.

"Let's go," he said.

Louis sighed heavily and offered his arms to heaven. "When I took this job I thought I'd be driving Wayne Gretzky around."

The Porsche sped west along the Gardiner Expressway. "The airport again," Louis sighed. "I'm beginning to know this guy."

Louis was right.

Ash Conlon drove to Terminal One, and left his car in the parking garage. Inside the airport terminal, Conlon, now carrying an attaché case, once again checked in at the American Airlines ticket counter.

Tom thought about it for a moment, then went over to the counter and purchased a return ticket on Flight 196.

"Better hurry," the clerk said. "They're boarding."

Conlon was sitting at a window near the front of the DC-10. He stared pensively out the porthole. He didn't even glance up as Tom whisked by him. The eleven o'clock flight was crowded with businessmen in gray uniforms carrying briefcases. Tom sat near the back of the aircraft, where he could just make out the curly top of Ash Conlon's head. He did not move from his seat for the duration of the fifty-five-minute flight.

The aircraft dipped down over Long Island Sound, then headed across the gloomy residential stretches of the Bronx, to the pier jutting into Flushing Bay that always caused Tom to gulp when he realized it was a runway, and they were landing at LaGuardia International Airport.

Conlon hurried off the plane and into the airport. Tom went after him. He dashed down a flight of stairs to the airport's arrivals level, and out the side door to the taxi ranks.

"You see that cab ahead of me?" Tom said to his driver when he got into the backseat. The driver was a small, bullet-headed man, with a thick accent.

"Sure, bub. Sure, I see the cab."

"I want you to follow that cab."

The driver turned and stared at him with suspicious peasant's eyes. "You serious?"

Tom handed him a twenty-dollar bill. "That's how serious I am."

"That's serious enough," the driver said, throwing the car into gear.

Conlon went into the city via the Queensborough Bridge. The skyscrapers of Manhattan sparkled under a hard midday sun. From the bridge sweeping over Roosevelt Island, everything was gold and silver, a city of dreams that disappeared into narrow streets and congested traffic as you got closer to it.

Once in Manhattan, the crosstown traffic was hopelessly snarled. Tom saw Conlon's cab turn left onto Fifth Avenue. A moment later his driver made the same turn. At Fifty-ninth Street, Conlon's cab pulled over and stopped at the Fifth Avenue entrance to the Plaza Hotel. Flags fluttered over the portico. The doorman rushed to open the rear door of the first cab. Conlon stepped out briskly, glanced around quickly, then went up the steps and into the hotel.

Tom paid his driver and followed Ash. The lobby of the Plaza is all breathtaking ersatz French renaissance, marble columns, hanging chandeliers, and lawn-green broadloom. Conlon walked briskly past the Palm Court, jammed with luncheon guests, and around to the registration desk.

Tom watched as Conlon chatted amiably with the clerk. She handed him a key, and he nodded his thanks, then walked over to the bank of elevators. Tom walked over and stood behind him, noting the neat way in which the dark curls of Conlon's hair fell along his collar line. He caught the whiff not of Pierre Cardin this time, but of Coppertone.

The elevator doors clanked open. A half-dozen people crowded inside. Tom stayed behind Conlon. He turned, and for a moment they were face to face. Conlon merely stared disinterestedly past him. Tom did an about face toward the doors. The elevator started to move up. Someone tapped on Tom's shoulder. He turned, and once again he was staring into the dark poker face of Ash Conlon.

"Excuse me," Conlon said.

Oh, Jesus, Tom thought. "Yes?" he said.

"Could you press twelve for me?"

Tom reached forward and pressed the button on the panel. "No problem," Tom said. "It's my floor."

When the elevator reached the twelfth floor, Tom allowed Conlon to disembark first, then followed him. The corridor was quiet, the discreet, weary elegance of the Plaza hanging heavily. Tom looked around distractedly.

"I always get lost in this place," he said.

Conlon ignored the remark and went to room 1229,

turned the key in the lock, and quickly closed the door behind him. Tom went up to the door. From the other side, he could hear Ash Conlon clear his throat.

The elevator announced its arrival with a quiet ping, and Tom moved hurriedly away from the door. Shit. He couldn't stand outside Ash Conlon's door for very long without attracting notice.

He went back down to the lobby, and approached the front desk.

"Mr. Coward," said the clerk, a young, amazingly groomed man named Antonio. "Good to see you again."

"How are you, Antonio?"

"Are we expecting you?" Antonio began punching keys on a computer terminal.

"You're not expecting me. Sudden trip. I need a room for the night, though."

"No problem, Mr. Coward."

Tom leaned on the marble-topped counter. "I need a particular room, Antonio. Twelve-twenty-seven."

The clerk hit some more keys. "Sure. Let me see here." He looked at the screen, and then up at Tom. "Nothing to it. But why the twelfth floor?"

"The Beatles stayed on the twelfth, Antonio," Tom said. "I stay on the twelfth and I'm young again."

He saw Ash Conlon stroll past, heading along the corridor that wound around to the twin Oaks — the dining room and bar. Ash Conlon opted for the bar. Tom went into the crowded room. Even with the sunlight pouring in from Central Park South, illuminating the faces of beautiful women who refused to get dressed each month until the new issue of *Vogue* arrived, the place had about it the reassuring dark feel of drinks at midnight. Conlon was making his way to the rear of the room.

Tom found an empty seat at the bar and ordered a Miller Lite. He turned in time to see Conlon bend to kiss a woman with sparkling blue eyes. He kissed her on the mouth. She smiled up at him adoringly, the eyes practically glittering across the room. She clasped his hand in hers as he sat down beside her.

She was not unreminiscent of Stormy. She was tall. Her hair was fair, casually parted at the right side, falling straight to her shoulders. She looked expensively professional in a tailored white sports jacket, dark blouse, and white skirt. There was a silk handkerchief thrown rather raffishly into a breast pocket, which gave the outfit a splash of style, and a single strand of pearls at her throat, which suggested there could be nonsense here, but not too much of it.

She leaned forward and kissed Ash again, then looked delightfully embarrassed at her own daring. Her face glowed. Sitting there clasping his beer in his hand watching this, Tom was again reminded of Stormy and the night he watched her with Ash at the Courtyard Cafe. This was not, then, a business lunch or a get-together of friends. This was a lovers' rendezvous.

A striking matron moved past his line of vision, and began piling shopping bags from Macy's and Saks Fifth Avenue. Her shiny gray hair was folded into a wave at the base of her neck, and she wore an unseasonably dark suit, which she carefully tucked against her knees as she slid onto the stool.

"I'd like a Negroni, please," she said to the bartender. "Campari. Gin. Dash of vermouth."

"Coming up," the bartender said.

She noticed Tom. "My father used to bring me here when I was a young lady, and he would order a Negroni. It was a drink he discovered when he was in Paris. Now every Tuesday, I go shopping in the morning. And around one o'clock I come in here, and I order a Negroni. Just like my father. I drink my Negroni, and I sit at the bar. Father would have approved of the Negroni, but he would be shocked to see me sitting on a barstool like this. Absolutely horrified. It's my idea of rebellion, I guess.''

Tom glanced past her, over to where Conlon sat with the blond. They sipped cocktails and sat very close together, their heads almost touching. Very romantic.

The waiter carefully placed the Negroni on the bar. The matron picked it up, held it for a moment, as though she were testing it for weight, then took a sip.

"Ahhh." She smacked her lips appreciatively. ''That's more like it.''

Tom now saw that she had the most amazing face. There were lines beneath her eyes, and at the corners of her mouth, lines that seemed artfully arranged so that the onlooker was at once reminded of age and amazed at how little it had affected the still-fresh serenity of her features.

''You're very beautiful,'' Tom said to her.

The woman glanced at him sharply, but there was humor dancing in the wide eyes. ''This is why my father didn't want me sitting in bars. I'm old enough to be your grandmother.''

Tom laughed. ''My father wanted me sitting in bars. He said I'd meet nice people like you.''

''Don't give me that. You're trying to pick me up.'' She winked at him and sipped more of her drink.

Ash Conlon signaled for one of the white-coated waiters. The blond opened a compact and employed its mirror like a scanning device, searching the surface of her carefully painted face for any signs of wear and tear. Ash came close to her, and she pulled the compact away so that they both were captured in its reflection. She looked lovingly at the compact, and they both laughed.

The woman sitting next to Tom finished her drink. ''There are some days when I think to myself, I'd like two of these. There are moments when I would enjoy getting the bartender's attention, and telling him to bring me another Negroni.''

''Why don't you let me buy you another Negroni?'' Tom said.

"Oh, no you don't, young man. You'll just get me drunk and have your way with me." She winked at him again. "Some other time." She collected her packages as the bartender approached.

"You come in here all the time, do you?"

"Every Tuesday," the woman said. "Like clockwork."

Tom said to the bartender, "Would you put this lady's Negroni on my account, please."

The woman looked at him, surprised. "Why, that's very kind of you," she said.

"My pleasure."

"You've made an old lady's day," she said with a merry laugh. "Free drink from a handsome stranger. I guess that's why you come to the Oak Bar." She collected up her parcels. "Thanks again." Tom watched her leave, impressed with the way she moved. He glanced back across the room as Ash Conlon and his companion rose from their table and started for the door. A moment later they disappeared. Tom gave the bartender a ten-dollar bill, told him to keep the change, waited a few seconds, then followed the couple into the lobby. They went to the bank of elevators.

He waited a few moments, then took the elevator up to the twelfth floor, and went to his room. There was a marble fireplace, a cut-glass chandelier, and a view of Central Park through gauzy curtains. There was also a door connecting his room with 1229. He lay down on the soft gray broadloom, his ear close to the air space between the door and the carpet. He felt ridiculous, but at the same time there was a certain voyeuristic excitement. He was now a matter of only a few feet away from Ash Conlon, his secrets, and his most private moments. Yet Ash Conlon had no inkling of it.

For a moment, he could hear only the hum of air conditioning. The sound swept up at him from under the door, and he feared it might drown out everything else. Then the low murmur of voices rose above the sound of the rushing air. Laughter. Then more silence. The silence now somehow suggested erotic tension. Next, there was the sound of clothing rustling. Covers were turned. The creak of a bed. More low laughter, followed by a murmur and a groan of pleasure.

"Oh, Jesus, Ash!" Her voice rose, sharp and pleading.

The bed creaked again. More violently.

Her voice again, low and sensual this time. "Oh, Jesus, Jesus, please."

The headboard slapped against the surface of the wall. Again. And again. She was imploring now. "Do it to me, do it, do it. Ohhh, do it!"

Silence. A scream. "Please! Fuck me. I love it when you do. *Please!*"

The bed creaked with a rhythm now, and the noise level of the two lovers increased dramatically as the two-backed monster got down to work. Toward the end, Tom finally heard clearly the voice of the man who would marry Stormy Willis. It was pitched high, at the moment of ecstasy. There was no mistaking what it said.

"Oh, darling, darling," Ash Conlon cried out, "I love you! I love you so much!"

16

On the return flight to Toronto, Ashley Conlon ordered a double Vodka. Tom watched him hand the flight attendant an American five-dollar bill. He had an aisle seat this time, and Tom watched him unscrew the cap of the miniature bottle and pour the contents over ice in a plastic glass. What was this, Tom wondered, the celebratory drink? The fiancé returning jubilant from his final afternoon fling with an old flame?

Ash and his New York blond had made love for three hours, raw, energetic fucking, that failed to end in the tears that might be expected if the lover was breaking off with his beloved. The last glimpse of them Tom caught was of Ash escorting her out the Fifth Avenue entrance a little after four o'clock, and waiting patiently while the doorman managed to rustle up a taxi. She leaned against him, her arm around his waist, and when the cab arrived, she kissed him lingeringly on the mouth, stroked the side of his face, burned her eyes deeply into his for another instant. They did not look like they were finished. They appeared to be just starting, and in a white heat over it.

After that, Conlon had hopped into his own cab. He was driven back out to LaGuardia, where he got the five-forty plane back to Toronto. Tom was genuinely scared, now, that Conlon would recognize him. But he sat on the plane, his face buried in a tent formed by his hands, and did not look up at anyone. If anything, he seemed to be hiding within himself, thinking. Thinking of what?

At Pearson International, Louis was beside himself.

"You just left me here, for Christ's sake. I've had to move the car about twenty fucking times because of the Mounties. Jesus Christ, Mr. Coward, you push a guy's patience too far."

"Be patient just a little longer, will you, Lou? Conlon is headed out of the airport. Let's see if we can catch up with him."

"Shit, shit," Louis said.

They caught up to the Porsche just as it turned onto Highway 427. The last streaks of sunlight were smeared across the western sky as the car sped south. Tom was sure Ash must be hurrying to meet Stormy. But then the Porsche, having turned east on the Queen Elizabeth Expressway, abruptly went to the right and off onto Lakeshore Boulevard. Conlon was not going to Stormy. His destination appeared to be the Lakelot Studio, and the meeting with Kelly Langlois.

Louis eased the limo off the ramp and onto Lakeshore. It was dark now. Then, a moment later, the darkness was cut by a red light winking from behind. Louis jerked around, his face frozen in anguish.

"Jesus Christ," he said. "That's the cops, Mr. Coward. The goddamn cops and I ain't got no driver's license."

"What? You're driving a limo around, and you don't have a driver's license?"

"I useta have one, but they took it away."

"You mean you've had your license revoked?"

"Naw. They just took it away. They said I was impaired. Which was a bunch of bullshit. I'd only had six or seven beers."

"What do you mean, you weren't impaired? They must have given you a breathalyzer."

"No way, man. I refused to take any goddamn breathalyzer. So then they said I was guilty anyhow. Fucking police state."

He pulled over to the curb. Tom looked back and saw

that the red light was on the dashboard of what looked like an unmarked police car. A large heavyset man in an ill-fitting suit approached.

Louis rolled down the window, and the heavy-set man leaned against the door frame.

"Any trouble, officer?"

The man showed Louis a badge mounted inside a leather billfold. "Mannery. Metro Toronto homicide squad." He looked back at Tom. "You Thomas Coward?"

"What is it? What's the problem?"

"We're looking into the death of Carrie Wayborn, Mr. Coward. I've got a sergeant back here wants to have a talk to you about it."

"How did you know where to find me?"

"License, Mr. Coward. We've been on the lookout for you all day. Our luck we happened to spot your car. Now would you step out, please."

"I'm late for an appointment," Tom said. "Can't we do it another time?"

"Won't take a minute," Mannery said.

Tom got out of the car and stood along the shoulder of the highway. The detective had a huge stomach that bulged out over wrinkled gray-flannel trousers. His hair was cut close to his head, and he had small sleepy eyes that now regarded Tom with unrestrained pleasure. He looked to Tom the way cops all over the world were supposed to look.

"You go back to the car there, Mr. Coward. I want to discuss something with your driver."

"Could we hurry this up?"

"Won't take but a jiffy," the detective said.

Tom walked back toward the car, a nondescript brown four-door Ford sedan. Behind him, the limo suddenly started up and drove away. Tom stopped and wheeled around. The detective with the huge stomach came up to him.

"Where the hell is he going?" Tom demanded.

"You won't be needing him any more tonight." Mannery gave him a shove toward the Ford. "Ain't that what you guys with limos say?"

The window on the driver's side of the Ford came down. Lincoln S. Malik stuck out his head.

"Good evening, Thomas," he said courteously. "I guess you've already met my friend Mike, here."

Mike stuck a gun into the small of Tom's back.

It would be a sort of reunion party, Kelly decided, a festive occasion requiring colored streamers strung across the little hovel of an apartment that hung like a cavity on the side of the dark gaping mouth that was the interior of the studio. She had also added candles, dozens of them in different colors and fragrances, their flickering light hiding the dank, unappealing corners of the apartment, the sagging, ruined furniture, the grimy yellow walls.

In the candlelight there was an ethereal sense about the room, a suggestion of the possibilities contained in fantasy. You could create scenarios and truths in this light that otherwise would not be possible. It was a light she found particularly appealing this evening.

She spent hours painting herself by the candlelight, turning her face into an explosion of color and design, yellow swirls against red streaks. Her face was no longer a face, but a bright mask from *Zoom-Zoom*. She pulled her hair tightly back, and tied it at the nape of her neck.

Finally, she dressed in the black jump suit with the turtleneck — nothing on underneath — so that her body was in darkness except for the exotic colors flaring on her countenance. She looked at herself in the mirror, and a black goddess stared back, her features burning in reds and yellows.

At about ten minutes to eight, she heard the door to the studio open far below and knew it was him, knew that tonight it finally could all be ended. Carrie would be avenged, the slate wiped clean. Then what? she wondered as she heard his footsteps coming up the metal stairs from the studio. Never mind that, she thought. Mind only this —the sound of him on the catwalk. He was almost here.

The knock was polite, which made her smirk. She called, "Come in, hon," and the door swung open. Ashley Conlon stood in the doorway, beautiful in a double-breasted suit.

"Good God," he said when he saw her. He edged into the room, his face in the uncertain light drawn and tense. He was scared. She knew him, and he was scared.

"How are you, hon?" She grinned at him lasciviously, crept forward, wrapped her arms around his neck, kissed him. He pulled away.

"What are you doing, Kelly?"

"It's a reunion party, hon. I thought I'd dress up for it." She tried to kiss him again. He moved away from her.

"I don't want to do this," he said.

"But you're here."

"I'm here," he said. "Where's Lex?"

"Maybe we don't need him."

"I don't understand."

"Hon, there are a few things you're keeping from me. You didn't tell me about Carrie. The last time you saw her."

"I haven't seen Carrie for years."

"Don't tell me that, hon. I'm the witch here, remember? I can see straight through you, into your innermost being. I can see when you're lying."

"I'm not lying about anything."

"Carrie was in bad trouble over money, hon. I know she went to see Lex, and I know she was threatening him, because she told me about it. She also went to you looking for help."

Ash Conlon moved farther into the room. The candlelight caused the shadows to shift constantly. Kelly moved with the shadows. She was close to him again, her fingers running over his face.

"You're older, hon. But, God, you look good. All the lines. The crevices. They're all in the right places. Just like I wanted them. I created you, darlin', and Jesus, I did a fine job."

He shook her off. "This is bullshit," he said angrily. "Don't try to scare me with this crap, Kelly. It worked twenty years ago when we were all getting doped to the eyeballs. It doesn't work now. The sixties are over. You're not Zoom-Zoom anymore."

Her fingers no longer were reaching for him. Instead, they held the .38 revolver. For a moment, because of the uncertainty of the light, Ash was not precisely certain it was a gun. But then she waved it at him, and there was no doubt.

"Jesus Christ, Kelly." Panic bubbled in those smooth cadences. "I didn't kill her. Okay. We saw each other a couple of times. I hadn't seen her for years. Then we met on the street one day. Accidentally. At least it seemed like an accident at the time. Maybe it wasn't. Maybe she had something planned all along. Anyhow, we ended up doing some crazy things in bed. It was a recreational thing. Nothing to it. But then she wanted money. She had met my fiancée. Stormy happened to live next door to her. She was going to tell her that we were having an affair. Christ. An affair. There was no affair. A few casual fucks. I was furious with her. But I never killed her."

"Then who did it, hon?"

"You said Lex. You said Lex had the motive."

"But so did you, hon."

"Carrie was seeing a lot of people." Now it was his turn to move closer. "She told me about some of the people she was seeing. One of them was a hood, if you can

believe that. A guy named Malik. Lincoln Malik. She even
introduced us. I think she liked that, she liked the power
of having two men with her that she had slept with. I've
even got Malik doing a little bit of work for me. A pretty
mean customer, let me tell you. Hell, it could have been
him."

His face loosened a bit, as though the denials provided
strength. A smile played around the edges of his mouth.
"Let's talk about this, let's think this over."

"Here it comes," she said, moving back from him, keeping the gun raised. "The return of the charmer."

"You know I could never refuse you, baby. Even after
that night. Remember that night at the cottage? The crazy
night. What you did to me with the razor."

"Craziness," she said. The gun was only inches from
his chest. He came closer and she moved back until her
shoulder blades touched against the wall.

"No hard feelings," he said gently. "We all got carried
away, that's all. That shit we were taking. That's what
did it."

He kissed her. She responded to the kiss.

"You killed her," she said, her mouth against his.

"No, baby. Never." He put his hands around her waist.
Now the gun was pressed somewhere between their bodies. The hands went up, found the gold zipper at the front
of the jump suit. Tugged at it. "Crazy Kelly. Still crazy
after all these years. All dressed up in warpaint." He
pulled the zipper down to her waist and ran his hand
inside, touching her belly, her breasts. "But as usual, nothing on underneath. All hot for action. My Kelly . . . The
old Kelly."

His voice was soft. He kissed her again. She cuddled
against him. He had her. As he kissed her, he opened his
eyes to inspect her face. As soon as he did that, he knew
he had made a terrible miscalculation. He saw her eyes,
staring, the deep terrible hatred glowing from her painted

face. In a moment, it would be too late to do anything. He grabbed for the gun, at the same time jerking away from her.

The explosion in that small, gloomy room shook the candles, bringing to an end in a single, unexpected moment both fantasy and possibility.

"Now, what we're going to do, Thomas," said Lincoln S. Malik, "we're going to drive north of Toronto, to this field that I know. We're going to take you out in this field, and we're going to kick the shit out of you. We're going to take your wallet, your watch, and any other identification you might be carrying. Then we're going to douse you with liquor and leave you there. We'll see how long it takes you to get back to Toronto in that state. I suspect that, given the conservative sensibilities of the populace, it will take you some time. That will give you plenty of opportunity to think."

Tom was squeezed into the backseat of the brown Ford beside Malik, who kept a .45 automatic pressed against Tom's ribs. Mike, the phony detective, was in the front, driving. They had turned off the Lakeshore and were now driving north along University Avenue.

Tom nodded toward the front. "If this guy isn't a cop, where did he get the badge?"

Mike let out a bray of laughter.

"That was a toy badge you could pick up in any department store," Malik said. "Your boy obviously thought it was the real thing."

"Some driver," Mike chortled. "I told him to get lost, and he got right the hell out of there."

"He hasn't got a license," Tom said.

"A chauffeur without a license," Malik said. "You sure are driving first class through life, aren't you, Thomas?"

Ahead loomed the imposing stone of the Ontario Legislature Buildings at Queen's Park, an old fortress trying to halt the march of the modern high-rises advancing up the boulevard. On either side of the street, Tom could see dozens of women making their way north toward the legislature and the wide crescent of lawn that ran before it.

As they got closer he could see that the crescent was full of demonstrators, most of them women, a lot of them waving signs that announced: "STOP PORN NOW," "NO MORE VIOLENCE TO WOMEN," and "WOMEN AGAINST PORNOGRAPHY."

"What's this?" Mike demanded.

"Some sort of demonstration," Malik said. "Can't we get around it?"

By now the mob had flooded across the street and was bottling up traffic. A chant was rising: "No more porn! No more porn!"

"What the hell is the matter with these people?" Malik demanded. "This is Ontario. There's no porn in Ontario."

"Are you kidding?" Tom said. "It's everywhere, Malik. In the underwear ads in Eaton's catalogue. It's even in the front seat driving this car."

Mike gave him a dirty look.

"See what I mean?" Tom said.

Malik jammed the gun more firmly into Tom's ribs. "Don't turn into a comedian on me now, Thomas."

Everyone was noisily taking up the "No more porn" chant, and taking a certain delight in the power of the mob to stop traffic. Tom leaned forward and rolled down the window.

"Don't do that," Malik ordered.

"It's sweltering in here," Tom protested.

"Jesus, Link, what're we gonna do?" Mike was sweating in the front seat. The crowd swirling around the car was making him nervous.

A middle-aged woman wearing a K-way jacket shook her sign in the air as she chanted with the crowd.

"Hey," Tom yelled out to her. "What you girls need is a good fuck."

The woman stared at him. "What did you say?"

"I'll bet you wouldn't be against pornography if you had a good fuck," Tom yelled.

"Hey," Mike said. "What's he saying?"

"Shut up, for Christ's sake," Malik growled.

Another woman peered down into the car. "What did you say?"

"If you weren't so goddamned ugly, you could get laid."

The woman in the K-way jacket had heard enough. She slammed her sign down onto the hood of the car.

"I think you all need a fuck!" Tom yelled.

Other demonstrators were turning, trying to see where the intrusive voice was coming from. The K-way woman swung her sign against the windshield.

"Son of a bitch!" she cried out. She turned to the others. "He's insulting us!"

"What you broads need is a good fuck!" Tom bawled.

Other women began to strike the car with their signs.

Mike looked wildly at Malik. "Do something, for Christ's sake."

Malik jammed the gun hard into Tom's ribs. Tom was knocked against the door. His hand caught at the handle, and he yanked up on it. A moment later he spilled out into the street. Malik attempted to come after him, but a score of howling demonstrators had descended on the car, blocking his path. They began to rock the car back and forth shouting out, "No more porn!" in rhythm with their rocking.

Tom rolled across the pavement. A woman hit at him with her picket sign. Another woman kicked at his groin.

"It wasn't me," Tom cried out. "It was the guys in that car." He was on his knees, pointing frantically at the Ford. The mob turned on the car. Tom could see Malik being

dragged from the interior. Then someone yelled "Oh,
God! He's got a gun! He's got a gun!" The crowd abruptly
folded back from the car like some giant wave thrown
into reverse. People began to scream as they stampeded
away. Tom was knocked over. He stumbled to his feet
and began running with everyone else.

He reached the sidewalk on the opposite side of the
street. A policeman mounted on a chestnut horse went
thundering past. From somewhere in the distance, he
could hear the sound of a police siren. He kept running,
heading south, away from the fracas.

Tom finally spotted a taxi. He slumped into the backseat,
gasping for breath.

"Jesus, did you hear about the riot up at Queen's Park?"
the driver said. "Bunch of goddamn anti-porn
demonstrators."

"I want to go out on Lakeshore Boulevard. There's a
movie studio out there. That's where I want to go. Okay?"

"Sure thing," the driver said. "Anything to get away
from that mess. Imagine getting into a fight over dirty
pictures. Jeez."

The cab dropped him in the parking lot adjacent to the
studio. He walked over to the side door and up the steps.
The metal door was ajar. Tom pushed at it. Was Conlon
in there? And if he was, what was he doing? Murdering
Kelly Langlois? If he was doing that, what was he, Tom
Coward, supposed to do about it? His heart started to beat
faster. He slipped inside, into the darkness. He could see
nothing. He paused, listened. The silence shouted out at
him. If Ash Conlon was murdering anyone, he was being
awfully quiet about it.

Finally, he decided to move. He felt his way along. The
blackness was an almost physical thing. He knocked
against something, scraped his shin, cursed. He found a
corridor and in the distance a thin light seeped back at
him. At the end of the vast interior of the studio, he could

see Alvin Jarvis's contribution to the art of cinema — the *Death Elevator* set. The thin light emanated uncertainly from the doorway along the catwalk, at least sixty feet above the floor. He thought of calling out. But call out what? To whom?

He reached the iron staircase that rose to the catwalk. He started up the hob-tread risers. *Clang.* Jesus. Go easy. He reached the top of the stairs and found that the catwalk was narrow, no more than four feet wide. It stretched into the blackness. The pool of light from the doorway filtered through the inkiness about forty feet away.

Okay, he thought. The logical thing was to go along the catwalk to the light. Wait, though. That was not the logical thing at all. The logical thing was to get the hell out of here, go somewhere and have a drink, forget all about this nonsense.

As he stood there debating this, the light in the doorway ahead of him went out.

Tom pressed himself against the rough bricks of the wall. Any moment now Ash Conlon would step through that door and come at him. In the darkness, the malevolent darkness, Tom would never see him coming. He would not see the *Titanic* coming. He thought of running, tried to dismiss the idea. He stood there, and stood there. And nothing happened. Maybe, he thought, maybe a gust of wind had blown the door closed. That could be it. Couldn't it? There was nothing to do but to go forward.

He began edging along the wall. When he dared breathe at all, air escaped in small, irritating whimpers. God! He must exercise more control than this.

His shoulder touched a door frame. He groped with his outstretched hand, clawed the wooden surface of a door. It was closed. He hesitated.

Silence.

He found the doorknob in the darkness and turned it. The door swung open with a creak worthy of any bad horror picture. Maybe Ash Conlon was in there. Waiting. What the hell, he thought. And wondered if it might not be his last thought. He pushed out from the wall, made a hard left turn, and stepped into the room.

As soon as he was inside, the odor assailed him. Rich incense intermingled with burning wax. He jumped to the right so that he had his back against the wall. There was just enough light from dozens of gutted candles to define the cramped space. The candles were everywhere. He stepped forward and whacked his leg against a piece of furniture, stumbled, fell against something else, tried to right himself. He almost gained his balance, except that his foot struck some sort of heavy object, and he tumbled to the floor.

He groaned and sat up, reaching out to support himself. His hand touched something warm and wet. He yelled and pulled his hand away. Then he saw the blood, and looked around.

He had fallen over a body. It was sprawled on its back on threadbare carpeting. There was a gaping hole where the stomach used to be. Tom stared in horror. He had put his hand into the wound. The face of the corpse was festooned with brilliant color, a grotesque death mask. Even so, he recognized Kelly Langlois.

Tom backed out of the room, taking it one step at a time. The little whimpers of air he exhaled before had become great, loud heaving gasps, as though there was not enough oxygen in the world to feed him. He bumped against the pipe railing running along the catwalk, reeled down along the hob-tread platform. He came to a stop only when it ended. He grasped onto the railing, gazing down upon the *Death Elevator* set.

The blow caught him on the side of the head. Everything exploded into a bright, electric pain, so acutely awful that for a moment it actually produced a kind of euphoria. Then came the numbness. Everything was calm and muted. No more bright lights. He fell gently into a chasm that he was convinced contained death. It was so pleasant. So easy. And Alvin would be pleased. Tom had expired on the set of his greatest hit.

17

H e was late. Lea Madison tried not to get excited about the visits, but somehow she always did. It wasn't that she particularly cared about him. She did not. It was simply, she conceded, as she perfumed herself in all the right places, and some of the wrong ones, that he was a fantastic lover. Sex with him was a sort of workout, like doing aerobics, and certainly during the latter days of her marriage to Lex, it relieved the boredom and the hurt. Now, there was nothing else. Or at least nothing else she was particularly interested in. He was better than catting around a gossipy town that did not easily allow for the prowling of separated women.

There was Tom Coward, of course. And there was Alvin. Tom was not interested at all. Alvin was perhaps too interested. Her luck. She was drawn to Tom Coward. If he only knew who was about to walk in through her door. She slipped into the sexy black negligee, all lace and silk, with a neckline that plunged to her belly button. She shook her hair loose, took a sip of wine, and glided across to answer the sound of the door chimes.

He came in looking ashen and drawn. His hair was uncombed, his suit rumpled. A mess. Unlike him. She embraced him, and he seemed to be trembling.

"Are you all right, darling?"

Ashley Conlon managed a wan smile. "I'm all right now," he said. "Let's just say it's been a crazy day at the office."

He bent down and kissed her.

Now how had they gotten in here? Lea wondered drowsily. She pressed her shoulders back against the wooden slats of her sauna. On the step below, Ash Conlon poured more water on the hot rocks. The heat rose, and the sweat broke out on their naked bodies. Oh, yes. She remembered. The tension, he said. A sauna was just the thing to relieve the tension. She could think of other things that would relieve the tension, but a sauna it was. Now, though, it was time for the other things. He twisted his head around to her, ran his nose along the inside of her thigh, then buried his mouth enthusiastically in the juncture of her legs, currently spread wide to receive him. She took his head in her hands, that beautiful head, and thought . . . *oh, shit!* She thought of Tom Coward.

She glanced down at the dark hair, wet and slicked back. Tom Coward thought this man, this man moving deep within her, was a killer? Poor Tom. The lovesick fool. If he only knew. Ash killed all right, but he did it softly, lovingly. She groaned loudly.

Later they both dived into the pool, and the cold water revived them. Lea swept her hair back as she came up beside him at the shallow end. He hoisted himself up on the pool's edge. She moved around so that she was between his legs, took his large penis in her mouth. He groaned. Tit for tat, she thought, as she began to use her tongue on him.

Finally, in the bedroom, having toweled each other off, she insisted he service her from behind, and she had a great roaring climax.

"Oh, Jesus, darling," she gasped. "There's so much of you tonight."

He grinned and rolled her over on her back. She looked up at him as he slid over her. Her voice was teasing.

"What is this, baby? The last fuck before you get married?" She had opened her legs, and he was going inside her as she said this.

"What?" he said.

"Come on, baby, give me," she implored, climbing up him.

He looked down at her. "Who told you I was getting married?"

"You mean you're not?"

He pulled out of her, leaving her exposed and empty. His face was darkening. "I didn't say that. I asked who told you."

"Someone who knows her. What difference does it make?"

"No one is supposed to know," he said. "What was this informant's name, anyhow?"

"Informant? Don't be silly. He used to go out with her." Lea sat up. She was suddenly nervous. She did not like his cold abruptness. Something was very wrong here.

He looked at her in amazement, working his jaw around. "Not Tom Coward."

She said nothing. He grabbed her by the shoulders and shook her hard.

"You know Tom Coward?"

She was scared now. "Ashley, please. You're hurting me."

"Are you working with Tom Coward? Reporting back to him about me? Is that it? Is that what you're up to?"

"Ashley, you're overreacting. For God's sake. He's an acquaintance. That's all — "

"You cunt!" he screamed. He slapped her across the side of the head. She flew across the sheets, and he was on her, his strong fingers closing around her neck.

The voices came to him before anything else. They seemed to float above him. For a moment, he thought the angels were descending to fetch him. There really was a heaven. There would be some explaining to do on his part, of course. But nothing too tricky, he thought. And maybe now he would get to meet Elvis. One of the angels began to talk. ''Jesus fuck. Have you been in there? What a mess.'' He was vaguely surprised that angels would talk like that. But then what did he know about angels?

Next came the pain. It started in his head, sharply undulating waves that flowed down the right side of his body, providing oddly numb and prickly sensations. He was not at all sure he could move his right arm, and he was not at all sure that he wasn't going to throw up because he hurt so much.

He was not lying on the floor as he first imagined. If he was lying on the floor, he would not be imagining anything. Instead, he was sprawled in the dust and the grime on the platform that topped the elevator set, about eight feet below the catwalk. Bless Alvin Jarvis, he thought, whose aesthetic vision had made all this possible.

He moved, and everything hurt more. Above, he could hear feet falling against metal, and more voices. Must be police, he concluded. And here he was on display, literally under their noses, a prime suspect in the murder of Kelly Langlois, complete with her blood smeared on him.

From below he could hear the grind of machinery starting to life. ''That's got it,'' someone called out. They were coming up here. He pulled himself to the edge of the platform and looked over into the darkness. He imagined it to be more than fifty feet to the ground. Tom painfully eased his feet over the side. Across the platform, the elevator slammed to a halt. Tom's legs dangled, groping for purchase along the metal struts. Finally, he found it, and he slipped down over the side of the gantry, just as a couple of police officers emerged out of the cage and onto the platform.

''Nothin' up here,'' one of them said.

''Better take a look around, just to make sure.''

''There's nothin' here, I tell you, Hal.''

"I'll do it."

Footsteps started for Tom. He abruptly lost his footing on the struts, and his body weight shot him downward. Frantically, he grabbed the struts. His fingers closed around the metal, and held. His feet wildly peddled the air.

"Did you hear something?"

"Hear what?"

Then there were three gunshots.

They exploded in the cavernous interior of the studio, reverberating like great thunderclaps that once again almost caused Tom to lose his footing. On the platform the two cops stopped dead in their tracks. "What the hell?" one of them said. They both ran back for the elevator.

A voice screamed for an ambulance. Someone demanded, "How is he?" Another shouted question: "Is he dead?"

Tom eased himself painfully back onto the platform, rolled under the protective shadow of the catwalk's overhang, and lay on his back. For the next hour, sirens wailed, voices hollered orders, confusion welled and spread. Nothing transpiring above him seemed to have any form or order about it. A madness had entered the studio, and it thudded off the walls as though desperately trying to escape.

Eventually the chaos seemed to wear itself out. Or perhaps it was that Tom tired of attempting to understand what was happening. Besides, the hurt was increasing, and it smothered out anything else. His body demanded sleep, and he drifted off, wondering dully if they had found Ashley Conlon and shot him. Whatever happened, he dimly concluded, he would not be the night's hero, only its fool. He slept.

When he awoke, it was with a loud, frightened groan he was certain could be heard across the studio. Only there was no one to hear him. A single light spilled weakly down from the catwalk as he hobbled across the platform. He looked up and saw that the door above was once again closed tight, as though to shut out the nightmares of the past few hours.

If there were controls up here that operated the elevator, he could not find them, and he could not hoist himself up onto the catwalk. There was nothing to do except begin the climb down along the struts, an agonizing and dangerous process that at other times, in other circumstances, he would never even have contemplated. But these were not other times, and his circumstances had altered dramatically. So he gritted his teeth and climbed down, trying to forget the pain and the fact that if he slipped, that would be the end of it.

He reached the ground. Undoubtedly, the police had sealed off the studio. And officers probably were left behind to watch the place. He found his way down another narrow corridor, fumbled along the wall until he discovered a light switch. There were cubicle-sized dressing rooms on either side of the hall, each outfitted with a latched window. He pushed a folding metal chair against a wall in one of the rooms, stepped up on it, and found himself staring out into the parking lot. He unlatched the window, unhooked the screen behind it. There was no one in sight. He knocked the screen forward with the edge of his palm. It clattered onto the pavement. He waited for the cops to come swarming. When they didn't, he hoisted himself up and through the window.

Where to go now? He couldn't go back to the hotel looking like this. Not with the blood of Kelly Langlois on him. He thought of Alvin. But Alvin was pissed off. There was only one place. The first sickly light of dawn was seeping across the sky as the taxi deposited him at Lea Madison's door.

"Sure you're all right?" The driver was youthful, concerned.

"Yeah, sure," Tom said. "Got beat up in a bar, that's all. My wife's gonna kill me."

The driver smiled sympathetically. "Good luck, man."

Tom rang twice, heard the bells chiming through the interior of the house. Rang again. And again. He was beginning to think she would not answer when the door opened, and there was Lea Madison, fully dressed, the side of her face black and blue.

"Oh, Jesus," she said, when she saw him.

"Can I come in?"

She stepped back to allow him into the house. He looked at her face.

"What happened to you?"

"I slipped. Fell against the side of the pool." As Tom went past her he stumbled. She held him. "What happened to *you*?"

"I'll explain everything — in a moment." He sagged into one of the sofas. "I think the police — they shot Ash Conlon."

Lea shook her head slowly. "No."

"He murdered Kelly Langlois tonight. I tried to stop it. Got there too late."

She sat next to him. He saw now that in addition to the battered face, her eyes were red, as though she had been crying.

"What's wrong?"

Her eyes grew wet and she buried her head against small knotted fists. "The police shot him."

"Shot who?"

"Lex, for Christ's sake. They say Lex murdered Kelly Langlois."

PART TWO

18

'M other?''
     He had called her name again, standing there *in the darkness beyond the door frame, facing the light. The fierce white light. He remembered that. It was perhaps his first real memory. He remembered the long sliver of light, his mother's voice, gentle, reassuring. And the explosion. More like a single loud clap, actually. And a moment later, the sliver of light was wider, and he had stepped into the bedroom.*

    "Mother," he called again.

    She turned to him, and he remembered that she was not wearing many clothes, and she was sitting astride his father. The light had become an incandescent glow drawing him in. Lyn Lisa Conlon rose and hurried to him, blocking the view across the room. She held something in her hand, a metal object that looked like a wonderful toy. He grabbed for it, but she held it out of his reach.

    He did not immediately know his father was dead. And he doubted it would have meant much to him. What was death anyway? That would come later. He would know about death, and he would know that his father was dead. Or gone away, as they insisted on putting it. But then he never liked his father much. His father was loud, and sometimes violent, and very unpleasant. His mother on the other hand was always gentle and loving, just like a mother should be.

    She ushered him to the door and told him to go back to

his room, that everything would be fine. She would be along in a few moments. Then the white light was just a sliver again as she shut the door.

But he didn't return to his room. He stood at the crack of light and he peered in. He could see his father across the room, without any clothes on, slumped back in his chair. He could see the awful bloody mess of his face. He could see Lyn Lisa Conlon kneel down beside his father and carefully place the gun into the slightly curling fingers of his right hand. Then she stood, and moved back a couple of paces, and buried her head in her hands. He wanted to run to her then. But he thought better of it. She turned and came toward the door, and on desperate tiptoe he ran away from the light, back to the safety of his room.

A moment later she was beside him, comforting him, holding him tightly against her warm body. It was going to be difficult for a long time, she whispered to him, as though it were a secret only they could share. Daddy has gone away, and there would be a lot of people asking questions. He was to say nothing. Did he understand that? No matter what, he was to say he was asleep in his bedroom, and heard nothing. Did he understand?

Yes, he understood. He would not say anything. All sorts of people did come, and they did ask lots of questions. He kept his word. He said nothing. He was never quite sure in those days what was going on, although he got to the point where he understood these people were accusing his mother of taking father away. But away to where? And what was wrong with taking him away?

It was years before he fully comprehended events. By that time his mother had been acquitted of the murder of his father, although of course he knew better. It was a subject never discussed, though. Not a hint from her of guilt or innocence, just the silent assertion that he had been a good boy, just as she had wanted. He was mother's boy. A beautiful boy. A good boy. And she would never forget that . . .

There was Gable. God, they didn't make stars like Clark
Gable any more, not with Gable's nonchalant masculinity, that self-assurance. What he would not give for Gable's self-assurance. Look at that profile, for God's sake,
the way the skin dropped smoothly over those incredible cheekbones. Of course, they had to be careful how
they photographed him, because he had big ears that
stuck out alarmingly. But he looked great. Just great.

He picked up another photograph, this one of Gary
Cooper. He loved the way Coop's hair was pushed back
from that sharp widow's peak, loved his lean, placid countenance, that thin cynical line of a mouth. The mouth and
the eyes. They always suggested humor, that Coop knew
this was all a bit of joke, that it wasn't to be taken too
seriously. The eyes suggested that when Coop got up in
the morning he didn't climb on a horse. Instead, he got
out one of the expensive suits tailored specially for him
in London.

He flipped through the other photographs, the pictures
of stardom he had been collecting since childhood. Tracy.
Bogart. And Cary Grant, possessed of a male beauty so
overwhelming that he could only get away with it by being
funny. Cary Grant knew how to take care of himself. He
didn't drink much, and he didn't smoke, and he got lots
of sleep each night. His was a life devoted to self-preserv-
ation. You could not be a star, Cary Grant concluded long
ago, unless you took care of yourself. You could not survive into longevity without developing a harsh self-dis-
cipline.

He studied those pictures, all the young gods captured
forever in their own mythology, and tears came to his
eyes. He yearned to be like them, to transport himself
away from mere mortality as they had been able to. He
wanted to be bigger than life. He wanted to be special in
the way they were special. And he knew that was impossible, that the moment he stood in the doorway and
watched his mother, his life was altered forever. There

were black demons that would have to be dealt with. There would be no mythology for him. He was forever shut out from the physical greatness he so much wanted. It was the tragedy of his life.

Ash Conlon closed the book of photographs. Tears spilled down his cheeks, the cheeks that at certain angles, and in just the right light, reminded him of Clark Gable's.

Later he went to the gym. Not a gym, actually. A health club. That's what they called them. He used the outdoor track on occasion. But otherwise he stayed in the weight room. He worked on the pectoral muscles of his chest, doing the bench presses, working on form, concentrating on lowering the barbell slowly, making use of the negative resistance factor as much as possible to help build the muscles. Inhale going down. Exhale going up. Ten repetitions. Then lateral raises for the side and rear deltoids. The sweat was breaking out on his body now. He watched himself carefully in the full-length mirror as he worked. The raises were followed by some barbell curls for biceps. He was really starting to get into it, looking like a winner.

Then Lincoln Malik appeared behind him, and it broke his concentration. He lowered the barbell to the floor.

"You're in great shape," Malik said. A cigarette dangled from his lips.

"Yeah, well, I work at it." Conlon grabbed a towel and ran it across his face. The weight room was empty at this time of the day. "Would you mind dousing that cigarette while you're in here?" Conlon said.

Malik looked at him. "Cigarette smoke bother you, does it?"

"Yes," Conlon said. "It bothers me."

Malik removed the cigarette from his mouth, carefully snuffed the end of it with his fingers, then put it in the pocket of his leather jacket. "We seem to have solved the problem of your friend."

"What does that mean?"

"It means he has left town."

"You're sure?"

"One of my people followed him to the airport this morning. He took a flight to New York."

"That would make sense," Conlon said. "He works a lot out of New York. Any trouble?"

"Some. More than I expected, actually. But that's what makes the job interesting. Trouble when you don't expect trouble. However, I think the matter is taken care of. What was the problem with him, anyhow?"

"He was bothering me."

Malik smirked. "I see."

They went into the locker room and Conlon got his wallet.

"Say," Malik said, "did you see they arrested someone a couple of weeks ago for Carrie Wayborn's murder? Some sort of famous movie director."

"I saw it," Conlon said. He counted out fifteen one-hundred-dollar bills and handed them to Malik. "What happens if he comes back?"

"The job carries a six-month warranty. Any problems, give me a call." He counted the money and shoved it unceremoniously into his pants pocket. "Did I tell you the cops came around to see me after Carrie was killed?"

"What did you say to them?"

"I told them the truth. I said she was a great fuck. And I would never kill off a good fuck, let alone a great one." He cackled with laughter. "Besides," he continued, "I had a terrific alibi. I was at the racetrack with about twenty people. Even had my picture taken. The date's on it and everything."

Malik looked at him again. Conlon turned away from the stare and that smirking arrogance Malik flashed every so often, an arrogance based on the knowledge he could break Conlon's arm without thinking twice about it.

"Sure was a shame about Carrie though," Malik said. "That asshole director. I hear he's in a coma. Knocked off some other broad, and the police got him."

"That's what I read in the newspapers," Conlon said.

"Christ, you can't read anything else." He nodded at Conlon. "Well, be seeing you, Ash."

Malik sauntered out of the locker room without glancing back and Conlon immediately felt better. The depression that had dogged him all morning was beginning to dissipate with the good news that Tom Coward had left the city. The way Coward started nosing around had made Ash furious. Telling Stormy those things about his mother. Asking her questions about his work. Then there was that bitch Lea Madison. Coward even got to her. Ash could have finished her off right there in her own bed, he was so angry at the way she had double-crossed him. But all that was behind him. Malik had taken care of Coward, just like he promised. Too bad it was not as simple where Stormy was concerned. All this had the effect of making her more possessive. But then maybe he shouldn't have given her the engagement ring in the first place. That may have been a dumb move on his part. Stormy was turning out to be just like all the women he had known. As soon as he had them in bed, gained their love and their devotion, they invariably began to bore him. He needed something different, and he needed it constantly.

Not to worry, though. There was New York. Things were definitely hot in New York. And they would get hotter. The thought excited him. Alone in the dressing room, he stripped off his gym shorts, socks, and sneakers. The excitement had made him semierect. He went to the mirror over one of the sinks. He touched at the contours of his face, ran his fingers along his hairline, checking for signs of receding, a hint of gray. Nothing. He gave himself a big sunny grin in the mirror, and admired the straightness of his teeth, their glistening whiteness. The light fell nicely across his jawline, giving him a pleasantly rugged look.

"You could have been in the movies, Ash," he said to the reflection in the mirror.

19

"Oh, shit," Lea Madison said.

"Something appears to be missing." Tom Coward trailed in through the door of the apartment, weighted down with her sleek Gucci luggage and his worn leather carryall. He allowed the bags to drop onto the Oriental rug. The walls of the vault-ceilinged living room were done in creamy yellow, and a bright-red settee was pushed against high windows that looked down onto West Fifty-Seventh Street and the Russian Tea Room. The settee was at right angles to the fireplace and the only other piece of furniture, a wing chair covered in white-on-white crewel fabric. Otherwise, the room was empty, the walls showing smudged light patches where paintings once hung.

"We are missing Bonnard," she said indicating one of the light patches. The heels of her leather boots clicked harshly on the parquet floor before moving onto the muffling surface of the rug. She wore form-fitting suede slacks, and a light knitted cotton sweater. As she moved, Lea raked her fingers through her hair, flinging it away from her shoulders, showing off a face now turning dark and bitchy. "He's sold the furniture," she pronounced.

"What?"

"You heard me. The bastard sold my furniture." Exasperation was tearing at the edges of her voice. She moved toward a heavy antique telephone that perched atop the mantelpiece on the far side of the room.

"Who sold the furniture?"

She picked up the brass receiver, once again threw back

her hair, and placed the receiver against her ear. "This works, at least. He sold the furniture. But he didn't disconnect the phone. Jesus."

Tom flopped himself down on the settee, feeling tired and grungy. They had flown out of Toronto that morning, had spent the better part of an hour trapped in traffic trying to get into Manhattan. Now he wanted a shower, a drink, and some lunch. And perhaps some sense from Lea Madison.

She finally provided it: "My husband, silly. It's just like him. I said he could use this place if he needed it. Naturally, he would translate that into selling the furniture." She started to dial.

One thing was certain: Lex Madison was not the husband in question. Several weeks after the shooting, he remained in intensive care, still in a coma, a police guard on duty twenty-four hours a day. One had only to turn on a television set or open a newspaper to discover those facts. Lex had made CBS News twice; and ABC World News Tonight once. While there was not an *entire* cover of *People* magazine devoted to him, there was a color-photo insert on the front with a throw to the story inside (it made up the week's "In Trouble" section). No, Lex was not involved in anything except the attempt to stay alive. And there was much speculation that, what with a police bullet lodged in his head, he was not going to be successful with the attempt.

"Which husband?" he inquired.

"The first one," she said, as she finished dialing.

"The actor."

"No. That most dangerous of all species, the *unemployed* actor." She held the receiver and listened. "Derek. Derek Shower. Former Carnaby Street wonder boy. Mod star of the sixties. International fucking furniture thief."

She was trying to be light, as she always tried for lightness with a little toughness added. But he noticed her

face, the pale, drawn quality it had taken on lately, the
sharp worry line that etched itself between eyebrows running gracefully back from the elegantly long nose; the
dark smudges beneath the eyes. The last couple of weeks
had been difficult. There were the police, of course. The
charge against Lex for the murder of Kelly Langlois. The
publicly voiced suspicion that he was also responsible for
the death of Carrie Wayborn.

Then there were the reporters, the camera crews. They
had hounded her everywhere. It was quite amazing. The
local scribes ordinarily wondered at the newest Royal
Commission appointed to investigate the latest social
and/or political malfeasance. They hemmed and hawed
over the advisability of summer road repairs that pre-
vented the Firenza owners from reaching the suburbs after a day's hard toil downtown. Occasionally, they sniffed
around the mysterious death of a local socialite. But life
in the news trenches seldom got close to anything like
glamor. The glamor came in dispatches from Liz Smith,
which the newspaper's syndicate paid for. It came from
People magazine or *Entertainment Tonight*. Glamor had
nothing to do with Toronto news. Glamor did not sit on
Metro council. And thank heaven for that.

But now here was a Hollywood director, albeit one who
had grown up in Toronto, accused of the murder of his
former girlfriend, who also happened to function as the
star of that weird sixties cult flick, *Zoom-Zoom*. There was
also the attractive owner of a sexual-aids retail outlet. The
Hollywood director had been involved with her as well.
And she too was dead. There was speculation about a
love triangle dating back twenty years. The police let it
be known they had information blackmail might be involved. The innuendos, as usual, were even more juicy
than the facts. And the facts themselves were plenty juicy,
including the beautiful estranged wife of the famous
Hollywood director.

Whatever ambition the locals had to cover the story was bolstered by the arrival of the out-of-town Yankee press. The cameras came first from Buffalo, and then, much more impressively, from New York. There developed not only a certain civic pride that Toronto was capable of this sort of internationally newsworthy story, but also a blood lust to pursue it. They knew now this was a big story. If it wasn't, surely Dan Rather would not be talking about it. Why, Mary Hart herself had come up to Toronto with an *Entertainment Tonight* crew. The local newspapers were so impressed they sent their television critics to interview her. Hart politely declined the interviews, stating she was a reporter here to do a story.

The only black mark against the whole episode was that it did not make the front page of the New York *Times*. Disappointingly, it was relegated to eight paragraphs on page fifteen.

In any event, it all got to be too much for Lea. Tom was fed up as well. He had tried repeatedly to get in touch with Stormy, but he had to settle for the recorded voice on her answering machine. She refused to return his calls. And she was not jogging along the boardwalk.

There was, at the same time, pressure from his syndicate to produce, in light of events, a Lex Madison story. To avoid having to do that right away, he grabbed at the Lacy Bergen assignment that had been hanging fire for some time. It was irrelevant fluff, therefore totally worthy of him—the premiere of Lacy's first adult movie. She was making her move out of the jeans commercials, for which she was famous, and into the nude scene the critics who lamented her adolescent exploitation said she was headed for anyway. Lacy would be available for interviews in New York. Tom would go to New York.

That being the case, Lea suggested, they might pool their resources, so to speak. She in order to get out of town, Tom so that he might bring a starving world the news of Lacy Bergen. Strictly platonic, naturally. After all, Lea did not want to do anything that would tarnish the armor of the knight errant. He merely made a growling noise at that, and agreed it might be fun to be in New York with her.

Lea's grip abruptly tightened on the receiver. "Derek? It's Lea. No, I'm not in Toronto. I'm here. In New York. I'm standing in the middle of—I'm fine, yes. I'm all right. You heard about it? On newscasts. I see. Since when did you listen to newscasts? Well, I came to New York to get away. It was incredible chaos up there. No, darling, nobody connected me with you. You sound disappointed. One thing though, Derek. There is nothing to sit on. Yes, I do realize the furniture isn't here. That's the goddamn point of this call. Yes, I am pissed off. No, I do not believe you didn't sell it."

Tom collected their luggage and dragged it back along the corridor. French doors opened off the living room into a long dining room. Beyond the dining room there was a narrow kitchen with wide linoleum counters and cupboards that reached up to the ceiling. Farther along he found a white-tiled bathroom with a big old-fashioned tub that sat curled on marble paws. There was also a bedroom done in lush apricot tones with matching pleated window shades, and a queen-size mattress covered by a Duvet quilt. He threw the bags down on the bed, found a towel in the hall closet, and went into the bathroom.

He wondered again how Lex Madison managed to end up at the Lakelot Studio, and concluded yet again that Kelly Langlois must have called to arrange a rendezvous. He doubted very much Lex murdered Kelly, not because Tom had any evidence of his innocence, but because he badly wanted the killer to be Conlon. Besides, if Lex was planning to get rid of Kelly, why would he have admitted to Tom that Kelly considered him Carrie's murderer? It didn't make sense.

Tom stripped off his clothing as he replayed this, then tried the shower nozzle that hung ancient and accusing over the tub. He was rewarded with a trickle of rusty water that eventually gained some strength. A thin slice of soap was offered up in a tray at the side of the tub, and once he had soaked himself under the uncertain and lukewarm shower spray, he used the soap to wash himself.

No, Conlon must have driven from the airport to the Lakelot, where he murdered Kelly. If only Malik had not intercepted him, Tom might have been able to stop the murder. In any event, Lex would have walked in after the killing, found Kelly's body, realized that he could well be implicated in her murder, and panicked when Tom arrived. It must have been Madison who slugged him over the side of the railing. And it was Madison who could not get away from the studio before the police arrived. He must have hidden in Kelly's apartment, finally been spotted by a trigger-happy law-enforcement official, and for his trouble got himself shot in the head.

There was the question of motive. Lea herself told the police about Kelly, and Kelly's suspicions that Lex killed Carrie Wayborn. Certainly Lex was in Toronto when Carrie died. He had closed down an entire movie ostensibly to save his marriage. Except the night Carrie was killed, Lex was not with Lea. That pretty much closed the case for the cops. They concluded Lex had gone to Kelly's apartment, an argument had ensued over his culpability in the Carrie Wayborn murder, a struggle, and Lex had ended up shooting his former girlfriend.

Tom turned off the shower, and stepped onto the cold tile of the floor, his bare feet slipping a bit. He got the towel and was wrapping it around himself when Lea opened the door and stepped in, arching that eyebrow when she saw his nakedness.

"I'll dry your back," she offered.

He playfully turned his back, and she grabbed at the

end of the towel, lifted it up, and used it to pat along his shoulder blades, causing, he had to concede, a sensation that tingled. It was, suddenly, quite close in here, only the sound of a dripping shower nozzle, the water smacking with great plonks against the marble surface of the tub. There was soft heat along his back, her lips touching at his skin.

"That's drying my back?"

"I'm doing it with my lips," she said. "Manual labor."

Then she wiped at his back more brusquely with the towel's end. "There you go." She moved away from him. "Derek wants to have drinks in an hour or so."

"I thought he'd stolen your furniture."

"He denies the accusation. He says he merely put the stuff in storage for me."

Tom went out of the bathroom and into the bedroom. "Do you want to have a drink with him?"

"I want to get my furniture back. He wants to meet us at the Palm Court at the Plaza. Apparently he's being interviewed there." She sauntered after him, watching the little pools of water on the hardwood left by the soles of his feet.

"That's going to stain," she said.

"What's going to stain?"

"Your feet on my hardwood floor."

"Oh, Jesus," he said. Hopping awkwardly on one foot, then on the other, he dried his feet. "I thought he wasn't working."

"He is now. He's making his comeback in the Lacy Bergen movie."

"We could check into a hotel," Tom said. "I'm only going to be a couple of days."

"I'm going to stay longer. The natives aren't quite so restless in New York."

"What about Lex?"

"What about him?"

He pulled a cotton shirt out of his carryall. "Shouldn't you be there in case he comes around?"

Her mouth curled, as though something distasteful had found its way inside. "The dutiful wife, eh? Sticking by her hubby. Hell, we can pose for pictures together."

"That's not what I meant."

"Tom, for Christ's sake, he killed two women. I'm just fortunate he didn't kill me."

"The trouble is, I don't think he did it."

"Do you think I enjoy the idea of having a killer for a husband? For God's sake, this is going to haunt me for the rest of my life. Every time I do anything, every time I walk into a room, meet someone — Christ, every time I shit — there is going to be this whisper: 'Oh, yes, that's Lex Madison's wife. You know Lex Madison? The director who murdered those two women."

"You're not listening to me."

"I am listening. I've done nothing but listen. I know what you think. You think Ash was on his way to the Lakelot Studio that night. But he wasn't, believe me. Don't you understand? Ash didn't kill anyone."

"How do you know that?"

She took a deep breath. "Because he was with me that night."

He was in the midst of making a messy knot with the tie. He had never been any good with ties or knots so it was an appropriate time to stop, and narrow the eyes. "What?"

She turned away from him. "It's at moments like this I wish I still smoked."

Tom came over to her. "You were with Ash?"

"It was nothing particularly serious. What used to be called recreational fucking. It's been going on for about six months. We met at a party. He took me home and threw me over the couch. It was marvelous."

She turned to him, and there were tears in her eyes. "I

was having a terrible time with Lex. I didn't know he
and Ash knew each other. I just enjoyed the physical thing
with Ash. He'd come over every two weeks or so. I'd
open my legs, talk dirty for a couple of hours. Wham,
bam. Thank you, sir. Lex found out. He didn't know who
it was, but he knew it was someone. That's when we
separated.''

He had given up on the knot. He watched a tear drip
out of the corner of her eye and start a run for the edge of
the cheekbone. There was a numbness in him. He had
the distinct feeling he was mounted high on a rickety platform, and that platform was beginning to collapse.

''I mean,'' he said, ''there are times involved here. We
have to consider times. What time did he get to your place,
for example. That sort of thing. He could have murdered
Kelly, then have gone to your place. That's possible.''

''Oh, Jesus,'' Lea said. The tears increased.

''Isn't that possible?''

''I suppose so. Yes. He was late. He didn't get there
until after ten.''

''Lots of time then,'' Tom said, ''Lot's of time. How
was he?''

''What do you mean?''

''What sort of state was he in? Mentally. Emotionally.''

''He was okay until — ''

''Until what?''

''Until I made a joke about the fact that he was getting
married.''

''Then what did he do?''

''He got furious. I mean really angry. Until then, the
Ash I knew was this very sexy, cool, controlled lover. He
was like this fantasy figure come to life. That's what made
the affair so exciting. I half-expected to look out the window and find his white charger waiting outside for him.''

''What did he say to you?''

''He wanted to know how I knew about the marriage.''

"And?"

"And I told him. I told him that particular piece of gossip had come from you."

"How did he react?"

"He reacted very badly. He grabbed my throat."

"He grabbed your throat?"

"Yes," she said. "He tried to kill me."

20

The Killer spent the morning shopping, then decided to have lunch at the new French restaurant just around the corner. The *pâté de Gibier dans sa croute* was wonderful. So was the grilled bass. It was washed down with a glass of the house white, and the Killer felt quite marvelous. The *gratin de fruits frais* was considered, then rejected.

After that came a pleasant sunny stroll back to the apartment. A lengthy consideration of what was to come, and a final decision to go ahead with the plan. There was no sense of madness in this. The Killer was surprised to discover what a truly rational act murder was. There were no demons, no voices from heaven urging vile deeds, such as the murder of twenty-five drifters. That truly was murder emanating out of madness.

This was murder as a method of solving certain problems, the killing of people who did not deserve to live in the first place. It was also murder as a rather delightful challenge; a hobby if you will. If one could commit murder successfully, then one joined a small and elite club, at least in this society. In El Salvador, say, the membership of the club would be considerably larger, the getting away with murder not nearly the accomplishment.

The Killer returned to the apartment, nodded to Jake the doorman, and went up to the sixteenth floor, turned on Mozart's piano concerto in E flat. Mozart, the Killer long ago concluded, was best at the concertos. Thus, only the piano concertos were played. As the music filled the high-ceilinged room, certain necessary items were laid out: the hair dye, horn-rimmed glasses, kid gloves, a floppy hat, a trench coat. And the murder weapon. Oh, dear. The murder weapon. Now what to use? There was the gun, of course. The gun was the necessary element of surprise. But something was needed to get the ball rolling, to signify hurt without causing everyone to run for cover. The rug cleaner would hardly work this time. That had been a weapon of necessity, anyhow. Something employed on the spur of the moment. The kitchen. That was the best place for the tools of death. A knife was the simplest, most appropriate weapon. The Killer chose one with a wooden handle and a long, thin stainless-steel blade, its edge serrated. This was laid out beside the other items.

When the Mozart concerto was finished, the Killer snapped on the television set and watched *The Young and the Restless*. There was also a promo urging viewers to watch the *Six O'clock "Live Eye" News*.

Yes, thought the Killer. We certainly must watch the news.

They strolled across Sixth Avenue. The late-afternoon light was hard, rising up from somewhere in Central Park, flooding south, burnishing the crowds pouring along the street.

"So why didn't he kill you?" Tom demanded.

"He didn't kill me because he's not a killer." Lea made the statement simply, as though it were the most natural conclusion in the world. "He was angry, he was hurt. He felt I had betrayed him. He hit me, and he hurt me. And when he had his hands on my throat I honestly thought for a moment he might kill me. I thought of you. I thought of what you had said about him. Your suspicions. And I was sure he would do it. But he didn't."

A vendor waved a copy of the New York *Post* and announced loudly that eleven were dead in a school-bus crash. Tom took Lea's arm and hurried away.

"Maybe he thought it was too dangerous," Tom said.

"He wasn't thinking rationally. He was just really angry. I think if he could have, he would have killed me. But he couldn't."

"What did he do?"

"Called me a lot of vile names, and, like I said, he knocked me around. But then Lex knocked me around. So that's nothing new. After that, he stormed out, and I haven't heard from him since."

"Why didn't you tell me you were seeing him?"

"Because it was none of your business. It wasn't anyone's business."

They were heading east along Central Park South now. They walked past the horse-drawn hansoms and the limos, the expensive hotels and fashionable apartment buildings, gimlet-eyed doormen, and mean-faced bag people.

"Okay," Tom said, "maybe he didn't kill Kelly with any premeditation. Maybe it was her gun. Maybe they fought over it and it went off. That's possible."

"But that doesn't explain who killed Carrie. If you think Ashley killed her, too, then you've got to believe he killed two women accidentally. That doesn't seem very likely."

"Oh, shit," Tom said. "I haven't come this far in order to discover your husband is the goddamn bad guy."

She stopped him outside the entrance to the Plaza. "Look, if you go poking around in anyone's life, Tom, you're going to find out things that aren't very pleasant. Ash fools around. He screwed me. According to you he comes to New York and screws some mysterious blond. He quits his job, and he doesn't tell anyone. He even has a mother who was indicted for the murder of her husband, and he had a pretty traumatic experience with a crazy woman when he was in college. But none of those things makes him eligible for murder. Ash may need a psychiatrist, but then so do we all."

She brushed a hand gently through his hair. "Can I make a suggestion? You forget about this. *Really* forget about this. We have a drink with Derek. We go to the premiere, get a little high, we come back to the apartment, and we'll just blot everthing out with a lot of sex."

He shook his head. "It doesn't work," he said. "I've tried it. Believe me."

"You haven't tried it with me," she said quietly.

"Let's go and find Derek," he said.

Inside the lobby of the Plaza, everything was as usual. The Japanese businessmen argued about car imports. The blond-haired, dark-suited security guards, were on lookout for the gorgeously dressed models who met middle-aged businessmen in a spray of expensive perfume and a kiss on either cheek.

Tom and Lea floated along the pastel-green carpeting to the Palm Court where a piano player and a violinist engaged in a politely contested Gershwin medley. The captain stationed at the entrance took one look at Lea, all cool and casual elegance in Italian linen, and smiled admiringly. Across the restaurant, a gray-haired man lifted an eyebrow, fluttered a greeting.

"Derek," she said.

"Lea, you look wonderful." He was on his feet, shorter than Tom expected. But then actors always were shorter than anyone expected.

"This is a friend, Tom Coward." Lea was crisp and formal.

Derek Shower turned limp blue eyes and a small too-pretty mouth toward Tom. A shock of hair fell across his forehead. Youth was disappearing quickly off his face, being replaced by nasty, unattractive pouches and lines that were developing in the wrong places. He offered a hand and the winning charm of a smile that had made him the hit of the London mod scene in the early 1960s.

"How are you, old man?"

Tom shook the small, white hand. "I'm fine," he said. "Let's have a drink."

They were seated, fussed over by a waiter; drink orders were taken. "How are you?" Derek repeated the question to Lea.

"More to the point," she said, giving him a cool eye. "How are you?"

"Working, darling. All that counts, isn't it? In this new movie, I'm the older man admired by Lacy Bergen. God! Who would ever have thought the day would come when I would be the older man?" He glanced at Tom. "In the sixties we all thought we would be young forever." He turned to Lea for support, and she issued the ghost of an affirmative smile. "We had all the money in the world, and thought we could never spend it all. We stayed out all night, and we drank everything in sight. I crashed around with Petey O'Toole in those days. And Burton, of course. They were both making the Beckett movie. We'd go pub crawling together, wenching together. Great times."

His eyes lowered for a moment, as though in salute to great, bygone days. He brushed at the surface of the tablecloth with his hand. "Now Burton's dead, and Petey doesn't dare touch another drop." His curious little mouth made an ironic smile. "And yours truly is making his comeback playing the older man. Ah, well. There you go."

The smile got bigger and grew fonder as he looked over at Lea. "Lea was only about nineteen when I met her. At Peter Lawford's beach house, actually. I was just off the boat from England, as was she. Hollywood was going to make a star out of me. What a laugh. I had seen her around London, of course. She was moving with a fast crowd. I was moving with a fast crowd. But they were different crowds. Anyway, we met at Lawford's place over brunch, and I thought she was the most wonderful woman on earth.'' He leaned forward and squeezed her chin. ''Still do.''

''So will you have the furniture delivered? Or do you want to give me the name of the storage company, and I'll take care of it?''

He flashed another winning smile. ''Luv, don't worry about it. I told you I would take care of it.'' Drinks arrived, and Derek abruptly straightened his tie.

''Uh-oh,'' he said. ''She's early.''

''Who's early?'' Lea demanded.

Derek was rearranging the pouches on his face under a glow of welcome. ''Julie Keene,'' he said out of the corner of his mouth. ''The entertainment correspondent for *Live Eye News*. She's the one doing an interview with me.''

Julie Keene swept over, tall, blond, professionally confident, every feature painted and enameled into a perfection that would allow a television camera to photograph it. Tom looked at her, looked again, and realized that he knew Julie Keene. She was the woman Ash Conlon met in the Oak Bar. She was the woman who had gone with him to his room, spent the afternoon making love to him.

Derek introduced her to Lea and Tom.

''Gee,'' Julie said to Tom when she was seated and had crossed long, slim legs. ''You're the journalist, aren't you? I've read your stuff. I admire anyone who can write.'' She targeted Tom with those startling, intense blue eyes that he had noticed even from across the room at the Oak Bar. The eyes were her charm, and she didn't waste them for long on any one man. Their trajectory moved on and focused on Derek Shower.

''Gosh, I rented a whole bunch of cassettes of your movies last weekend. I spent the whole time curled up with a cup of herbal tea watching your movies. You were wonderful, Mr. Shower. All that stuff about England, and the whole mod scene. I didn't know anything about it. It was very educational. Carnaby Street. Is that, like, is that still in London?''

"In a manner of speaking, yes,'' said Derek. "Not like it was, of course."

"Because I've been to London. A couple of years ago. And I thought I visited all the landmarks. But I never saw that one."

"Well," said Derek with a brave smile, "it's hard to fit everything into one trip. Can I get you anything? A drink?''

"Just a Perrier, thanks. Anyway,'' she continued, "I'm really looking forward to doing this piece. What we'd like to do is talk to you here for a little while. I've got the camera crew outside. I think it would be kinda neat to do it right here in the Palm Court, don't you?''

"Certainly,'' Derek agreed.

"Then we're going to be at the theater tonight. We'd like to film you there. And at the party afterward at Hisae's. You know, kind of get you on the biggest night of your career, sort of thing."

"I wouldn't precisely say it's my *biggest* night,'' Derek said. "Important, yes. But I remember the premiere of my first film. Now that was — ''

"I know what you mean," Julie Keene said. "I wasn't trying to imply anything.''

Derek Shower nodded reassuringly. "Of course not, m'dear. Why don't we get on with it then? Bring on the cameras. I want to tell the world what Julie Christie was really like.''

Julie Keene looked confused. "That's a sixties person. Right?''

Derek Shower's young-old face was crestfallen.

When she left the Palm Court to get her camera crew, Tom followed her, watching that plump behind turning against the tight tangerine skirt, picturing Ash Conlon's hands cradling it.

"Julie," he called out. She stopped at the French doors leading out to the Fifth Avenue entrance. He caught up to her. "Can I talk to you for a moment?"

"Uh, I think I know what you're going to ask," she said.

He looked surprised. "You do?"

"You see, I'm not dating right now. I mean, I am dating but this one guy, you know? He's out of town, a lot. But he's the only guy I'm seeing."

"It isn't Ashley Conlon, by any chance?"

Her blue eyes grew wider. "You know Ash?"

"That's, ah, what I wanted to talk to you about. We're — we're old school chums. He mentioned that he, ah, was seeing a television reporter."

"Oh," she said. "I'm sorry. I thought you were going to ask me for a date. I'm from the Midwest. A lot of guys here are constantly hitting on me for dates."

"But not Ash."

"Ash didn't *hit* on me for a date, exactly. He was a lot more subtle about it. Not like most of the other men I've met here. I got my view of New York men out of the *New Yorker* magazine. It's all wrong."

"I saw him recently," Tom said. "In Toronto."

"Toronto. That's Canada, right? I know he travels a lot. But what was he doing in Toronto?"

"Isn't that funny?" Tom said. " I would have sworn Ash said he was living in Toronto."

"No, no. He lives right here in New York. With his mother."

Tom blinked. "His mother. Are you sure?"

"I haven't met her, not yet. She isn't very well, apparently. But as soon we make the announcement, he's going to introduce me to her."

"Announcement? What announcement?"

The blue eyes warmed and lost much of their intensity.

"We're very much in love, Mr. Coward," she said. "Ash has asked me to marry him."

"And what did you say to that?" Tom asked.

"Why, I said yes, naturally. What girl wouldn't say yes?"

"I'm beginning to wonder," Tom Coward said.

21

At five o'clock, the Killer took a long hot bath in one of those huge tubs where you can really stretch out. Then the Killer spent an hour using the hair coloring, getting it just right. What a difference a little dye made. The years dropped away. Satisfied with the results, the Killer dressed in the faded jeans, the sneakers, the white cotton shirt, and then gave the whole outfit a little pizzazz with the addition of a narrow leather tie. Whoa! Pretty hot stuff.

Then the Killer set about putting together the second set of clothes, packing them neatly into the carryall. It took only a few minutes to get the change of clothes ready. In the living room, the wall clock said it was six o'clock. On the television set, the *Live Eye News* was on. The anchorman, white-haired, solid jaw, reassuring demeanor, was introducing the night's lineup: the possibility of another vigilante killer, this one in the South Bronx; angry taxi drivers unhappy about rate increases; a jewelry robbery on Fifth Avenue. And, on the lighter side, a report from Julie Keene on a new star and an old one getting together for a movie.

The camera angle widened to include Julie, sitting pert and chipper at the anchor desk. "Sounds as though it's going to be quite a night, Julie," the anchorman said in the avuncular fashion that earned him nine hundred thousand dollars a year and made him believe that if things had gone just a little differently, he could have been another Cronkite.

"It certainly is, Brett," Julie agreed."Tonight is the premiere of the new Lacy Bergen movie."

"That's the young lady who does all those jean ads?"

"Now she's trying to branch out, Brett. This is her first adult movie. The interesting thing is, she is co-starring with Derek Shower. Remember him from the 1960s?"

"I certainly do, Julie. The British star."

"Right, Brett. Derek is making something of a comeback with Lacy. In fact I met him this afternoon. He's an interesting story. I'm going to be reporting from the theater and the premiere party at Hisae's restaurant."

"We'll look forward to it, Julie." The anchorman turned back to the camera. "Okay, at the top of the news tonight. Police in the south Bronx say they may have another vigilante killer on their hands . . . ."

The Killer turned off the television set and went to a hall closet and removed the shoe box. Inside was the handgun that the courteous and informative gun salesman had called the Undercover.

"This is new," the salesman explained. "One hell of a piece of weaponry. It's a .38 caliber special developed by the Charter Arms Corporation. Weighs only sixteen ounces. You can hold it in the palm of your hand. This one " — he held out the gun—" features cylinder, frame, hammer block, cylinder latch, and trigger of Chrome-moly steel. It's known in the trade as the pound of prevention. The price is right, too. Just three hundred and fifty-five dollars."

The gun with its walnut panel grips was placed on the coffee table, and the Killer sat back for several minutes just looking at it admiringly. What was it De Maupassant once wrote? "There is nothing more beautiful and honorable than killing"? Precisely. For such a memory, a drink might be in order. A little cognac to sooth the nerves and to pass the time until Julie Keene made the last television report of her life.

Derek Shower arrived with the black limousine at 7 P.M.
He was decked out in a tuxedo, with a rose in the lapel.
A bottle of champagne was open in the back. Imitations
of renewed glamor bounded around the pearl-gray smoked-
glass interior.

"The interview went just great," Derek reported as Lea
and Tom crawled into the car. "I was smashing. Absolutely smashing." He failed in his delight to notice that if
there was anything smashing inside the car it was Lea.
She wore a slinky black something, cut up to the thigh,
spaghetti straps holding up a bodice cut low to demonstrate the awesome power of cleavage. She was dressed,
not to kill, but as a kind of revenge. Tom, upstairs in the
apartment, had taken note and had saluted revenge with
an admiring kiss. Her lips shifted hotly under his and
the kiss started to gain momentum. He cooled things off
by telling Lea about his conversation with Julie Keene.

"He's lied through his teeth to her. He says he lives in
New York with his mother, for Christ's sake."

"What about his mother?"

"His mother has been dead for ten years. But here's
the kicker. He's asked her to marry him."

"I truly am amazed," Lea said. "God, he is certainly
weird enough. I grant you that. I don't know that any of
this makes him a killer, though."

"It doesn't make him anyone Stormy should marry,"
Tom said.

"So that's it," Lea said coolly. "You've won. Don't you
see? You can go back to Toronto now and tell Stormy what
you know. Of course, she can't marry him. How could
she? No one in their right mind would. Maybe she'll even
have you back. That's what you want, isn't it?"

He said nothing. He didn't know what to say. He concentrated on chewing at his lower lip. "Julie Keene is
going to be at this thing tonight," he said finally. "I'm
going to talk to her some more."

"I think you're enjoying this, Tom. You like being the voyeur, snooping into people's lives. Gives you a little buzz, doesn't it? Gives you power. Watching people who don't know they're being watched, learning secrets about them they don't want learned."

It was at that moment that Derek had arrived, providing Lea with the dramatic exit, and saving Tom the necessity of defending himself against what perhaps was not defensible.

"This is a big night for me," Derek said. He held his glass aloft, and in the changing light from the traffic on Fifty-seventh Street, his face shone white and scared.

"To big nights," Lea agreed. She, too, held up her glass.

They had no sooner toasted Derek than the limo was in front of the theater on Second Avenue, the street awash with light, the crowd held back behind police barricades. The chauffeur bounced out, hyped up for the occasion. He swung open the door with a certain elan, and Derek virtually flew out of the car. He was high on his own future career possibilities, waving at a faceless mob and at the *Live Eye* camera crew recording the moment along the sidelines. Tom caught a glimpse of Julie Keene standing just behind her crew.

Derek stood there momentarily in the white lights, his gray hair tousled, his tuxedo unwrinkled, his arm raised, his mouth open. He almost fooled the paparazzi hunting in front of the theater. They lunged for him. The chauffeur's elan and Derek's enthusiastic confidence had made them think he was somebody. Cameras were up and ready to shoot before the silent signal that is sent constantly on such occasions was flashed: *Nobody*. The cameras went down as abruptly as they had been raised; indifference emanated like heat from the pack of photographers. The crowd, primed for celebrity, ready to roar out a welcome, was oddly silent, as if embarrassed.

Lea, the pro in these instances, stepped up smartly and

took Derek's arm, moved him toward the theater entrance. Lea might not be famous, but she was dazzling, which in the photographer's limited lexicon amounts to about the same thing. The paparazzi could appreciate, if not always sell, dazzle, and so they avidly photographed it. Tom brought up the rear, feeling merely exposed.

They reached the lobby where the security guards did battle with the richly dressed customers. It was a class fight as much as anything: the poor pushing around the rich and enjoying every mean-minded moment.

"Come on now! Move back! Move back!" one of the guards, a burly black man, was yelling at the top of his lungs.

"Jesus, there's Andy Warhol," someone announced. Reporters scribbled hastily into notebooks; photographers fired off a halfhearted volley of flash guns. Andy Warhol and a token would get you a ride on the New York subway.

Derek came to a stop somewhere deep in the milling throng. His forehead had broken out into a cold sweat that dampened the hair flopped across it.

"Have you seen Julie?" he asked.

"Outside," Tom said. "With the cameras."

"She said she wanted to follow me around," Derek said lamely. He was aware that his arrival had not been a success.

"Get the fuck back," yelled the security guard.

"Let's sit down," Tom said.

"I think I'll wait for Julie," Derek said. He mopped at his forehead with a large pale-blue handkerchief.

"I want to see Lacy Bergen," Lea said.

"You're still mad at me," Tom said.

"I want to see Lacy Bergen." She paused. "And maybe I'm still mad at you." Someone knocked against her. "This is like being in a clothes dryer," Lea said.

"Then let's sit down," Tom said.

"I don't want to sit down," Lea said.

The crowd began surging toward the door. Lacy Bergen was arriving. She squeezed through the entrance amidst the photographers, keeping the smile glued to her face as the security guards trampled her in their enthusiasm to protect her. She wore a tiara in her hair, and her round young face glowed. She was the princess at her first prom. Except she was the star of a fourteen-million-dollar movie, and a small riot.

She spotted Derek Shower and her face lit up even more.

"Derek darling," she called out. A moment later they were embracing, and the photographers now were fighting each other to get the shot. Derek looked as though he had died and gone to heaven. And in a sense, he had; the heaven that for just another moment saves an actor from obscurity.

Three hours later, the determined party people and the good liars retreated to Hisae's restaurant.

"If God wanted Lacy Bergen to grow up he wouldn't have allowed her to make this movie." Tom tried to squeeze by the author of that statement, balancing a champagne glass in either hand. He failed. Some of the wine splashed on the author's arm. He didn't notice.

Someone else was saying to the movie's director, "You know in that final cut? When you shift back across the Manhattan skyline and down into Central Park, and the camera comes to rest on that ice rink, and the kids skating? What did it mean?"

"Life," the director firmly avowed. The director had dark hair and a beard trimmed so neatly it seemed more a work of art than mere facial hair. "When Lacy walks away from her lover the last time, I wanted to reaffirm that no matter what happens to her from here on in, life goes on." The director paused solemnly. "It's a message of hope," he continued. "It's a message that I think has a great deal of relevance for today's youth."

The post-premiere atmosphere was heavy with wilted excitement, falsely induced by publicists working overtime, knowing that nothing would flow naturally in the wake of a freshly discovered turkey. Considering this was New York, the audience had been unusually polite. It had given the movie twenty minutes before the first snickers escaped. An hour elapsed before full-scale laughter broke out. But there were surprisingly few walkouts, considering the universally held opinion that this was one of the most boring movies ever to open in New York.

"I've attended worse premieres," said Tom as he and Lea walked over to Hisae's. "Not many. But some."

Now Derek Shower was directly in front of him, blocking the way with a countenance weary but hopeful.

"Wasn't Lacy brilliant?" It was more demand than question.

"Interesting," Tom amended.

"She's got a great future," Derek gushed.

"As an adult," Tom said.

Derek looked at him sharply. "You didn't like the movie."

"That's one way of putting it, I guess."

"I intensely dislike the cynicism of the press."

"I'm sorry to hear that," Tom said.

"And I don't think I like you very much, Coward."

"There is a long line, and it's growing."

"I don't know what you're doing with Lea," Derek continued. He had more than a few drinks in him, and those, combined with a night quickly plunging toward failure, made him nasty. "I hope you're not taking advantage of her."

"I don't have a single stick of her furniture."

Derek moved threateningly at Tom, and Lea was there between them.

"How gallant," she said cryptically, "two young swains fighting over little old me."

Tom saw Julie Keene come into the room. "Derek doesn't

like me," he said to Lea as he moved away. "He thinks I'm going to steal your furniture."

Derek gave him another dirty look, and Lea took the actor's arm.

"Take it easy," she said. "That's not the way to get your picture on the front page of the New York *Post*."

"I don't like his attitude."

"Yes," Lea said. "He seems to have a great deal of trouble with that."

Tom approached Julie Keene, and she presented him with one of her most dazzling professional smiles.

"Ash's friend," she said by way of identifying him to herself.

"I think we should talk about that," Tom said.

"I don't have much time. In fact, I'm getting a trifle nervous. I'm supposed to do a live spot with Lacy Bergen and she hasn't shown up yet. I've got a camera crew all set to go and everything."

"Julie, there are a few things about Ash that I don't think you know."

She regarded him with a quizzical expression. "What do you mean?"

The field producer, a harried-looking man, frantically chewing at a wad of gum, touched Julie on the shoulder. "Okay. I just got word from her people. Lacy's on her way."

"I have to go," Julie said.

"I think we should talk," Tom said.

She was looking genuinely concerned now. "I don't think there's much to talk about."

"For one thing," Tom said, "as far as I know Ash lives in Toronto, not New York. His mother isn't unwell. She's dead. In Toronto he's involved with a woman named Stormy Willis."

"What are you talking about?"

"He's asked Stormy to marry him," Tom finished.

She just stood there in the midst of the party, the confusion, and the noise. The producer was tugging at her
arm.

"Julie. Please. We're right on the line."

She shook her head. The blue eyes cleared and recap-
tured some of their former intensity. "Okay, John. I'm
with you." She pulled in a deep breath and showed Tom
a strength he didn't think she possessed. "You're right,
Mr. Coward, I think we should talk. I don't know whether
you're crazy or what, but I think we should talk. Not here,
though. I have to concentrate on this, I really do."

"Later then."

"Can you meet me at my place?" She was fishing for
something in her purse.

"Sure."

She scrawled an address on the back of a business card.
"I'm at Gramercy Park. I have to leave right after this.
Every night at eleven-thirty, rain or shine, I walk Arnold.
Arnold is my mutt. He's all I have in the world. I never
miss the date. Why don't you meet me afterward at the
apartment? Say in an hour?"

"I'll be there."

"She's coming in the door," the field producer said.
"All set?"

Julie Keene nodded tightly. "All set," she said.

22

J ulie Keene reported on the "dazzling" arrival at the post-premiere party at Hisae's of "America's newest young star, Lacy Bergen." Lacy gushed into Julie's microphone that she was "delighted" with the response to her first adult movie. Then it was back to the studio and *Live Eye's* Mel Dickerson with the weather. If it was not already drizzling out there in Manhattan, Mel genially offered, it was about to.

The Killer rose from the easy chair, snapped off the television, feeling warm and confident and not a little excited. The drinks helped. There had been two of them. No more. Discipline must be exercised. The trench coat was put on. Then the floppy fedora. Pulled down sharply over the face. This was followed by the eyeglasses and the pair of kid gloves. Finally, the weapons. The kitchen knife was shoved into the left-hand side pocket of the trench coat. Into the right pocket went the Undercover— "the pound of prevention." All set.

The Killer went out the back way so as not to attract the doorman's attention. Outside, the air was moist and threatening, making blurry the lights from the oncoming traffic. At Sixth Avenue, the Killer dropped down into the graffiti-scarred netherworld of the New York subway system. There was a wait of twenty minutes before the B train to Forty-second Street appeared, a rusty finger crawling out of hell.

In the car, there was an advertisement that read "WCBS-88 AM The Best in the Business." There were perhaps thirty other passengers, everyone grim faced, keeping resolutely to themselves. When you rode the New York subway, especially at night, you stared but you looked at nothing. It was the law of the jungle down here.

There was a change of trains at Rockefeller Center, and a hike to the upper platform for the number-seven train to Grand Central Sation. There was spray-painted graffiti announcing lost love: "Cheryl, I will never forget. Ernest." At Grand Central station, The Killer got off the train and walked past a plump black woman seated on a chair that looked dangerously small for her. She held a Bible and chanted unintelligible words.

The Killer waited on the platform for only five minutes before the Lexington Avenue local arrived. On board the clattering train, the Killer, investigating emotional responses, felt wonderful. There were no nerves at all. But then the murder was not a matter of nerves. It was, this evening, a matter of getting off at Twenty-third Street.

Tom intended to leave Hisae's with Julie Keene, but one of the public-relations people had cornered him and the next thing he was being shunted over to a corner where Lacy Bergen radiantly held onto a glass of soda water and a grin that would make an orthodontist quiver. She exuded youth and vitality. When you looked at her, Tom thought, it made you want to buy jeans. It made you want to do other things, too. He shook her hand; her smile grew even brighter.

"You're supposed to interview me," she said.

"I hope so," Tom replied politely.

She made a face that betrayed the child still lurking on the edges of the hastily emerging adult. "I don't like doing interviews," she said. "Everyone asks me about my mom."

"I won't ask you about your mom," Tom said.

"Good," she said. "Ask me about world peace."

"What about world peace?"

"I'm in favor of it," Lacy Bergen said. She said it in a way that suggested she might be able in short order, to make it possible.

"And the seal hunt," she added.

"You're for the seal hunt?"

She laughed and slapped him on the arm. "No, silly. I'm against *that*."

When he finally made his escape, Julie had already left. He went through the restaurant in the wake of a fleeing Lacy Bergen, flash guns going off to mark her departure. On the street, Lacy had disappeared, leaving behind miserable autograph hunters. She had taken with her the tiara, her youth, her orthodontist's dream teeth, and perhaps any hope that her entry into adulthood would produce a hit movie.

A thunderclap sent a doorman scurrying into the street frantically hailing passing taxis. In a few moments, Tom thought, as soon as the rain started, there would not be a cab available in Manhattan. He decided not to wait, but try his luck farther east on Madison. He thought of Julie Keene, her unexpected grace. He wondered how much more he should tell her. He thought of Stormy, and how blond and alike the two of them were, and how he was about to ruin both their lives with the truth.

The first splash of rain hit him as he neared Madison. The truth. He had spent most of his life avoiding what was customarily, if usually inaccurately, known as the truth. Now, for once, he was the messenger bearing truth. He should have felt better about it than he did.

By the time Julie Keene had completed the ritual of opening the locks of her apartment door, Arnold, her tiny champagne Shih Tzu, was yapping frantically. He leapt into her arms before she was halfway inside.

"Hello, baby," Julie said, nuzzling at the dog as it

squirmed happily. "How's the only man I'll ever love?" That brought the tears, and Arnold licked at them frantically as they rolled down his mistress's cheeks. The depression also hit her then, a force that almost caused her knees to buckle.

She put Arnold down, his claws scratching frantically against the hardwood floor. She tried to stifle the sobs. There was no use crying, she told herself. You knew something was wrong. Everything was totally right. Yet something was wrong. You could feel it deep down. This was all too passionate, too crazy. He was too wonderful, too mysterious. Ashley had reminded her of Maxim de Winter in *Rebecca*. This wasn't a novel, though. It was life. And life always ended badly, even for chipper blonds who did bubbly celebrity reports on local television newscasts.

Julie snapped the leash onto Arnold's collar. "Ready for your walk?" The dog was leaping up on her legs, threatening her nylons. She had never been a happy person, and God knows there were a lot of reasons for that. But Ash had made her happy. Deliriously so. He was gentle, kind, funny, and vulnerable, too. Beneath that dark beauty, there was the scared boy who needed help. Just as beneath the dumb dipstick blond she felt everyone always saw in her, there was this intelligent person trying to get out. Ash saw that. He understood that because she was trying so hard to say the right thing it often came out wrong, and she sounded so silly. And of course that breathy cheer-leader voice of hers did not help matters.

She shoved Arnold away from her legs. "I hope you don't mind pooping in the rain."

Julie pulled Arnold into the hall, carefully relocked the apartment. Now a stranger was coming to tell her that Ash was someone else entirely. He was coming to tell her that she knew nothing about him at all. She wondered if she should listen to him. What difference did it make what Ash was to someone else? It was what Ash was to her that counted.

Except that man said Ash was going to marry someone else. The tears started again.

Little Mrs. McPherson emerged from the rattling old box the super laughingly called an elevator, and Julie wiped a hand quickly across her eyes. Mrs. McPherson looked disapprovingly at the dog and her mistress.

"I saw you on television tonight," she said in a tone that suggested Julie had been caught doing something particularly dreadful. "I must say I deplore what they've done to that Lacy Bergen. The exploitation of that young girl is shocking."

Julie said nothing. Just nod, smile, and slip past into the safety of the elevator, close the gate. She looked down at Arnold, busy sniffing out the secret delights contained in the corner. "I don't think Mrs. McPherson approves of us, Arnold." Arnold looked up at her attentively with his little pushed-in face.

It was beginning to rain as Julie reached the street. Arnold bounded ahead, straining at the leash, anxious for the first fire hydrant. Gramercy Park was swathed in mist. When she first arrived in New York from Detroit, where she was the weather girl and host of an afternoon women's talk show, she could not believe her luck getting an apartment in this area. She adored the neoclassic town houses, their windows shuttered, their little wrought-iron balconies looking out onto the park. Tonight, in the rain, the park was deserted. The dark, hulking statue of the actor Edwin Booth stood forlorn and lonely, waiting to play his Hamlet for a crowd that would not arrive.

This night, the crowd, such as it was, congregated as usual at the corner, not far from what was once Booth's red brick house. Les Gals were stationed here. At least Julie chose to refer to them as Les Gals. As many as a dozen of them gathered at the corner on any given night, curious eyesores amid the carefully maintained old elegance of the neighborhood, but somehow unmovable, having discovered a tiny piece of turf where for the moment the cops did not bother them.

It initially had amazed Julie to find them there, but then pockets of prostitutes could be found in the most unlikely neighborhoods. They were basically harmless, even good-natured, working women with whom she could not help but share a curious bond. Besides, like everyone else, they were starstruck. They wanted to know all about the celebrities she interviewed. "Honey," one of them called out a couple of months before, "any time you wanna bring that Tom Selleck around, we service him for free. Understand?" And Julie had gotten up the nerve to reply, "Oh, no, if anyone services him in this neighborhood it's me." They all laughed at that. The ice was broken.

"Hey," called the tall black hooker Julie had come to know as Emmeline. "It's the TV lady. How you doin', girl? Who you interview tonight, anyhow?"

"Lacy Bergen," Julie said, thereby avoiding the question of exactly how she was. She was tempted to go over and cry her heart out to those women. Maybe they knew something about men she didn't know.

Most of their faces were familiar to her by now. They were outrageously painted, much like theater actors made up for the back row of the balcony. Only they were decked out to catch the eye of passing tricks, broadcasting sexual availability with lavish wigs, awesomely tight spandex pants, short shorts or leather miniskirts and fishnet stockings. Tank tops and lacy see-through blouses showed off exotic breasts. The whole show was mounted on high-heeled spikes, which had the effect of transforming even the smallest whore into a goddess of amazon proportions.

"Shit, Lacy Bergen ain't nothin' but a goddamn kid," Emmeline observed. "Man wants a real woman, he should drive right over here. Never mind that Lacy shit."

Julie laughed. "It's going to rain in a couple of minutes. You'd better find some cover."

"We're out here rain or shine," Emmeline said merrily. "We's here to serve the public, honey. Little rain don't bother us none." Emmeline bent over and proceeded to tickle Arnold in his favorite spot, just behind the left ear. The little dog's eyes crinkled appreciatively. A few more drops of rain splattered against the sidewalk.

"Goddamn," one of the other hookers said. "This is a new wig."

"I'd better get going," Julie said. "Arnold doesn't like to poop in the rain."

Everyone laughed, and that made her feel better. People usually took her so seriously. These women treated her as a woman. If she said something funny, they laughed. If it wasn't funny, they didn't laugh.

She started for Lexington Avenue, Arnold trotting ahead, pulling the leash taut. He stopped to investigate one of the wrought-iron guard fences surrounding a tree. "C'mon, Arnold," Julie urged. "Do your business so I can get back home." Arnold pranced on, ignoring both Julie and the rain. Ahead, there was a fire hydrant he had not sniffed at for at least three nights.

Farther south, in the shadows along Lexington, a figure in a trench coat emerged and began walking toward the woman and her dog. The Killer saw them, and smiled.

Finally, Tom managed to hail an empty taxi. It was pouring rain, and he was soaked as he climbed into the backseat.

"I've got to go over to Lexington at Gramercy Park," he said to the driver, leaning forward and speaking through the change vent in the Plexiglas barrier.

"Downtown? Right!" the cab driver cried out. According to the license shield propped up beside the meter in the front seat, the driver was an anemic, dangerous-looking hombre named Manuel Orzano. A real hotshot. In retrospect, it did not matter what Manuel was on. He was definitely on some sort of illegal substance, flying through an airspace that he had mapped out for himself, and into which no one else was able to penetrate. No one could keep up with Manuel Orzano this rainy night. That was for sure.

He skidded across rain-slicked Fortieth Street just as the light turned red and the mass of traffic heading west bore down on them. A metallic monster decked out in bobbing lights just missed them as they bounced across the intersection.

"Jesus Christ," Tom said.

"*Whooooooo-Weeeeee!* cried Manuel Orzano, baying at his own moon.

Tom looked at his watch. It was nearly twelve-thirty.

Julie placed the plastic glove on her right hand, and got into position so that when Arnold decided to go, she was ready for him, and the streets of New York could be spared his poop. Arnold, not particularly civic-minded, did not give much warning when he was about to perform essential canine duty. But by now she had the timing down, so that Arnold's ears had only to move twice, his bottom hint at lowering itself toward the pavement, and quick as a flash she had her gloved hand down, cupped and waiting to receive the mutt's waste. Friends from her home town, who heard descriptions of this procedure, were invariably appalled: "Warm shit? In your *hand?*" But this was New York. Along the jungle trails, you adapted.

Abruptly, Arnold made his move. Or so she thought. Julie's hand swooped down under the tiny bottom. But perhaps because of the rain or because the previously neglected fire hydrant lay ahead, Arnold changed his mind and danced on. "Goodness, dog," Julie muttered, as the leash jerked in her grasp. "Will you please hurry up?"

The rain was truly lashing down now, a real old-

fashioned New York thunderstorm. She glanced back at
the corner. Amazingly, Les Gals remained in place. They
had erected umbrellas for protection, but they continued
to man the corner; commerce apparently could not be
interrupted by mere inclement weather.

She watched Arnold with mounting impatience, then
caught a glimpse of someone in a trench coat and a
fedora striding toward her through the rain.

Manuel the cab driver swung east onto Twenty-ninth
from Madison headed toward Lexington. The cab was
sailing along at fifty-five miles per hour, an awesome
speed for this narrow street. The windshield wipers
worked, but only halfheartedly, so that the world outside the windscreen was a watery blur broken occasionally by opaque lights.

Ahead, the Lexington light turned red. Manuel hit the
breaks, and the car broke into a long skid, fishtailing into
the intersection. A van headed south barely missed them,
it's horn howling anger.

"*Whoooo-weee!*" Manuel yelled. "These streets some-
thin' else."

There was the rain, the figure indistinct in a halo of
light, a flash of steel, and something arching through the
air toward Julie's face. After that there was pain. Straight
down along her forehead, attacking her right eye, nose,
moving across the cheek, to the earlobe. There was the
realization she had been badly cut, and there was blood.

The Killer stepped back, knife in hand, its serrated
edge now dripping blood. Julie dropped the dog leash,
screamed, reeled back on the street in the rain. She looked
ludicrous, as though she were dancing alone, holding her
hands to her face. The Killer turned and shouted to the
women bunched beneath umbrellas at the corner.

"Hey, someone's being attacked here."

Julie punctuated the call with yet another scream.

Up the block, Emmeline, hard-nosed capitalist though she was, considered calling it a night. She was fairly new to this line of work, but surely to Christ no one wanted to get fucked in the rain. Her friend Jewel pulled at the sleeve of her drenched blouse.

"Is that your friend?" she asked.

Through the wind-lashed rain she could just make out Julie staggering in the street. There was someone beside her in a long coat. The figure called out but she couldn't make out the words. Arnold, the Shih Tzu danced around the pair.

"Shit," Emmeline announced. "Some fucker's jumpin' on that girl." She reached down into her boot and pulled out a slim knife. She flicked a button and a six-inch blade gleamed blue and murderous. "Let's go."

Up the street the Killer saw the women breaking and nodded with satisfaction. The gloved hand closed around the .38, the Pound of Prevention.

Emmeline got only a fleeting glimpse of Julie's attacker. She had the knife out and ready. But then she saw the assailant's hand go up, noted the gleam of what surely was a gun, and knew the knife wouldn't do her any good. She was shot in the leg, right through the fishnet stockings she had bought just that day, and went down quickly. That stopped the other women in their tracks. The Killer swung the gun hand around and fired again; another girl screamed and went down on the pavement. Another gunshot and everyone was scattering, screaming in panic.

The Killer walked calmly over to where Emmeline lay on her back in the street, groaning, holding on to her leg.

"We don't want your kind around here," the Killer said to Emmeline. "Do you understand that? When the police come, you tell them that there is someone out here fed up with whores taking over the streets. There is somebody who has decided to do something about it."

For the moment, Julie was ignored. She continued her slow panicky spin in the street, trying somehow to come to terms with the pain, the blood, the rain. Then, the alarm bells began to go off, and the fog swirled in. A voice, tiny but insistent, rose up from somewhere in the back of her head: *Get the hell out of here!*

She began to run.

The Killer turned, spotted Julie fleeing and raised the gun. Fired. Julie kept running, propelled by some deeply intuitive survival instinct. The Killer fired again. And missed again. Damn! It was no fun when distances and accuracy were involved.

Amazingly, even on Lexington, speeding south past Twenty-sixth, Manuel kept the cab pushing sixty. He screeched left around a slow-moving Chevy, narrowly missed an oncoming truck, just made the light at Twenty-sixth. He was jerking around in his seat with the excitement produced by his own craziness. He slammed ferociously at the steering wheel.

"Comin' up to it," he screamed into the back seat, as Gramercy Park came into sight.

"Thank Christ," muttered Tom.

The next instant, and it seemed only an instant, Manuel was hitting the brakes. Through the windscreen Tom did not so much see a form as he got a split-second impression of a dark shape against the cab's hood. the rear of the car swung wildly to the left as the brakes took. Manuel wrestled with the wheel, trying to control the vehicle. He could not do it.

Next thing there was a terrible *whumph!* and for an awful moment the dark form had a face, covered with blood pressed against the glass of the windshield. Then it was gone, and the side of Tom's head was being driven into the Plexiglas shield as the taxi careened into a parked car.

Tom grabbed at the door handle, and the door creaked

open. Somehow he crawled out onto the street. It was then that the cab and the parked car into which it had smashed erupted into flames. No explosion, at least none he could remember later; just a *whoosh*, as though someone had poured more starter fluid on the barbecue.

Tom got to his feet, the rain splattering against his face, dampening momentarily the intensity of the heat. He noticed bodies in the street and residents beginning to emerge from the town houses. Between the two cars, amid the erupting flames, a figure struggled to get free. The face turned toward him. Julie Keene was dying before his eyes.

In the eerie flickering light from the fire, a small dog pranced and barked. For the first time in his life, Arnold was ignored.

23

Tom Coward eased himself into the apartment using the key Lea had given him. Light from Fifty-seventh Street slanted unappetizingly through the windows across the Oriental rug, showing him the limp wisp of a dress and the suit jacket thrown carelessly into the wing chair. Lea and Derek were in the bedroom, reliving old times.

He slumped onto the settee, and the night's events closed in, collapsing him into a tiny black box of horrors with Julie Keene burning in hell in the midst of it. The sound effects were provided by police sirens and screaming women writhing on the street.

Tom had escaped the box, running through narrow side streets reproduced from some Orwellian nightmare of the industrial state, frantically searching for — what? Ash Conlon. On these streets he would discover Ash hurrying away from the scene of the carnage he surely created. But there was no Ash. Just an elderly woman moving nervously along, wearing a windbreaker, carrying a shoulder bag. "You haven't seen —"And he stopped there, not sure what to say.

The woman was shying away from him. "Seen what?" She said, sounding scared.

"A man," Tom said. "A tall man. Uh, dark."

"Black? I ain't seen no black man," the woman said. "Ain't seen no one. Except you. And you're scaring the hell out of me."

Tom apologized and stood there on the deserted street feeling foolish, running after things that were not there.

Then a light fell into the black box of his memories and Lea emerged from the back of the apartment, gliding across the carpet in a negligee. She carried a blanket for him, threw it down onto the settee.

"I'm afraid the bedroom's in use," she said.

"Consoling the wounded?"

"Something like that. Don't be nasty. After tonight, he's hurting badly."

Tom sat back on the settee. "So am I." She saw the gash across the side of his face, turned without a word and went into the kitchen. She returned with disinfectant and cotton batting, administered to his wounds and listened to the story of what happened.

"You mean she's dead? Julie Keene is dead?"

"That's right," Tom said. "She ran right into the cab. Everyone was babbling something about a gunman out to get prostitutes. There were women lying in the street. They had been shot. It was an awful mess."

"What did you do?"

"I got the hell out of there. What was I supposed to do? Stick around and explain to the police I was coming to see Julie because I thought her boyfriend was a killer? Besides," he added, "I was trying to find Conlon."

She studied him with growing incredulity. "You think Ash Conlon was responsible for what went on there tonight?"

"I don't know. I do know all the women he's been involved with are dead. I know that much."

"I'm not so sure about that," Lea said. "I'm still alive. So is Stormy."

"I'm worried about Stormy," Tom said.

"And you're not worried about me?"

"Derek can save you from a fate worse than death."

"I'm not so sure about that," Lea said dryly. "Anyway, you'd better get some sleep. Then you can fly back to Toronto and save Stormy. That is, if she wants to be saved."

In the bedroom, Derek Shower stood at the door, heard Lea returning, and jumped beneath the bedcovers. She entered the room, dropped the negligee and slipped back into bed beside him. "What's going on?" he asked.

"Go back to sleep, darling. I'll tell you about it later." He had not heard it all, but he heard enough.

The next morning the Killer had bagels and cream cheese for breakfast, and considered turning on the television set. But the Killer adamantly refused to watch television in the morning. It was a sign of laziness, an indication that there was nothing else to do. The radio would do just fine. The Killer switched back and forth to various stations catching the newscasts. The voices were different but the story was the same: three women gunned down, a fourth killed, as the result of New York's newest vigilante killer. This one had announced he planned to rid the streets of prostitutes.

The fourth woman, television reporter Julie Keene, was an innocent bystander. She had been out walking her dog at the time and attempted to flee the gunfire. In her panic she apparently had run into the path of an oncoming taxi. She was killed instantly. So was the taxi driver.

The smell of percolating coffee was beginning to fill the kitchen. The Killer poured coffee into a big white porcelain mug, added a touch of cream, sipped at it for a few moments, then picked up the telephone and dialed.

"Hello, Ash," the Killer said, dropping into tones of gloominess. "I'm afraid I have some bad news for you about your friend Julie Keene."

The next thing Tom knew, Lea was shaking him awake. The blanket she had thrown over him had slipped to the floor. The day was forcing itself upon him.

"I have coffee for you," Lea announced tersely. She wore no makeup, and her face looked drawn. She handed him a cup. "This is a real mess. It's all over the afternoon

papers." She showed him the front page of the *Post*. There
was a huge photograph of the blackened remains of the
cab that killed Julie Keene. The headline awkwardly
blurted the news: NEW VIGILANTE KILLER HUNTS N.Y.
HOOKERS: CAUSES DEATH OF TV REPORTER.

Lea continued:

"The story says the police are looking for a passenger
in the cab who was seen leaving the scene."

"But they don't know it's me."

"They may know it's you by now. That's why I woke
you up."

Tom put the paper down. "What do you mean? Jesus,
Lea. You didn't call the police."

"I didn't call the police. But I think Derek has. He just
called, told me I'd better get out of the apartment because
the cops would be coming around for you. He said he
was just doing his duty as a citizen. I think he sees head-
lines, though. Something to the effect that a washed-up
actor turns in Julie Keene's killer."

He got off the settee. "I'm getting out of here."

"And going where?"

"Back to Toronto. I've got to talk to Stormy."

"Do you think it's wise to start running away from the
police at this point?"

"I think it's less wise to stop to answer too many questions. Will you do me a favor?"

"I'm afraid to ask what."

"Talk to the police."

"And what do you suggest I tell the police?"

"Stall them."

"And how do I do that?"

"Tell them I've gone out for cigarettes."

"But you don't smoke."

"Lie a little bit."

"Jesus Christ," Lea said. "How did I ever get involved
in this?"

When he got to LaGuardia, Tom went to a pay telephone and called Louis the chauffeur at home.

"Lou," Tom said jovially. "How are you?"

"Mr. Coward? I don't think I'm supposed to be talking to you."

"Why not?"

"The company's really pissed off at you, Mr. Coward. You owe them all sorts of money." Louis sounded hurt, as though the unpaid bills reflected badly on his character.

"Look, Lou, I need your help. Just this once. Please. Pick me up. I'll clear everything up with the company. So help me I will."

Louis hesitated. "My supervisor doesn't want me to have anything more to do with you, Mr. Coward."

"There's a hundred dollars in it for you, if you meet me, Lou. You pocket the hundred no matter what. Anything else, that's between the company and me."

"Gee, I dunno, Mr. Coward, I could get in big trouble for this."

"One hundred and fifty."

"Two hundred. You got yourself a deal."

"Two hundred. Christ. It'd be cheaper to get a taxi. Okay, Lou. But make sure you're there. I may have to leave the airport in a hurry."

"You're not in any trouble or anything are you, Mr. Coward?"

"Me? Don't be ridiculous."

"You're a weird guy, Mr. Coward. If you don't mind my saying so. Weird but interesting."

"Just be at the airport."

24

At Lester B. Pearson International Airport, Tom breezed through the customs inspection and went up the escalator into the arrivals area. He expected the Mounties to pounce. But there were only scores of milling passengers eyeing the long, rubberized tongue that spit their baggage out into lazily revolving stainless-steel kiosks. He watched the crowd pressing against the glass that divided the arrivals area from the airport concourse. No sign of any police.

Fate gave up his leather carryall quickly. He yanked it off the kiosk and somehow its weight, with the tape recorder, the Typestar Six typewriter, and an emergency magnum of Mumm's, was reassuring. Now there was only the customs officer at the exit taking the entry cards. If he could get past him, he would be out through the automatic glass doors into the airport concourse itself. Now if only Lou was waiting for him . . .

Tom shoved his piece of cardboard into the officer's disinterested fingers. He went to step past.

"Hold on." The official, a mannequin suddenly come to life, waved his card off in a direction that vaguely indicated he should go to the left. "In there," the officer instructed.

Straight ahead. That was the exit. Those glass doors that made the hissing sound when you stepped on the rubber mat in front of them. To the left, though. Damn. That was baggage inspection, a series of yellow partitions, more officers in pale-blue short-sleeved shirts, standing beside long metal beds, carefully going through suitcases open like white wounds to reveal the dirty underwear and the undeclared whiskey. Tom moved along, noticed one of the officers glance around. Did he look nervous? Jesus. Jesus. *He looked nervous!*

Someone touched him on the shoulder. He swung around and was confronted with a thick, neatly trimmed mustache. The mustache dropped straight down to a long, full mouth. The mustache had been grown to hide that mouth, Tom was willing to bet. Each of the mustache hairs was clipped off precisely at the top of the upper lip. It was quite amazing.

Above and below the mustache was an RCMP officer. His face was smooth and stern. He wore a cap pulled firmly down over his forehead, a khaki shirt, and chocolate-brown trousers. There was a yellow stripe running straight down the side of each leg. There were bright yellow sergeant's stripes on the sleeves of his shirt. He looked very neat, an admirable authority figure if there ever was one. Now that mouth the mustache was designed to camouflage was opening, and words began tumbling out.

"Mr. Coward?" The mouth said with official courteousness. "Would you come along with us, please."

It took a moment for the words to register. Tom bent closer, as though to better hear. "I'm sorry. Could you repeat that please?" The old high-school trick, employed when you were in trouble in class. Stall for time.

"Would you mind coming along with us please?" The Mountie moved a step closer, and now Tom could see there were other Mounties. That made sense. They would not send one officer to pick up a dangerous criminal like himself.

Tom thought no more about it. He simply swung his heavy carryall into the sergeant's groin. The Mountie, obeying the macho code of the force, did not cry out. A sharp burst of breath was all that marked his surprise as he folded in half.

Tom leaped atop one of the metal tables, not quickly enough, though, to avoid a customs officer, who managed to grab at his knees in an approximation of a football tackle. Tom kept moving, taking the tackler with him, big enough and heavy enough to overcome what really was a halfhearted grab. Not so halfhearted though that he could avoid losing his balance and tumbling into one of the yellow partitions behind the table. It went crashing over with him. Someone yelled. A woman screamed. Tom rolled across the downed partition, caught a glimpse of what appeared to be approximately half the human race coming toward him.

He scrambled to his feet. The automatic exit doors lay directly ahead of him. He burst through them into the main concourse. People whipped around as he came charging through. He looked back long enough to see Mounties herding behind him. Then it was actually quite funny. Onlookers, not knowing what was wrong, but realizing instinctively it was not good, shrank away from this crazy running man. Tom could hear people yelling. A warning? Maybe the police were about to open fire. The crowd was turning away from him as he ran for the exit doors.

Outside, he saw Louis waiting for him, leaning against the limo. Tom tried to slow down, look natural as he approached the car.

"How are you, Lou?" His breath was coming in gasps. Louis looked at him. "You all right?"

"Yeah, sure. I'm fine. Let's get out of here."

Behind them, the Mountie sergeant burst onto the sidewalk as though fired out the end of a cannon.

"Halt!" he cried.

Louis looked around. "I wonder who they're after."

Tom pushed him toward the car. "Let's go!"

And then it dawned on Louis. His eyes grew very wide. "They're after you!"

Tom opened the back door and pushed him, protesting, inside.

He leaped behind the wheel of the limo. More mounties were crowding onto the ramp. The sergeant fronted them, crouched in a shooting stance.

"Holy shit," Tom said. He threw the limo into gear. The tires shrieked against the pavement as the car sped off.

Concentrating on the road, Tom only vaguely heard the explosion.

"Jesus Christ," Louis moaned from the back. "They're shooting at us. Mounties are shooting at us! This is a goddamn 1985 Cadillac Fleetwood. It's the top of the line. If they hit it, I'm finished!"

Tom kept driving.

They managed to get out of the airport without further incident. The traffic on the southbound 427 was thick, a momentarily reassuring camouflage for the limo. At the first exit ramp Tom got off the highway.

"What are you gonna do?" Louis's white face loomed in the rearview mirror.

"I don't know," Tom said. "To tell you the truth, I never expected to get this far."

"Why were they after you?"

"It's a complicated story, Lou. Let's just say I'm an innocent man."

"Listen, pull over for a minute, will you, Mr. Coward? I gotta see whether they hit the car."

Tom stopped the limo adjacent to a field. Rows of town houses, drawn into neat ranks, were visible in the distance. Louis jumped out and inspected the rear of the car.

"Those Mounties must be lousy shots," he said with

obvious relief. ''Not a scratch on her.'' Now that the car was safe, the excitement began to rise in him. ''Jesus, Mr. Coward. That was like something out of *Miami Vice*. I felt just like Sonny chasing a bunch of dopers or something. It was great.''

''But this isn't television, Louis,'' Tom reminded him. ''And the fact is, an awful lot of police are going to be looking for this car.''

''That's true,'' Louis agreed, and the seriousness of the situation sobered him. But only for an instant. ''Look, I know this area real well. There's a GO-transit station not far from here. I can drop you there. Train'll take you downtown in twenty minutes. The cops will be looking for you in a limo, not on a train. Not for a while, anyhow.''

''What about you?''

''What about me? I went out to the airport to pick you up. You forced me into the backseat and drove away. What could I do?''

''You're a good man, Lou.''

''Like television. I tell you it's just like fuckin' television. You know who we are, Mr. Coward?''

''Who are we, Lou?''

''We're fucking Simon and Simon. That's who we are.''

At the transit station, a deserted platform atop a high embankment, Louis shook his hand and patted him on the arm.

''I don't know what the hell you've gotten yourself into, Mr. Coward. But I hope it works out all right. You're a real character, let me tell you.''

''I'll be okay, Lou. Don't worry. It's not as bad as it looks.''

''Well, they were shooting at us, Mr. Coward. That looks pretty bad to me.''

''Anyhow, I appreciate your help, I really do. You're a terrific guy, and a great chauffeur. We'll be in touch. I promise.'' Tom turned to go.

"Ah, Mr. Coward?"

He looked back at Louis.

"There is the matter of the two hundred dollars, Mr. Coward."

"Jesus, Louis," Tom said. "I thought with all the two of us had been through, you wouldn't want the money."

"We did make a deal, Mr. Coward."

"I'll bet Simon and Simon don't take money from each other," he grumbled, fishing into his pocket with great reluctance to bring forth his billfold. He spent a moment inspecting its interior. "I don't have two hundred. How about one fifty?"

"You said two hundred, Mr. Coward. Remember, I'm the one who's going to have to deal with the police."

"Lou, for God's sake. This is blackmail." He handed the chauffeur the money.

"Like I always said, Mr. Coward. You're quite a character."

"Get lost, Louis," Tom said.

When he reached Union Station in downtown Toronto, he telephoned Stormy. He got her answering machine: "Hi. This is Stormy Willis, I'm not in at the moment. But if you'd like to leave your number and a message, please wait until you hear the sound of the tone."

Tom said, "Stormy, it's me. It's important that we talk. Look, I don't know where I'm going to be for the next little while. But when you get in, please, stay put."

Next he placed a call to Ashley Conlon's house. The phone rang twice before it was picked up.

"Hello." The voice was deep and well modulated. A real nice telephone voice.

"Ashley, it's Tom Coward."

There was silence at the other end.

"I just thought you should know I'm back, Ashley. I know everything. Or just about everything."

More silence.

"You're finished. You should understand that, Ashley. I know about all the lies, all the deceptions. I know you killed Carrie, and you killed Kelly Langlois. You probably also had something to do with Julie Keene's death —"

"I don't know what you're talking about." Ashley Conlon's voice interrupted calmly. Then the line went dead.

At his house, Ashley waited a couple of moments before he picked up the receiver again. Calm down, he told himself. Just stay calm. He inhaled deeply a couple of times, then picked up the phone again.

"Malik?" he said into the receiver.

"Speaking."

"You said he wouldn't come back," Conlon said, trying to keep the nervousness out of his voice.

"That's what I said, all right."

"Well, he's back. He just telephoned. He's making all sorts of stupid threats. I don't want him making all sorts of stupid threats."

"I'll take care of it. But I need a little more information. What's your beef with him anyhow?"

"He used to date my fiancée Stormy Willis. He's trying to reach her. I don't want him to do that."

"Is he with her now?"

"I don't think so."

"Do you have any idea where he is?"

"No. There's a woman named Lea Madison, she might know something. I'll give you her address."

"You had better tell me where this Stormy Willis lives, as well."

"All right," Conlon said. He paused for a moment. "Malik, remember we talked about certain possibilities."

"I recall that, yes."

"It looks as though something a little more extreme is going to be required here."

"That's going to cost a lot, and it requires some planning."

"We don't have much time for planning. He's got to be stopped, and stopped now."

"All right, don't get upset. I'll see what I can do for you."

"Please hurry," Conlon said.

Tom took a cab over to the house Alvin Jarvis was renting and waited in the backyard where not long ago the big marquee had stood and he had first sipped champagne with Lea Madison. When Alvin finally arrived home, driving a battleship gray Mustang GT, it was long after dark. Alvin jumped when he climbed out of the car and Tom called his name.

"What the hell are you doing back there?" Alvin demanded when Tom separated himself from the shadows.

"I'm hiding out," Tom said.

"From what?"

"From the cops," Tom said.

"You still acting crazy?" Alvin regarded him with narrowed eyes.

"I'm afraid so," Tom said.

Alvin sighed. "I guess you'd better come on in." They went up the back steps and into the house. "I've got a tag team of female mud wrestlers coming over in an hour or so, but in the meantime, you can drink my Scotch, and tell me why the cops are after you."

Alvin switched on lights, threw the car keys on the kitchen table, uncapped bottles, tinkled glasses, rattled ice cubes, and presented drinks, while Tom told his story. He ended with New York, and the death of Julie Keene.

"Holy shit," Alvin said. "You've been around the block a couple of times."

Tom nodded. "A couple. Can I use your phone for a moment?"

"Sure."

He tried Stormy's number again. He got only the cheerful monotone of her answering machine. Then he called Lea Madison in New York.

"Are you all right?" she asked.

"I'm okay," he said. "Did the police show up?"

"Two of them, Detectives. Cute guys. They both looked like Matt Houston."

"What did they say?"

"They said they wanted to talk to you. I did my best to stall them. I told them you had gone out for cigarettes. I don't think they believed me."

"Thanks, Lea. I appreciate this."

"It's just about over, isn't it?"

"Just about."

"Don't do anything foolish, Tom."

He hung up the receiver. Alvin was pouring another drink.

"Do you still think I'm crazy?" Tom asked him.

Alvin took a big swallow of his drink. "Somebody's certainly crazy. I'm not quite sure whether it's you. One thing, though. I don't think you should be holding onto this stuff. You should be talking to the police."

"Not until I've talked to Stormy."

"You think Stormy's in danger?"

"I think Stormy should know about this guy."

"Then talk to Stormy."

"I've been trying. There's no answer at her place. She's probably out somewhere on assignment."

"It's a fucking crazy business," Alvin said. He swallowed more Scotch. "I'm very tired, Thomas. Tired and miserable."

"You must be just about finished shooting."

"The giant rats," Alvin sighed. "As soon as Bobby Put-

nam gets his giant rats. Three more days." He drank more
of his Scotch. "Let me tell you something, Thomas. I'm
beginning to think maybe you're not all wrong about this
Stormy thing. She's a good woman. You should hang
onto a good woman. There aren't that many of them
around. Do you know what I'm thinking? Do you know
what I want to do?"

"What do you want to do, Alvin?"

He looked tired and beaten down, a lumpy little fire-
plug in a windbreaker, pouring more Scotch. "I want to
make a movie with David Lean. That's what I'd like to
do."

"Jesus, Alvin, don't get delusions of respectability on
me."

He handed Tom a fresh glass and then went over to the
sofa and sagged down onto it. He spilled some of his
drink, and he shook the liquid from his hand.

"Lately, I've been asking myself, what contributions
have I made? Where is my *Places in the Heart* or *Terms of
Endearment*? How many times have I lifted the human
spirit? And you know what the answer is? The answer is
I have never lifted the human spirit. I have lifted some
teenager's cock sitting there in the dark, and I've scared
the shit out of a lot of kids. But I've never lifted the human spirit, Tom. That's what cinema's all about. It's about
lifting that human spirit."

He drained half his drink. "I'm getting older. I'm not
going to last forever. I want to settle down." The statement slipped out quietly, loosened by the whiskey and
the exhaustion. He looked over at Tom and blinked a couple of times. "I like this house, Tom, you know that?
I like living here. I like the feeling of security."

"What about the middle class? You said you never
wanted the middle classes to get you. You're a free man.
You go where you want to, live the way you want to."

"I'm lonely, Tom," he said. There were tears in his eyes.
He rubbed the back of his hand across his face, and put

his drink down on the floor. He stretched out on the couch. "Jesus Christ, I'm tired. I'm gonna shut my eyes for just a couple of minutes, Tom. Then we can talk about your problem. We can solve your problem."

"Sure, Alvin," Tom said gently.

He got up and poured the remainder of his drink in the sink. When he came back, Alvin was snoring loudly. He sat there for a few moments. He studied Alvin, watched the rising and the lowering of his belly.

He walked through the house to the study. The gun remained where Tom had hidden it the day of Alvin's party, lodged behind the *Reader's Digest* condensed books. It was a Smith and Wesson .22 caliber magnum in gleaming stainless steel.

He lifted it out from behind the books, pushed at the thumb piece at the left side of the gun's frame, then knocked the cylinder free, revealing six empty chambers. He found a box of cartridges in the desk, filled each of the chambers, then pressed the cylinder back into its frame.

Back in the living room, Alvin shifted violently on the couch and smacked his lips loudly. But he kept on snoring. Tom picked up Alvin's car keys from the kitchen table. He shoved the .22 magnum into his belt under his jacket. It felt oddly reassuring pressed against his stomach.

There was light showing at a couple of the windows in Stormy's house, making it look warm and inviting. Alvin would love this house, Tom thought as he parked the car. He could be cozy and safe here. No more lonely nights. Except you got to the point where you wanted lonely nights, and you didn't like to be cozy and safe. That was were the trouble started. Tom could testify to that.

He went up onto the porch, which still showed traces of the gray paint he had grumpily applied at Stormy's insistence. Did Alvin want to paint porches, he wondered.

Somehow he doubted it. He knocked on the screen door, and waited. No answer. He pounded again.

"You're looking for Stormy, are you, Tom?"

He turned and Laura Crawford Dougall was standing at the bottom of the steps. She held a carton of milk under her arm.

"Hello there, Mrs. Dougall. As a matter of fact I am."

"She's gone for a run down on the boardwalk. She was over visiting me all evening." She indicated the carton. "She drank my milk. I was telling her that I'm leaving tomorrow for Florida. I've been asked to appear in a new production of *I Remember Mama* at the Burt Reynolds Dinner Theater. Burt himself is directing, and personally asked for me. It's quite an honor, I must say."

"You say she's jogging?"

"I told her it was awfully late to be out alone. But she was so tense, she said. She just had to get some exercise. It's been quite a traumatic night. She's terribly upset, Tom. You should have a word with her. She phoned this Ashley Conlon gentleman with whom she's involved, and told him she didn't want to marry him. Told him that everything was happening too fast. That they both needed time to think things over. Poor dear, she really is torn about him. But from what she's been telling me, I don't think he's for her. I really don't."

"I'd better find her," Tom said. "You say she's running alone?"

"Well, there is the other gentleman."

"What other gentleman?"

"He came along perhaps ten minutes ago. He said he was a friend of Ashley's. He had an important message for her from him. I thought it would be all right. In fact it sounded rather romantic, sending a messenger with a message of reconciliation. I didn't think young people did things like that these days."

Tom raced down the street toward the beach.

25

The night was lit by a full clear moon, and the wispy light thrown off by the street lamps stationed along the boardwalk. Tom came to a halt at the grassy rise that fell off to the beach. The pavilion where he had tried once again to win Stormy was in the distance. He thought of the number of times they had walked here, talked, dreamed here. Now he was back, perhaps to save her life. He wondered if she would appreciate the gesture.

A figure was moving along, darting into the pools of light from the street lamps, then out again to be captured in shadow by the moon, a lithe ghost in gym shorts, white hair flowing behind her, skin the color of ivory. There was no sign of any romantic gentleman bearing messages of reconciliation. But perhaps such a gentleman was not far off.

"Stormy," he called out to her.

She looked up. He waved an arm at her and started down the incline at a trot. He reached the bottom with a thud. Ahead of him on the boardwalk, Stormy had come to a halt, standing tall and confused in one of the pools of light.

He was running along the boardwalk when God's fingertip reached down and whacked him in the right shoulder and sent him spinning into the sand. It must have been God's fingertip, he concluded, for there was no sound. Just a racking pain shooting through his arm and along his back. It took him a minute to realize he had been shot.

He heard Stormy call out to him. He tried to raise his head out of the sand. It hurt to do that. The top of his shoulder was covered with blood. He managed to twist around in time to see Lincoln S. Malik come around one of the park benches from out of the darkness and saunter down the incline. He carried a long-barrelled semiautomatic pistol with silencer and a night-scope mount.

"Whoa-boy," he said as he approached the place where Tom lay sprawled in the sand, "did you go spinning ass over teakettle. This infrared scope works great."

"Glad to hear it," Tom said between gritted teeth. He struggled into a sitting position.

Malik held the gun casually, at ease with himself, cocky in the knowledge that the prey was down and not about to provide more trouble. "When you left town, Thomas, you should have stayed out. Now certain people are really pissed off." He nodded in the direction of Stormy, who stood rooted to the spot, as though on display in the moonlight. "Someone doesn't want you messing around with his girl. Can't say as I blame him. She's a real looker. Nice tits. The whole bit."

"What's going on?" Stormy's tremulous voice sounded unreal in the night air. She edged closer to the two men, moving slowly as though her joints had seized up.

"This has nothing to do with you," Malik said to her. "Go on back up to your house. I'll take care of this. He won't be bothering you any more."

"He's not bothering me," Stormy said. Her voice sounded stronger. "I want you to leave him alone. I know him. He's a friend."

Malik eyed her calmly. "Now that's not the information I have."

"I don't know where your information comes from," Stormy said. "But it's wrong."

"I think the information comes from Ash Conlon," Tom managed to say. His shoulder was numb, and he was beginning to feel weak. "Ash put him up to this. That's right, isn't it Malik?"

"It doesn't make any difference," Malik said. "I can't leave any witnesses anyway. So if the two of you are friends, you can both go off to the happy hunting ground together."

With a kind of insolent confidence he turned the barrel of the semiautomatic toward Tom. Stormy gasped, then leaped at Malik. She wrestled against him for a moment, and he looked almost bemused by her action. When she tried to claw at his face, he slapped her away into the sand. He might have put more effort into hitting a fly.

"Don't," she cried out. Then more quietly: "Please — don't."

"God," Malik said. "I hate these little dramas."

He stepped back a few paces, and then aimed his gun at Stormy. She saw what he was doing and her mouth hung open in a small, futile question.

"You should have kept quiet, sweetheart. You should have let me get this over with, and there would be no problem." He raised the semiautomatic up to shoulder level. Stormy's mouth began to work, frantically attempting to manufacture noises that refused to come out into the night.

Tom pulled his jacket open, and yanked the gun out of his belt. Malik caught the motion, turned toward it, but his confidence made him slow. Tom shot him in the chest. The boom of the gun seemed to shake the moon.

For a moment, Tom thought he had missed completely. Malik lowered his gun somewhat, but continued to point it in the general direction of Stormy. He shook his head a bit. That was the cue for Tom. He fired again. This time Malik dropped his pistol and stepped back, as though he was preparing to take a bow. There was an expression of quizzical surprise on his face.

"Didn't expect you to be armed," he said. "Jesus."

Tom looked at the gun in his hand and looked at Malik in dumb amazement.

"I can't believe it," he said, "I shot you."

Malik stumbled forward and then, taking long, straight-legged strides, began moving toward the lake, the blood pouring out of him, kicking the sand up in his path. Tom got to his feet, followed after him. They made a curious couple in the wash of the moonlight. Malik reached the shoreline where the water lapped gently against the glistening sand. He wheeled around. Tom thought for an instant that Malik was drawing another weapon. He raised his arm, ready to shoot Malik yet again. But Malik, expressionless, merely collapsed headfirst into the water. He didn't move.

Stormy came up beside Tom. Her eyes were wide. "Is he dead?"

"I think so," Tom said. "Jesus. They don't die like that in the movies." He sagged against Stormy, and she held onto him.

"You're hurt," she said. "I'm going to call an ambulance."

"No," Tom's voice was adamant. "There are things I have to say, Stormy. Things I came a long way to tell you. Things it took me a long time to find out. Ambulances. Cops. I won't be able to say anything. Get me up to the house. Please."

"But you're hurt."

"Not badly, really. There's more blood than anything else. I think it's what Roy Rogers used to call a flesh wound. He winged me, that's all. Will you take me back to the house, Stormy? Will you do that?"

"All right," she said.

The house was as he remembered it. The green corduroy couch, blotched with the red wine stain, still sagged beneath the front window. The eggshell white of the walls was offset by the chocolate-brown carpeting. The light pine furniture they bought was still neatly arranged around the room. There was the fireplace they had stripped down to its original wood, the iron utensils gathered against the grate. And there was the old pine hutch, stationed next to the entrance to the kitchen. However, the dieffenbachia, the schefflera, and the spider plants, all hovering near death while he was in residence, now flourished around the room. And instead of a photograph of Tom and Stormy atop the piano, there was one of Ashley and Stormy.

He chose not to say anything about the photograph as they came into the house. Besides, he was so weak. He put the gun down on the table that stood against the wall just inside the door. Stormy wrapped a towel around his arm, and lowered him to the couch.

"I'm going to have to go next door for some dressing," she said. "I haven't got a thing here. I'm not exactly equipped for the treatment of gunshot wounds."

"Stay here," Tom mumbled, "I want to tell you about Ash."

She tucked a pillow behind his head. "I already know about Ash. At least I know he's been lying to me. He doesn't have a job. I found that out yesterday. And I think he's been seeing other women. I had a long talk with him on the phone tonight. I told him the marriage plans are on hold. There are a few things that have to be straightened out."

"He's dangerous," Tom said. "Very dangerous."

She stood up. "I'll be right back, darling, I promise. I'll just get some stuff from Mrs. Dougall."

She turned and ran out of the house. Tom put his head back against the pillow. The room revolved slowly around him and a great feeling of fuzzy warmth washed through his body. Everything was blurry, and he realized he was about to lose consciousness. Vaguely, he heard the back door open. Ah, he thought, Stormy is back. He loved his Stormy.

A shape loomed in the entrance.

"Stormy," Tom said. He lifted his head off the sofa. Standing there was Ashley Conlon.

He stepped into the room, looking like a Fitzgerald hero, young and handsome and superbly tailored in a white linen suit that made his complexion all the more dark and rugged. His black hair was tousled and curled, heaving down in silky waves across his forehead. A beauty, Ash Conlon, Tom thought dimly.

"Where's Stormy?" he said quietly.

Tom flicked his hand weakly to indicate that wherever she was, she was not here.

Conlon followed the wave of the hand and glanced around the living room. "I came here to see her, to have a talk. There are some things she doesn't understand. Now I can see why. You're back in her life." He raised his eyebrows when he saw the blood seeping through the towel. "We're bleeding, are we? It looks as though Malik ran into you. What have you done with him?"

"He's down at the beach, taking some sun," Tom said.

"I'm just sorry he didn't finish the job," Conlon said. "But maybe we can do something about that."

He was standing directly over Tom now, glaring down at him. Hostility did not work well in conjunction with the handsomeness. It gave his face mean lines that pushed it unexpectedly toward ugliness. Tom liked the look of that face. It was the evidence he had interfered with the perfection of Ash Conlon.

He started to rise off the sofa, and Conlon stepped quickly forward and awkwardly slugged him on the side of the face. Tom was knocked back. Shards of pain jabbed through his shoulder. Everything went blurry again.

"You just sit there," Conlon yelled. "You just stay right there." The action seemed to have knocked away the thin veneer of calm. His eyes suddenly were wild, and his mouth was turning in all sorts of unpleasant directions.

"Everything's gone wrong because of you. Do you know what you've cost me? You've cost me my life, my happiness. I loved her. Don't you understand? She was going to be my wife, until you came back and screwed up everything."

Tom tried to talk. The words clunked out like heavy rocks tumbling from the mouth of a cave. "You loved them all, Ashley, but you killed them anyway. You bastard."

He leaped at Tom grabbing him by the shirt front. "I'll show you," he breathed. "I'll show all of you."

Tom was like a rag doll being shaken around by a particularly irritated child. He tried to raise his arm to protect himself, but didn't have the strength. Ash's fingers closed around his throat. They were soft for a moment, caressing. He thought of those fingers caressing Stormy, and grew angry. But then the fingers tightened and he couldn't breathe. He looked up and into Ash Conlon's enraged face.

Then Stormy crashed into view, lunging against Ash, pushing him away. Stormy cried out, and Ash smashed at her. She went skittering across the floor.

"You're no better than he is," Ash said to her between clenched teeth. "You were both out to get me."

"Ash, no," Stormy cried.

He came at her. They had destroyed his dreams, stripped away the facade he so carefully had constructed for himself, the star persona he had cultivated. Now he would destroy them. He knocked Stormy back against the pine table beside the door. Tom somehow got off the couch and threw himself at Ash's back. Conlon kicked out at him, and Tom sagged to the floor. Conlon spun around to the fireplace, grabbed the poker that leaned next to the gate, and swung it at Tom, cracking it against his ribs.

Ash turned to Stormy. She knew he was going to kill her right there with the poker. Her hand touched the gun on the table, and before she quite knew what she was doing she was grasping the stock. Then the gun was in her fingers, and Ashley was bringing up the poker. She ducked and the poker smashed into a picture frame on the wall over the table. Her finger involuntarily tightened on the trigger, and the gun jumped in her hand. She swore later she did not hear any report.

But the next moment there was a bright-red patch marring Ash Conlon's linen jacket. He looked down at the patch and his face registered disbelief, anguish, hate, all the emotions fighting for a last performance before death came in and canceled out everything. His face went blank, and a moment later sadness climbed across his features. He crumpled to the floor, and died with the sadness on his face. He lay very still, the white linen glaring up from the chocolate-brown carpet.

Tom watched as Stormy slowly lowered the gun. Her face was white, the eyes stony.

"Are you all right?" he asked. His voice sounded hollow and far away.

"Yes." She said the word tentatively, as though not quite sure what it meant.

"Good," Tom said, just before he lost consciousness. "I want you to be all right."

26

"It is a superb film," Bobby Putnam was saying. "*Buns* is a movie that will speak to today's youth. And you should see the footage involving the giant rats. They truly are frightening. You would never know we dressed dogs up in rat costumes. Of course, the producer didn't want me to do it. Raised a real ruckus about it. Even threatened violence. But I am an artist. I have a vision. I pursued that vision."

Bobby Putnam, a little drunk, laughed heartily, pulled one of the pert Bun-Bun girls closer to him, and leaned back against the railing that ran around the pavilion. Behind him, the surface of the lake was like a mirror in the deepening twilight. Someone said there was autumn in the rusts of the twilight, and on this late-summer evening, no one could disagree.

"What are you doing next?" The Bun-Bun girl inquired.

"Oh, Jesus," Bobby said. "Maybe a western in Australia. They say the western is coming back. Perhaps I can bring it back. I think it requires something different, though. That's why we have the kangaroos."

"Kangaroos?" said the Bun-Bun girl dubiously. "In a western?"

"Different, isn't it? Like injecting the rats into what essentially was a teen exploitation movie. It infuses what basically is a cliché with unexpected originality. That's what the *art* of cinema is all about. Finding those unexpected moments."

"God," said the Bun-Bun girl, "you really are an artist, Mr. Putnam. I mean I really am into the whole art thing at the moment. I hate the commercialism that pervades everything.''

"This western will be a statement against commercialism," he said. "That is, if I do it.''

"It sounds wonderful. Why wouldn't you do it?''

"Why else?'' Bobby laughed. "We can't get together on the money.'' Everyone laughed, and Bobby Putnam spotted Tom Coward coming through the crowd. He waved.

"Hey, Thomas, how are you, son?''

"Not bad,'' Tom said. "Congratulations. I hear the giant rats look wonderful.''

"Monumental. If I do say myself. Where have you been, anyway? Haven't seen you around much. Didn't I read something about you? Or hear something about you?''

Alvin Jarvis came over and wrapped his arms around Tom. He wore a starched safari jacket and trousers with a crease in them.

"It's good to see you, you crazy son of a bitch.'' He squeezed him again, and Tom noticed that he had lost weight. "We were worried about you for a while there.'' He turned and Lea Madison was standing there, looking hesitant in a simple summer frock. "Lea and I were both worried.''

He drew her against him, his arm wrapped around her waist.

"How are you, Tom?'' she said.

"I'm fine, Lea, just fine.'' Tom looked at Alvin. "You've lost weight.''

"A few pounds. Figured I needed it, you know? Went on the wagon for awhile. Nothing major. Just giving the body a little rest.''

Tom eyed the safari jacket. "A new wardrobe.''

Alvin shrugged elaborately. "A couple of things. I got

tired of wearing jeans and windbreakers all the time."
Alvin wanted the subject changed. "Is Stormy coming
over?"

"Of course," Tom said. "How could she miss the wrap
party for *Buns*? She just got held up on the phone and
told me to come on ahead."

"That's great," Alvin said. "It's great to see you two
back together. It's time we all settled down, Tom. We were
getting too old for this gypsying around. I'm making some
fairly major changes in my life. From now on I'm doing
good things. Quality stuff. Lea's got this terrific script.
We're going to do it together." He looked at her with a
proprietory smile. "Aren't, we, honey?"

Lea smiled quickly. "Yes, we are, Alvin."

"And I'm going to hang onto that house, Tom. I've got
an option to buy. I like this town. It's quiet, clean, a de-
cent place to put down some roots."

"You sound like you're a changed man, Alvin," Tom
said.

"A changed man," Alvin agreed. "We're all changed
men, right, Tom?"

"Right, Alvin."

Louis the chauffeur came over, carrying a big leather-
bound binder.

"Lou," Tom said, "you're not wearing your cap."

"Ah, come on, Mr. Coward. I'm off duty. Besides, I'm
quitting that job. It's just not for me." He held the binder
up. "This is for you. Sort of a memento."

Tom took the binder and opened it to page after page
of clippings and photographs.

"Everything that's been written about you for the last
month or so is in there," Louis said. "I knew you wouldn't
have seen a lot of this stuff, what with being shot and all
and in the hospital."

"Louis, this is really sweet. Thanks a lot."

"Hey, don't think nothing of it. You made me a hero, Mr. Coward. Honest you did. All the guys, they want to know what it was like dodging bullets."

"A bullet, Louis."

"Yeah, well, maybe I jazzed it up a little bit. I mean everybody's interviewed me and everything. I was even on *CityPulse News*. That's how famous I am."

Tom put the binder under his arm. "I couldn't have done it without you, Lou."

"Believe me, Mr. Coward," Louis said with a grin. "That's what I've been telling everyone."

Later Tom went to the railing. He could see Stormy strolling across the park. The last rays of the sunlight caught her hair. Coming through the dappled shadows thrown off by the trees she looked incredible, a golden dream girl in a short blue-and-white skirt that showed off long, slim legs. He was watching her come toward the pavilion when Lea Madison came up to him.

"Are you and Stormy officially back together?"

"I would hardly call it official. I've spent most of the last few weeks in the hospital or talking to police. Or both. But I suppose we're seeing each other."

"Dreams do come true then."

"I detect a note of cynicism there."

"A little wariness, that's all. Anyhow, I didn't come over here to rain on your parade, Tom. I just wanted to apologize. I should have called, come around and seen you, something. It was just so crazy here, though. I wanted to stay away from it as much as possible. Alvin's been a great help. Very protective."

"I'm the one who should be apologizing," Tom said. "I'm sorry I got you involved in any of this."

She shrugged. "I believe I was a willing accomplice."

"How's Lex?"

"Coming along. It's a slow process. Physiotherapy twice a day. That sort of thing."

"I hope he makes it," Tom said.

"I think he will. The doctors are optimistic. He won't be the same, of course. Nothing will ever be quite the same again, I suppose. How about you? How are you feeling?"

"Shoulder's still a little stiff. My ribs are still taped. I'm still tired, and I'm sick of all the questions they keep asking me."

"I hear you're writing the story of all this."

"They want me to," Tom said. "I suppose I will."

"What are you going to say about Ash?"

"That's an interesting question. The Toronto police are convinced he killed Carrie Wayborn and Kelly Langlois. Any number of psychiatrists have spent an awful lot of time on this. They're convinced he was suffering from a schizoid personality of some sort. He watched his mother kill his father, and the psychiatrists think he tried to compensate for this through a whole fantasy life he wove for himself. He was the movie star, the matinee idol. Women were crazy about him, that sort of thing."

"Which was true," Lea said.

"Exactly. In Ash's case he could actually live out his fantasies. It was Kelly who engineered that in college. Before he met her, Ash spent years with his mother, a recluse who would not go out in public because of her notoriety. He had only a fantasy life to fall back on, and the movies that fed that fantasy. People who knew him in those days remember him being cowed by everyone, lacking any self-assurance whatsoever. Kelly changed all that. She took the raw material and created her own fantasy figure—although she later tried to destroy it, which didn't exactly help Ash's overall mental state — and he fed off that image. He fabricated this character who was handsome, assured, articulate, and totally in control. He became the star of his own movie. He had photograph albums full of movie stars. The police found them in his house. He wanted to be those people, to live in real life the existence that ordinarily is only on a movie screen.''

''So what happened?''

''Well, if you want to believe the psychiatrists, Carrie became a threat. She knew that the Ash Conlon that Stormy was involved with was only a creation. She was trying to blackmail him with that knowledge. So he killed her to keep her mouth shut.''

''And what about Kelly?''

''Well, instead of solving his problem, Carrie's death just created more of them. Kelly came back to town to find out who had killed the woman who was her best friend and lover. She suspected either Ash or Lex was responsible for her death. Apparently at the beginning, she leaned toward Lex as the culprit. For Ash, though, she was a real threat, and one that had to be dealt with. If Carrie could tear down the facade, think what Kelly could do. And Kelly was a lot more lethal. Remember, she tried to kill Ash in university when she was strung out on acid. Over the years, she'd done just about everything under the sun. The police autopsy showed traces of heroin and PCP in her system. She was a real heavy hitter, and it had screwed her up badly. There wasn't much that she wasn't capable of. In fact, the police think she may have murdered a computer executive who apparently put her up for a time when she got to Toronto.''

Stormy was almost at the pavilion now. She saw Tom and waved up at him. He lifted his arm in response.

Lea said, ''So when you came back to town, you also became a threat to him. You were poking around in his past. When Ash found out, he hired Lincoln Malik.''

''That's right,'' Tom said. ''Malik was a former boyfriend of Carrie Wayborn's. The police questioned him after Carrie's death. They knew him as a small-time hood and professional enforcer. Ash had met him through Carrie, and apparently hired him to get me out of the way.''

"What about Julie Keene in New York?"

"There is a strong suspicion Ash is responsible for her death as well, although the New York cops aren't as convinced. Airline records show no sign of Ash arriving in New York at the time of her death. He was going to New York three of four times a week to see her, and he was a frequent flier on American Airlines. The attendants at the check-in counter in Toronto knew him very well, and they don't recall him flying out to New York the day Julie was killed."

"What about Stormy? Did she see him that day?"

"She saw him the day before Julie died. But not the day or the night of the murder."

"So he could somehow have flown to New York and killed Julie."

"Sure. It's possible. It's just that the New York cops aren't buying all the conjecture, that's all."

Stormy came up the steps to the pavilion. Lea watched her. "She's beautiful." She turned to Tom. "Was it worth it?"

"I'm not sure," Tom said.

"What are you going to do now?"

"I'm not sure about that either."

"You sound like the same old Tom to me," Lea said.

"Oh, no," Tom said with a straight face. "I'm a changed man."

Lea patted him on the cheek. "Good luck, changed man. Alvin and I are off to create great cinema. He's a changed man, too. At least he was until yesterday when I caught him on the telephone discussing the possibility of *Buns II*."

Stormy came into the pavilion and stood hesitantly in the face of the party that, as it got darker, was becoming more rambunctious. Tom went over to her.

"We don't have to stay," he said.

"Don't be silly," she said. "I'm not the fragile lily of

the valley. At least I'm trying not to be. Why don't you get me a big glass of wine?'' She nodded toward Lea. ''Is that Lea Madison?''

Tom said, ''Yes. Do you want to meet her?''

''Definitely. What's the book for?''

''Louis the chauffeur put it together for me. He clipped all the stories and mounted them in this binder.''

''Good grief,'' Stormy said. ''There were that many stories?''

''We're famous.''

''Oh great,'' said Stormy.

Lea wandered over and Tom introduced them, and the two women spent a few moments inspecting each other before Alvin arrived.

''Hey, the two lovebirds,'' he said, embracing Stormy and giving her a kiss on the cheek. ''It's great to see you two back together. You're quite a couple.''

Tom and Stormy duly smiled at each other.

He lay in the big brass bed they once had shared and were about to share again. While he waited for her to come out of the bathroom, he reached over to the bedside table and picked up the binder Louis had given him. He began flipping through the clear plastic pages with the newspaper stories mounted on them. The coverage was nothing like the international furor over Lex Madison. But it was extensive nonetheless. Tom, for convenience, was made the hero of most of the pieces. But there was great fascination with Ashley Conlon, particularly since he was unable to complain about the speculation and the pop psychology. Tom came across a weekend piece delving into Ashley's family history, and how his mother came to murder his father—there being no longer any doubt, at least in print, that his mom killed his dad. There were photographs of the young Ashley, taken from various high-school and university year books. And there was a photograph of his mother, Lyn Lisa Conlon, in the full flower of youth, an ice queen from Ohio with a lovely oval face and dancing eyes.

Tom looked at that photograph for a long time, until the bathroom light snapped off, and Stormy came into the bedroom.

She was nude except for a pair of bikini panties, her big movie-starlet breasts parading in front. They were the bane of her life, but a bane she knew how to employ to effect at the right moments.

"I'd forgotten all about *those*," he said.

"I'll bet." She came over to the bed, hair tumbling around her shoulders, and laid *those* into his waiting hands.

He groaned, and kissed the nipples. "I missed these" he said.

Again the dubiousness. "Oh, sure." She fed one of the starlet breasts into his mouth. "I'll bet there were lots of women, with lots bigger," she said.

"No," he protested, except it was somewhat garbled. She giggled and wrapped her arms around his head, drawing him closer.

He closed his eyes, transforming his reality into fantasy, then opened them again and fantasy was reality, blond lashes coming down over smoky hazel eyes, moist red mouth opening to meet his, slim fingers fumbling between his legs. "Ohh," she said. "Oh, Tom." He had waited a long time to hear her say that again. He opened his mouth to say something. But say what?

She straddled him, rubbed the dream tits across his face, then settled back on him, and he slid deeply into her. She threw back her head, bared her teeth, arched her back so that the breasts were great defiant orbs above him. Then she shook her hair, lowered her mouth to his, blew hot breath against him.

"Good, baby," she said. "Good, baby. So good."

He rolled her onto her back, and went down between those endlessly long legs, his mouth and tongue licking softly at the juncture of her. Just like the old days. All those months wrapped between her thighs. The sounds remained the same as well: the small, satisfied moans rising to snorts, and then the long piercing scream. Something different this time, though. Tears. He cradled her in his arms, and she was saying "Oh, Tommy, Tommy, Tommy."

She shook her head again, regained some composure, and said, "Oh, boy. Oh golly gee whillikers." She took him in her hand, sucked him, then fucked him, lying on her back, legs pitched wide, her small white teeth digging into her lower lip, slamming that body with the rosy flush spreading across its paleness, up to meet his.

"I forgot about that." She stared up at him, wearing a cat's smile.

"Forgot about what?" He breathed.

"I forgot you made those funny little noises."

"I do not . . . make . . . funny little noises," he said, beginning to make funny little noises.

They both fell into an exhausted sleep. Tom dreamed. He dreamed of sons and mothers. He dreamed of Lyn Lisa Conlon.

In the morning he awoke early. He lay there for a long time watching the sunlight from the window spreading across Stormy's naked back. He touched her spine, ran a finger gently along its furrow. She shifted somewhat, the blond hair soft on the pillow. Eventually, he rolled over and retrieved the binder from the floor where he had dropped it the night before. He flipped through it until he found the photograph of Lyn Lisa Conlon. No, he didn't think he was wrong. He was studying the photograph when she awoke, stretched, rolled over on her back, and held out her arms for him.

Later, they went for a walk along Queen Street, stopping to stare into the windows of the shops, picking up the morning papers — which for the first time in a long while did not feature them on the front page — stopping for coffee and croissants at a bakery. Autumn was in the air, just a hint of it in the clean nip of the wind. They did not say much. The small talk was minimal. Tom drifted far away, until finally she snagged him back, pressing against him, her arm through his.

"Tell me about it," she said quietly.

"I have to go to New York," he said.

She nodded. "Aha."

They walked in silence for a few moments, and then she said, "Even when I was with Ash, I used to think about you a lot. I hated myself for it, because I thought I was so nuts about him. If I was so nuts about him, why was I thinking about you? I used to wonder about that. But I would go right on thinking about you. It was involuntary."

"And what did you think?"

"I thought you'd never ask. I thought, well, you were hurting, but in the end that it would work out for the best. Because although your intentions are good, you really don't want to settle down. I think it's going to take awhile for you to understand that about yourself. Once you do, I think you'll be a lot happier than you are right now."

"Which means?"

"It means that I understand you. Let me see. It means you know and I know that this is not going to work. At least it's not going to work in the traditional Protestant way you think it should work. It means you and I will always be friends. It means I will always think about you, and kind of miss you. That's what it means."

"It's just that I don't think this is finished yet."

She stopped, and her eyes searched his.

"Yes it is," she said firmly. "It's over."

"There is still something missing," he said. "Something that's not quite right."

"I think something's missing, Tom darling. But it's in you. When you find that missing piece you're going to be a wonderful, solid, dependable guy. What you are now is merely a wonderful guy and I'll always love you in a certain kind of way. Now come here and kiss me."

He took her in his arms there on the street, this tall, statuesque blond woman, this creamy dream with the lush mouth dipping deeply into his. They kissed. It was a goodbye kiss.

27

T om spent the morning in New York arguing with his editors over when the Lex Madison story would be delivered. It was pointed out that newspapers across the country where clamoring for it. It was further pointed out that there was a book in the offing. Perhaps even a television movie of the week based on the whole incident. The phrase "big bucks" was employed several times. What was lacking, it was pointed out, was a story. That, Tom said, was because the story was not yet finished. When would the story be finished? They wanted to know. Perhaps after lunch, Tom said. Perhaps never. It was pointed out that Tom Coward was seldom this enigmatic about anything. Tom replied that it was seldom in his life that enigma was necessary.

At noon, he took a cab over to the Plaza Hotel.

The lobby was jammed, as always. He inspected the bulky-knit Cesarani sweaters in a glass display case outside the tiny men's shop. He wandered into the gift shop and browsed through magazines for a few minutes. Then he walked around to the Oak Bar. He looked at his watch as he entered. It was just after one o'clock.

He took a seat at the bar, and turned to the woman next to him.

"Hello, Mrs. Conlon," he said. "It's Tuesday."

She put down her Negroni and turned to him. Her face showed nothing. "I beg your pardon?"

"You are Lyn Lisa Conlon," Tom said. "Ashley's mother."

"You're the young man who bought me the Negroni a few weeks ago."

"I'm Tom Coward."

"Yes," she nodded, "you're Tom Coward." She finished her drink and put it on the bar. "Now I'll tell you what, Tom Coward. I think today is one of those days when I'm just going to have myself another Negroni."

"Let me buy it for you."

"I shouldn't let you," she said. "But I think I will."

Lyn Lisa Conlon wore an expensive velvet jacket over a blouse with a silver broach pinned at the throat, and a white pleated skirt. She looked older than he remembered. Perhaps it was because she had cut her hair since the last time he saw her. Now it feathered and curled more closely to the oval face. He now noticed the lines around her mouth, crevices beneath the wide, slightly surprised eyes, and age had made the chin terribly fragile. But the beauty refused to die out of her face. The pilot light still burned somewhere deep within, recalling the Ohio ice queen, the vivacious young woman who had come to New York years before and married first a rogue, and then a killer.

"How did you know it was me?"

"I saw a photograph of you," Tom said. "Why don't we find a table, so we can talk in private."

She nodded and gathered up shopping bags from Bloomingdale's. Tom was aware of her assertive walk, the still-sensual turn of her hips, as they moved through the tables. They sat at a banquette by one of the large windows glaring out at Central Park South. A couple of tourists climbed out of a hansom carriage, laughing together, as Tom ordered a Negroni for her, and a Miller Lite beer for himself.

"How long have you lived in New York?"

"Since I had myself declared dead ten years ago. You

can do just about anything in Mexico, as long as you have the money. I had the money.''

"And a son to help cover up any loose ends.''

"And a son to cover up any loose ends,'' she agreed. "He was also a son whose life I had helped to make pretty miserable, Mr. Coward. I am not unaware of my shortcomings in that regard.''

The coquettishness from their first meeting had disappeared. This was a tall, severe woman. Only the chin was fragile. Tom was beginning to understand how she could have done what she did.

"So when Carrie Wayborn tried to blackmail Ash, you decided to see if you could give him a hand.''

"When you're dead, Mr. Coward, you can move about pretty freely, I've discovered. I didn't think it would do any harm to go up there and see if I could knock some sense into that young woman's head.''

"That's one way of putting it,'' Tom said. The waiter placed a fresh Negroni before Lyn Lisa Conlon, and poured beer into a tall glass for Tom.

When he had gone, she said, "I followed Ashley out to her apartment. Honestly, he was such a fool for women. He wanted to be a ladies' man, have all the girls falling for him. That's all right, to a point. But it got him into an awful lot of trouble. Sex usually does. I discovered that for myself.''

Tom wanted to keep her on track. "You followed Ash to Carrie's apartment, waited until he left, and then knocked on her door.''

"That's right,'' Lyn Lisa agreed. "They had been drinking, making love. She was pretty tipsy when I got there. She thought it was Ash coming back for more, I guess. She only had these panty things on. She was pretty surprised to see her lover's mother come stomping in there, let me tell you. The whole place smelled of sex. Quite animalistic. Disgusting. She was belligerent. I said to her I couldn't understand how anybody could be sleeping with a man she's trying to blackmail, although I guess I could understand. Women tend to use the weapons that are handiest."

"In your case, though, it wasn't sex. It was an aerosol can of rug cleaner."

"I brained her with a Cutty Sark bottle first. I became so furious with her," Lyn Lisa said with some satisfaction. "She was an insolent, drunken bitch. I just couldn't stand her. The carpet cleaner was right there. Handy. I just squirted it into her gaping, stupid mouth, and held her nose for a couple of minutes. Worked like a charm. I'm not sure whether I intended to kill her. But by the time I left that apartment she certainly was dead."

"And no one the wiser."

"Definitely no one the wiser. Not even Ash. He never did know."

"Everyone thinks Ash killed her."

"I suspect you are responsible for that perception, Mr. Coward. Besides, my son is dead. What anyone thinks at this point isn't going to hurt him. I presume you killed him."

"No," Tom said. "I didn't kill him. He tried very hard to kill me, but I didn't kill him."

Lyn Lisa seemed to consider this at some length. "Life was never easy for Ash," she concluded.

"What about Kelly Langlois?"

She looked taken aback by the question. "I never had anything to do with Kelly," she said. "I would like to have. But I didn't."

"Then who killed her?"

"Ash was terribly upset about that. I spent an hour with him while he sobbed on the telephone. Kelly apparently had gone completely crazy. She had a gun, and was threatening to use it on Ash. She accused him of having murdered Carrie. Ash tried to wrestle it out of her hands. It went off, and Kelly was dead. I prefer to think that Kelly killed herself. That's how I told Ash to look at it. He was quite reassured.''

"I can imagine," Tom said.

Her Negroni was almost finished. Tom signaled for the waiter. The Oak Bar was quickly emptying out now, like water draining from a lovely paneled old tub. The drinks provided an intimacy. The young man and the older woman talking by the window about the impending Broadway season, Pavarotti at the Met, the new French film sensation at the Beekman theater. Anything but the subject of murder.

"All right, then." Tom pushed his beer glass to one side. "Let's talk about Julie Keene. She's the one I don't understand. It was you on the street that night. You were the woman in the windbreaker."

"That was me, all right. Pretty good disguise, don't you think?" The second Negroni had made her more cheerful, and when she saw the waiter coming along with a third she looked quite delighted. "I really shouldn't. Goodness, I'm not a drinker." The waiter put the glasses down. "But they do taste so good. And I'm not sure when I'm going to be back here again."

She took a sip from her drink. "Now that involved some planning. That was what they call a premeditated murder. I followed her for a couple of weeks, established that, no matter what, she took the little dog for a walk each night. It was quite fascinating, actually, watching someone who doesn't know she is being watched. I came to the conclusion that the best way to do it was so that no one knew she was the intended victim. The prostitutes were just perfect. Julie became the innocent bystander who died accidentally. It wasn't murder at all. The police are still combing the city for the Hooker Vigilante. That's what they call him. In fact, there have now been a couple of other episodes, involving the shooting of prostitutes. People are fed up with them cluttering up the streets. They really are. They're beginning to fight back."

"But why? Julie was a harmless dip, a TV entertainment reporter. She wasn't trying to hurt Ash. Far from it. She was crazy about him."

"Let's just say I didn't like her." She was fidgety now, tapping a fingernail against the side of her glass.

"Maybe you were jealous of her."

"I wondered when we might get around to the pop psychology." She gave a secret smile to her glass. "But maybe you're right. I think she would have ruined his life. She wasn't a problem, but she would have become one. Ash was involved in such a web of lies and deceit with his life. I don't think he loved any woman. He just used them to make himself believe he was a man."

"So you killed Julie Keene to get her out of Ash's life."

"Something like that."

"Jesus," Tom said.

"Of course," she continued, "there might have been something else."

"Like what?"

The look on her face was impish. The drinks once again had made her the coquet. "Perhaps it was fun. Perhaps it kept me entertained. There was excitement. There was risk and danger. Why do certain people race cars or climb mountains? Why do people murder? You can't go shopping every day, not even in New York. And I am an experienced murderess, Mr. Coward, as you know."

"It's that simple?"

She shrugged. "Or that complicated. It's not something to which I have given a lot of thought. All this started because I thought my son was in trouble. I was his mother. I wanted to help him out. I felt Julie Keene was part of that trouble. One thing seemed to lead to another."

"What was next?" Tom wondered. "What did you have planned for Stormy Willis?"

She made a grimace. "To tell you the truth, I knew nothing of Stormy until after Ash was dead. I read about her in the papers. I thought he was involved with Julie Keene."

"He never told you about her?"

"No," she said. She was reflective for a moment. "I can't understand why. He told me everything. But he never mentioned her."

"I wonder if you might have had something to do with that," Tom said.

"Oh, dear," she said. "Here we go with the pop psychology again. Think what you will, Mr. Coward. Whatever simple explanation best serves."

She finished her drink, and smacked her lips together, savoring the final tasty drop. "As I understand it, though, none of this would have started if Ash had not taken your girl away."

Tom smiled. "Well, it's that simple. Or it's that complicated."

"In any event, the jig seems to be up. Isn't that what they say in detective fiction?"

"That's what they say. But why have you told me all this?"

"Because, Mr. Coward, I quite frankly don't think anyone will pay much attention to you. You must now go and ask the authorities to believe that Ashley Conlon's dead mother is responsible for all this. They are going to be dubious, to say the least. There is absolutely no evidence of any involvement on my part. At the same time there are a lot of people around who have convinced themselves Ash was responsible. By the time anyone comes to believe otherwise — if they ever do — I'll be long gone. I've disappeared before. I'm a wanderer in this world, Mr. Coward. I've been unhappy for a long time, and I rather enjoy it. My life is tragic, but it's my life, and I must survive it. So you see, there is no harm satisfying your curiosity. Besides," she said, "you're rather charming. And you did buy me a Negroni that day when I was keeping an eye on Ash.''

She began gathering up her Bloomingdale's bags.

''Suppose I prevent you from leaving,'' Tom said.

''Then you'd be molesting an elderly woman in a public place. That never goes over very well. Not even in New York.''

She got up from the table, hoisting thc bags with her.

''You've forgotten one thing,'' he said.

''No doubt,'' she said.

''I'm going to write about this. I'm going to tell the whole story. If the police don't believe me, maybe a lot of readers will.''

''Fair trade,'' she said. ''I have my freedom. You have your story. And perhaps Stormy.''

''No,'' Tom said ruefully. ''Not Stormy.''

''Then we have both lost something.'' She nodded a farewell. ''Thanks for the drinks, Mr. Coward. Each time I have a Negroni, wherever I am in the world, I'll think of you.''

''Goodbye, Mrs. Conlon.'' He watched her leave. The Oak Bar was empty. The waiter approached.

''Everything okay, sir?''

''I'm not sure,'' Tom said. ''I'm not really sure.''

In the late afternoon a couple of black kids in spotless white sneakers were break-dancing to music blaring from a ghetto blaster. The raw hip hop carried across Grand Army Plaza and landed on the steps of the Plaza's Fifth Avenue entrance, barely jarring the beautiful women and handsome men who hurried inside. Here beneath the marble-columned portico, there was no pain, no poverty. Only hip hop music to interrupt the rustle of luxury. The world was a better, cleaner, simpler place here, Tom Coward mused. No wonder the rich traveled in limousines with the smoked-glass windows rolled up. That way nothing unpleasant could get to them. They were wrong, of course. Something unpleasant always could.

"Tom. Tom Coward." He swung around to see Lacy Bergen emerging from the swinging doors. Her hair fell dark and thick to the collar of the knee-length white fur coat draped around her shoulders. It was coolish, about seventy degrees, but hardly fur-coat weather. She stood beside him, the world's smoothest and best-paid complexion beaming. A plump little secretary and a fey, pained-looking publicist waited impatiently on the landing above the steps.

"You look as though you're freezing to death," he said.

She slapped him on the arm. "You're always kidding. I just got this. I always wanted to walk around Manhattan in a fur coat. Mommy hates it, of course. All the more reason to wear it." She leaned toward him conspiratorily. The smell of her was intoxicating. "Edmond doesn't think I should be talking to you."

"Oh? Why not?"

"He thinks you're unreliable."

Tom sighed. "It's my season to be unreliable."

"I love unreliable," she said. "Everyone in my life is *soooo* reliable. It makes me sick. Listen, I thought you were going to interview me."

"I forgot," said Tom. "I'm unreliable. Remember?"

Her laughter was surprisingly throaty. "Everyone is begging to talk to me, and you forgot. You're so funny, Tom. You really are."

"Sure," Tom said. "I'm a riot."

"I'm on my way to Paris," she said.

"Why are you going to Paris?"

"They're going to take a picture of me in this fur coat."

"You're going all the way to Paris to get your picture taken in a fur coat?"

"That's the kind of girl I am," she said. "I've got an idea. Why don't you come to Paris and interview me."

"In your fur coat?"

She gave him her best sexy ninteen-year-old's smile. "In my fur coat. If that's what you want."

"Let me think about it," Tom said.

"Please come," she implored. "Promise you'll come."

"Okay," he said. "I promise."

She kissed him on the cheek. The publicist cleared his throat and announced that Lacy's limo had arrived.

"We're at the Ritz, of course," she said. "Ring me there. Don't forget now." She leaped down to the limo. The chauffeur rushed to hold the door open for her. She paused before she got in, and turned back to him.

"Say, someone told me you were in Toronto. What are you doing here, anyhow?"

"Business," he said.

"Oh." She made a little pout. "I thought you might have wanted to see me."

"Well," Tom said, "I was just in the hotel there solving a couple of murders."

She laughed again. "Tom, you really are funny. Does anyone ever tell you that?"

"Constantly," he said.

"Paris," she said.

He gave her the thumbs-up sign. "Paris it is."

He stood on the Plaza steps under the portico after she departed, and thought about Paris. He would have to talk to the police naturally. At least try out the Lyn Lisa Conlon story on them. And there was writing to be done. But Paris with Lacy Bergen. Strolls along the Seine. Drinks in Montparnasse. Dinners at La Coupole. You could do worse. Life, he thought, with a rueful smile. You can only get on with it.

Tom stepped down off the Plaza steps and began strolling toward Fifth Avenue.